T0302637

# The
# MIDNIGHT MECHANIC

"An unflinching depiction of 19th century London, and a vividly evoked and fast-moving tale of promises kept-and-broken, brotherly love, and fortitude."

— VIRGINIA BAILY, WINNER OF THE MCKITTERICK PRIZE, AND AUTHOR OF THE SUNDAY TIMES BESTSELLER, *EARLY ONE MORNING*

"*The Midnight Mechanic* is a pacy, Dickensian foray into the sewers of Victorian London. Brown's hardscrabble characters carry a heady ponk of corruption and unbridled ambition, ultimately revealing humanity's wormlike striving for sunlight above soil. With its rival brothers, industry bosses, and double-crossing gangsters, Brown has created a weird, dirty, wild world."

— ROB MAGNUSON SMITH, AUTHOR OF *SEAWEED RISING* AND *SCORPER*. WINNER OF THE FAULKNER-WISDOM GOLD MEDAL FOR FICTION, AND THE INTERNATIONAL ELIZABETH JOLLEY SHORT STORY PRIZE

"*The Midnight Mechanic* is both vividly original and scrupulously researched. Andy Brown recreates a little known but fascinating segment of London's Dickensian past, imbuing it with clear implications for our present environmental concerns."

— VESNA GOLDSWORTHY, FRSL, AUTHOR OF *GORSKY*, *MONSIEUR KA*, AND *IRON CURTAIN*

"*The Midnight Mechanic* takes us into the impressively conjured world of Victorian England's crippling poverty. I love this book for the sheer tactility of its portrayals of characters and urban cityscapes, and the way the reader is immediately sucked into the drama of the novel. Brown imbues his characters' lives with resilience, hope and the kind of drama that sweep us up from the very first page. *The Midnight Mechanic* is an imaginative triumph."

— JACOB ROSS, FRSL, AUTHOR OF *PYNTER BENDER*, SHORTLISTED FOR THE COMMONWEALTH WRITERS' PRIZE; *THE BONE READERS*, AWARDED THE JHALAK PRIZE; *BLACK RAIN FALLING*; AND THE COLLECTED SHORT STORIES *TELL NO-ONE ABOUT THIS*

By Andy Brown

*The Tree Climbing Cure*

*Apples & Prayers*

*A Body of Work*

# The MIDNIGHT MECHANIC

ANDY BROWN

Sea Crow Press

*The Midnight Mechanic*

Published 2024 by Sea Crow Press
Barnstable, MA
www.seacrowpress.com



Paperback ISBN: 978-1-961864-04-7
Ebook ISBN: 978-1-961864-05-4
Library of Congress Control Number: 2023947924

Cover Image by John Atkinson Grimshaw, *Westminster Bridge by Moonlight*, 1880
Cover Design Design by Mary Petiet
Interior Design by Mary Petiet

*for my Mum, Ruth Brown,*
*with love and gratitude*

# Author's Note

At the time of the publication of *The Midnight Mechanic*, London is rebuilding its crumbling Victorian sewerage system with a £4.9 billion 'super sewer' to deal with the perennial problem of the capital's waste in this new age of the mega-city. Meanwhile, around the UK, there are over 4,000 unscheduled sewage outfalls annually, into rivers, estuaries, and the sea, resulting in a boom in the number of environmental campaign groups and activities. Water quality has become a major national and global concern. Post COVID-19, stringent water treatment and testing have become vital in the struggle against water-borne disease, just as in the Victorian era Dr. John Snow diligently made the painstaking case for the water-borne nature of cholera — a disease which killed many millions in a wave of epidemics across the $19^{th}$ century. And just as in Victorian times, when multiple 'fake' theories about the mechanism of cholera abounded in the public consciousness, so during the COVID-19 pandemic, contesting theories, counter theories, and conspiracy theories abounded about the nature of the disease. Little, sadly, seems to change, save for our ability to contain disease through engineering programmes, treatment programmes, vaccination roll-outs, and international public health programmes. *The Midnight Mechanic* uses historical fiction to explore pressing environmental issues around sewerage and human waste that are still pertinent today, just as they were in the middle of the nineteenth century.

'If being swallowed by the earth is terrible on the seashore,
what is it in a cess-pool?'

Victor Hugo, *Les Miserables*

# One

*London, late 1830s*

MIST ROSE off the Thames in dismal wafts. Foggy yellow turning pewter grey. Across the bridges, the city's workers had long since hurried back to their terraced homes and courtyards.

By the dank wall of his own unlit yard, Silas Hunt watched a chink of light appear between post and planks as he pushed the rough boards of his backyard gate. He peered both ways along the street. Behind him, his younger brother Arthur, and the youngest of the three, George, waited for his signal.

Like many boys from these streets, Silas was scruffy with holes in his boots, a shabby serge jacket over a grubby vest and knee-length shorts. His stockings made an ill-matched pair. His brothers looked much the same, prone to scrapes and misadventure and too many days hopping off school. But Silas's features were sharp. His eyes were keen and full of purpose beneath his short dark hair. Anyone passing by that night might have seen those eyes peering out through that widening crack. But no one was abroad. Little moved in the streets but the mist itself. Silas knew this was their moment.

Darting from the breach into the moonlit lane, they hit the kerb like a trail of mice. Silas led his brothers, clutching a rough gunny sack beneath his arm. Between the high walls of the alley they ran, the bricks black with grime and soot. Behind them the battered gate hung squeaking on its hinges. Under their feet, the cobbles shone wet with muck.

By the streetlamp on the corner, he brought his brothers to a halt. Even the lamplighter was at home by now, he thought. Often, he'd watched the fellow pass through here as evening fell, cutting wicks and candles for the streetlamps, topping up the oil and raising the taper at the tip of his pole, before shuffling on to the next dimly glowing lantern, its flame barely alive in the choking air. Silas had watched him climbing his steps, then descend, up and down, up and down, all along the street, like a little rubber balloon.

Standing beneath the lamp now, his own face was lit from above, casting long shadows beneath his eyes.

'You look creepy,' George whispered, his unbroken voice like some small creature's. 'Like a ghost.'

'Don't be daft, there's no such thing, Georgie,' Silas replied. He checked the street again. 'Come on,' he said, 'this way.'

Silas turned them through the archway at the bottom of the lane. Here was a maze of blind, unnamed cul-de-sacs that led to places where faceless people did thankless jobs. Yards where dirty mothers dunked their children's clothes into old wooden basins of filthy water on dreary washdays. Where wizened old grandmas turned in fits of rage on any child hapless enough to cross them. Where shouting mothers lashed out at the light-footed, shoeless children who ran between their feet. Where resigned mothers picked up fruit skins and scraps from the gulleys and overflowing gutters. Mothers who were now, Silas thought, thankfully indoors with their hordes of bawling children. He was glad for his own mother's sympathies. He thought of her, back in their room, finally asleep.

'Follow me,' he said. The cul-de-sacs were nothing but silent basins of mist.

'You sure, Si?' said Arthur.

Silas looked back at his younger brother and snorted. 'Course I'm sure! Dog kennel's this way.'

'If you say so.' A year younger than Silas, Arthur would soon be catching up with him. In the meantime, that year's difference echoed in almost everything they did together. Silas knew Arthur was reaching for his coattails, trying to catch him up, but other than this small rivalry, the boys were thick with each other.

'Quit arguin' you two, won't you?' said George. 'Ma'll wake up soon and wonder where in hell we are. We ain't got long.' He was several years younger than both his brothers, but what he lacked in years he made up for in spirit. Often he gainsaid them, simply to see where he stood, to test his place in line.

'George is right,' said Silas. 'Got to be quick.' He indicated the direction with a flick of his head. The boys nodded in unison and took the arched alleyway. Covertly they made their way towards the pound at the far end of Dog Kennel Lane.

Silas had it all worked out. If the foreman at the tannery wouldn't buy the "pure" from their mother anymore, or she was too ill to collect it herself, then perhaps the tanner would buy it from *them*? Pure – straight out of the mongrels' guts. It was the only thing strong enough to make the tanner's leather soft. They boiled it into a stinking soup – bate, they called it – heated with steam. It made short work of softening leather. It had ruined his father's body. Vile stuff. And the tanner would have no idea who they were, would he? To him they'd just be any old pure gatherers, selling their scavengings to the tannery. And Silas knew exactly where he could get his hands on buckets of the stuff. Here was the source that would put them in new shoes, in trousers and shirts, in warm clothes for his mother, with hot meals in their stomachs and a trip to the doctors to get her sickness sorted.

The kennels were owned by a man called Tattersall. A local tough, he knew that much. A bully businessman, ruddy faced and choleric. Everyone knew he was given to gambling and dog fighting and betting on bare-knuckle boxing. He'd been known to step into the ring himself. But daytimes he could be found dealing in strays in the back lanes and courts, dressed in his working breeches and long boots; his barrel-like body and thickset legs. The man's shirts were clean but coarse, Silas had noticed, always with a bright cravat knotted at his throat. An old bowler hat of stained and shabby purple felt marked his arrival in the crowd. Silas knew he'd have to be silent, stealthy too, to avoid the kind of beating he'd once witnessed the man mete out to a mongrel on the street.

By the back wall of the pound a painted sign hung out from the wall on a rusted bracket. It made tiny, animal-like squeaks in the breeze. *Tom Tattersall, Dog Catcher and Impounder, Appointment to the Borough.*

'This is it,' said Silas. His brothers looked up, then pulled themselves tight into the shadows.

Here was the home of runaway pets. Of lapdogs who'd slipped their leashes in the park or wriggled from a collar and bypassed the garden gate. There were other dogs inside too: rabid ferals, victims of dog fighting wagers, injured curs. Once strong, loyal dogs, maimed from pulling carts the whole of their working lives. He'd seen such creatures tied to costermongers' carts when they worked for pocket money after school down at the market. The city's dogs were like the city's people, he thought. Like his father had been. Ill-used and knocked about by bad luck.

'Easiest way in's over here,' he whispered.

'How d'you know?' said Arthur.

'Because I been here to check it out, you eejit.'

'Alright!' said Arthur. 'Just asking...'

Silas saw the sneer on his brother's lips. 'Here, give us a leg up bruv,' he whispered more agreeably. 'Can't do it meself.'

'What about the dogs?' George looked suddenly worried. Inside it might be packed with animals.

'I don't care how fierce the dogs are!' Silas boasted. He lowered his foot from Arthur's clasped hands and slid down to George's level. 'You pigeon-hearted, or what?'

'I ain't scared.' George lifted his shoulders and chest.

'Leave him alone,' said Arthur.

Silas closed his eyes and gritted his teeth. 'Can't we quit the squabbling?'

Arthur and George shifted uneasily. Silas put his hands on their shoulders. 'There's a good supply of pure in there, George, you unnerstand? Littered all over the yard. Just waiting to be gathered. D'you want to eat next week? D'you want me to get a doctor for ma?' He paused for effect. 'You want me to go in and fetch the shit, or not?'

'S'pose so,' muttered George. 'If you're sure we should.'

'Course we shouldn't! But we *are*.'

'But it's stealing, ain't it?'

'Now's not the time George.' Silas rolled his eyes. 'Look, it's just collecting pure. Like any other day. Just like ma used to do. It ain't stealing. It don't belong to no one, not even the dogs, not once they've done their business. It's just that the pure *we* want happens to be on the other side of *this* wall.' He banged the heel of his palm against the damp brickwork.

'He'll be fine, George. The dogs are all caged-up overnight.' Arthur smiled weakly. 'Ain't they, Silas?'

Tattersall kept a team of Bull Terriers. Stout-bodied, long-legged fighting dogs. Aggressive too and not without intelligence. He used them in the rat ring and dogfights.

'Hope so,' Silas said.

'But what if *he* gets you?' the youngest brother said.

'Don't mind if I do get caught,' Silas bragged. 'The lock-up's only a few days and there's more regular food than we ever get. I'd kill for a piece of meat. I ain't eaten nothing but bread all day.' Since their father had died, they'd lived on nothing but charity loaves and parish tea.

'Stop talkin' about your stummuck and get on with it.' Arthur readied himself again to take his brother's weight.

'Promise you'll be quick,' said George.

'I ain't hanging about,' said Silas.

'Honour bright?'

'Honour bright,' the older brother replied, placing his hand across his heart. 'Anyways, you're not the one who's going over. *I am*. Now, gi's that leg up Arthur.'

It didn't matter to Silas how many dogs were inside. He'd been working this plan out for days. Over the wall, scoop up the pure and get it in the sack. Run. Hide it for a while where no one would find it, then sell it to the tanner. If his mother used to get two shillings a pail-full for it, then he'd shovel as much as ten pails from the kennels, bundle it into his gunny and earn them all ten bob. What you couldn't do with ten bob, he reckoned.

He sat astride the wall and whispered down. 'Chuck us the

sack. I'll be quick as I can. Keep watch. Give us a whistle if you see anyone...'

Beneath him, Arthur put his arm on George's shoulder and the two of them merged back into the shadows where a tall lime tree overhung the wall from the inside. 'Otherwise, keep mum.'

Silas thought of their mother back in the house. He'd had to lure her to sleep; he could be forgiven that, couldn't he?

'This is nice,' she'd said. 'Unexpected. What d'you boys want?' She'd laughed then and he'd laughed back with her. Had she noticed his unease?

On the other side now, where he clambered into the yard, the tree trunk branched at chest height. He lowered himself over the limb and down to the ground. The moon was still high and threw a dim light across the yard from behind a gauze of smog. He was trembling with cold and a healthy fear, although he'd have been happier with no moon at all – it was casting heavy shadows across the yard towards the sleeping dogs. He wouldn't stand a chance against a pack of bull baiters and rat killers like those.

Behind him, the tree and the brick wall dwarfed him. He looked around. Was that his brothers prattling in the street? Shut your traps you eejits, he thought. But, when he listened harder there was no sound, save for the common and indistinct noises of the city at night.

To his right the sleeping dogs were caged in wood and wire. He could smell them. Their hairy dampness. Their heavy musk. Their meaty breath and farting. He could hear their slow, laboured breathing, each outbreath rounded off with a rattle of jowls. One hound was making strange squeaking noises, the way George sometimes did as he lay dreaming in their shared bed.

To his left the compound opened onto a barren square, walled on each side, its edges overgrown with shrubs and nettles. He scanned it and saw what he wanted, lying there in neat little piles on the ground. Tons of the stuff spread out for the taking.

Within the confines of the wall, however, he saw there were two lines of barbed wire nailed to wooden posts – one at the knees, the other at waist height – to keep the dogs away from the walls and to give the keeper access from each side, he supposed. There was clearly no telling with pit dogs like these.

He hadn't counted on the wire being there and it was too high to step over. He'd have to crawl beneath it to get to the pure. Silas sank to his knees and flattened himself to the ground, wriggling his head and shoulders under. The ground scratched his knees where his shorts didn't reach his stockings. He made slow, uncomfortable progress, taking a mouthful of dirt as he crawled. He wiped his tongue across his sleeve.

Clear of the wire he stood up, rummaged for the neck of the sack and let it flop open in his hands. The rough fabric caught on his calloused fingers.

He picked his way between the turds, but the quad was strewn with cinders and clinker from the kennel-man's stove that crunched beneath his boots. Each footfall sounded like someone rattling a tray of marbles. He prayed for silence and quickly began to scoop the pure, not bothering himself with which pieces were dry and which still moist. The tanners liked them both ways anyway, for different kinds of leather. It was a foul task, and he pitied his mother for having had to do such a shameful thing by broad daylight.

Within a few minutes he'd cleared the ground and his sack was beginning to weigh heavy. He turned to the dogs, the dark mounds of their bodies inflating slowly then relaxing. Inflating, relaxing.

As he turned he noticed there, by the side of the kennels, a fixed scuttle. A wooden bunker with a loose, slatted grate. He slipped across the pound and placed his hand on the handle. It was cold from the night air. He grasped it and gently raised the cover.

The smell hit him like a wall of heat from a coal fire. It overpowered his senses and made him rock for a moment on his feet. The scuttle was piled with enough pure to keep a family in food and clothes for a year. *What a trove*! Tattersall was hoarding it to sell to the tanners. He must have been making a nice little profit, not only catching dogs, but selling their shit as well. This was the man, he reckoned, who'd put his mother out of work in the first place. Suddenly he didn't feel quite so guilty about taking it. Thank you very nicely, Tom Tattersall.

He began to scoop it with his free hand, dropping the remains into his sack. Soon it was almost full, although he'd only managed to empty out half of the scuttle. He'd have to come back for the rest. Quietly he slid the hopper's slats back into place.

With great effort he twisted the neck of the sack to a handle, tied it with a string from his pocket and swung it round, letting the momentum carry it up and over onto his back. As it landed across his shoulders, it almost knocked the wind from him.

He coughed loudly under the weight of the blow.

Somewhere to his side a dog grunted, roused itself from sleep and sniffed at the air.

'Lord,' he muttered.

Turning quickly he moved through the shadows towards the wires but, by now, the animal had awoken and had started to growl. Silas tensed himself as he reached the wires. With a great heave, he tossed the sack over. It seemed to hang in the air, then drop, becoming caught on the furthest wire on its way down. It teetered there for a moment, before overbalancing and tipping down on the other side. A few lumps of pure spilled out at the neck.

He lowered himself to the ground and began crawling. Behind him the growling swelled. The first dog was joined by another. And another. One of them started to bark.

A light flickered on at the back of the building. An oil lamp at the grubby window. A shadowy face. From inside the house came the clatter of furniture. The clacking of bolts on the back door. A disturbed voice.

Face down in the dirt, Silas thought of Tattersall's reputation: the bloodthirsty dog-baiter with little care for his own creatures, certainly none for children and definitely none for intruders. He crawled quickly, cinders in his mouth.

To the rear of the house the dogs were now jumping and rattling their cages. Silas raised himself onto his knees and felt a twist of wire suddenly rip through his sleeve. The pain tore down his arm from shoulder to elbow. He heard his jacket rip and saw a slip of fabric left hanging there upon the wire.

'Jesus Lord!' he cried, much louder now, a warm pulse of blood spreading on his upper arm. The pain shot through his muscle like a stroke from his schoolteacher's cane.

By now, the bearer of the oil lamp had made it outside. He was standing beside the cages. Tattersall.

From where Silas was kneeling in the shadows, he could make out the man's clumpy boots. His rundown bowler hat. In one hand he held the oil lamp. In the other a bludgeon. The man leaned over to the nearest cage and flicked up a latch. Two Bull Terriers came careening out, barking and sniffing at the air.

'What is it boys? What you waitin' for? Go get him!'

The dogs sped straight for Silas.

Tattersall held the oil lamp in front of his face. It sent a beam out through the mist. The dogs cut across the yard towards the wires, locked on Silas's scent.

He ran the last few yards to the tree and leaned the sack against the trunk, clambering onto the low-hanging branch. His feet searched for a foothold in the dark. He could feel the burning ache in his shoulder, the slipperiness of his wound. With his other arm he reached down and hauled at the neck of the gunny sack, hefting it onto the bough and pushing it overhead towards the top of the wall.

'Hey!' he called down to his brothers. 'There's bloody dogs loose here!'

It was then that Tattersall saw him clambering over the wall. 'Hoi, you there!' the man shouted.

From on high, Silas knew he was safe for the moment. The dogs would never get beyond the wires. He watched them pull up short of the barrier, their stocky front legs bouncing off the ground, their throats raising a fearsome din.

A moment later Tattersall joined them at the wires. He stopped and pulled at the bloodied scrap of fabric he found snagged there, rubbing it between his fingers. 'I'll have you yet you conniving little thug!' he shouted into the night.

From the wall Silas pushed the sack down into the street and threw himself forwards. When he landed, the gunny broke his fall.

'Grab the other end!' he snapped at Arthur and, between them, they lifted their haul. Pell-mell they ran into the shadows, urging George before them. Behind the wall, Tattersall's shouting was drowned in a clamour of barking.

The ground at their feet became a patchwork of black and white in the moonlight. A maze of obscure junctions. The cross beams of low passageways defined black squares and oblongs. The drainage downpipes from gutters and eaves caught glints of light and measured out the night in twinkling uprights. Occasional street lanterns glowed yellow in the mist, though the light they cast barely reached beyond the confines of their glass shades. Along the street the windowpanes reflected these sporadic glints. Save for some indistinct movement in the gutter, the night was almost motionless – the irregular stirrings of a tom cat or a street dog here, the shadow of a figure in a cloak and tall hat slinking down a side-road there, or was that just the play of light and silhouettes, as the breeze caused the mist to swirl in dreamlike patterns?

Silas knew their way home through the bye-ways and shadows like the back of his own hand – the principal routes and the little-known passageways, the rat runs and ginnels. As the brothers scampered away, they turned often to look behind themselves. Tattersall would surely soon be upon them. Yet they saw nothing but moonlight and shadow. Heard nothing but the silence of the streets and the beating of their own hearts.

Silas's arm was seeping blood and throbbing beneath his sleeve. He looked down to his left shoulder to see what the wire had done. As he did so, he caught Arthur's eye.

'Christ, Si, that's bleeding real bad. What the hell you gonna tell ma?'

'It's alright, don't fuss it,' Silas bit back, although he could clearly see the hole ripped out of his jacket and, through the vent, his badly bloodied shoulder. He winced.

Their mother would still be asleep, he prayed. A dim candle flickering on the table, her shawl still draped across her shoulders, the blanket tightly tucked around her midriff.

They left Dog Kennel Lane and turned into a siding. Skirting the minor streets, they reached the scrubland that passed for a green at the edge of their neighborhood; a stretch of low-lying quagmire, edged by ditches of stagnant water and decrepit buildings. The ground lay strewn with litter and castoffs that even the rag pickers and gatherers paid little attention to. On the higher parts stood a few meager strips of disused market-garden upon which some past neighbours had once grown vegetables, before trespassers and thieves had cleared the whole lot out and put paid to the enterprise. Now the ground wasn't used for anything, save for some travellers' horses occasionally grazing there before the summer markets. He'd stash the gunny here until it all went quiet. No one would bother to come looking here.

Silas took the sack and hurried into the bushes. 'Wait here.'

Arthur and George stood alone in the emptiness.

'Where's he gone?' George's nervousness was growing.

'Just hiding the sack,' said Arthur. 'He'll be back in a minute.'

Moments later Silas stood before them brushing twigs and leaves off his coarse serge jacket. 'Hidden it,' he said, gesturing towards a pile of bricks and rubble that lay at the heart of the covert. 'We'll come back for it in a couple of days. Ain't no one looking for it in there.'

'Who's the receiver?' said Arthur.

'Ain't no receiver... don't want to give it away! We'll lose half our money giving it to a receiver. I'm taking it down to the tanner myself.'

'You!' Arthur scoffed.

'Why not!' Silas stared his brother down.

'If you say so, Si.'

They left the scrubby green and, ducking back through the fence, picked up the streets again. There was still no sign of Tattersall.

'We've lost him.' Silas's confidence had returned. 'Let's get home quick.'

They stayed amongst the shadows. They mustn't slow down, he thought, sensing George's efforts to keep up. The smaller boy was beginning to tire, asking anxious questions about the terriers.

'They've long gone,' Arthur said. 'Just keep up, George.'

Was Tattersall behind them? Perhaps by now he'd also called the Peelers and there was a posse out looking for them? It never took long for a posse to come together around these streets. Silas had seen street gangs before and watched them give a thief a beating. But he consoled himself: they would be safely in bed before any band had time to come together tonight.

He led them past the back doors of the lodging houses in the labyrinth of streets behind their own, doubling back to retrace their steps, hoping to lay a false trail. From somewhere in the distance a church bell chimed. The moon threw a bruised light onto a setback doorway. Silas took his brothers into its screening depths.

'We'll see 'em from here,' he said, 'if they're still on our tails.'

'I thought you said they'd gone,' George complained.

'They have,' Silas said. 'Just gotta make sure.'

They let their bodies dip back into the darkness and cast their eyes out onto the street. For a minute all was utterly still. The street encompassed an unnerving silence. But then, just as Silas was on the verge of ushering them on their way, a man's shadow came into view at the street's end. A huge, dark shape crept up and across the brick wall. A man in boots and bowler hat, a truncheon casting long shadows from one hand and, from the other, two lines that attached themselves to the shifting shadows of two strapping dogs.

'Christ,' Silas whispered.

'What?' Arthur leaned in towards him.

'That's him.'

'You got to be bloody kidding...'

At the end of the street their tracker walked into the light. A lantern loomed above him from the end of a policeman's pole. His face leered into view, his cheeks and chin jutting forward, his eyes sinking back into darkened sockets.

Tattersall wasn't alone. Two policemen had joined him. Above their dark capes, their varnished hats caught the meager light. Both constables, like Tattersall, held truncheons. One held a lamp aloft. Silas recognised him – Bunce, the copper was called. He'd had to answer to him once when some street boys had stolen fruit from a costerman's barrow. It wasn't Silas's doing, but the policeman had made sure he knew who was who and what was what. Nasty bastard, Silas thought.

The two dogs pulled on ahead, their noses close to the ground. The men strode along, stopped to confer, then pressed on under Tattersall's lead. When they reached the junction, however, they seemed unsure which route to follow. Their voices drifted.

'Nothing but a gang of cadgers and lurkers down there, Fletcher,' constable Bunce said.

'Don't care nothing for law, nor society, nor property.' Tattersall's voice echoed from the brickwork.

'Thieves' kitchens, public houses and schools for pickpockets,' the other constable murmured to the darkness.

One of Tattersall's dogs barked and jolted George in his boots. Silas clapped his hand across his brother's mouth and pulled him back against his chest.

The constable named Fletcher walked down the side road to his left.

'Anyone down there?' Bunce inquired of his colleague in a raised whisper.

'I'll press on,' Fletcher replied. 'You take the other side.'

Bunce nodded and turned to the right. Tattersall followed Fletcher to the left. In that moment, Silas urged his brothers to make their move.

'Come on,' he said, pulling George beneath his arm. They sped through the dark alley in the opposite direction and soon reached a familiar passageway they often used as a short cut. At the far end, however, they found the gate was locked. 'We'll have to nip across the backs, two streets down. Behind the butchers' yard,' Silas said.

'That's the middens,' said Arthur.

'I don't want to go by the cesspools.' George folded his arms across his chest.

'And you don't want to get caught by Tattersall's hounds neither,' said Silas.

'He's right,' said Arthur. 'It's just a bit of a stink. Put your hand over yer mouth like this.' He masked his lips and nostrils with his sleeve.

George laughed quietly, and the brothers began to jog, their mouths covered by their sleeves. Arthur chivvied his younger brother along.

'We'll take this one,' said Silas, 'then it's just a minute to the cess.' He indicated a road to their left. The street was narrow, disappearing into blackness.

Behind them, quite suddenly, the shadows of the men and their dogs reappeared, turning the corner into the main street. Silas led his brothers into the dark.

In a few moments, they reached the back of the butchers' row and the boiler yard, behind which the night pails and middens were emptied. Hundreds of houses, hostels and lodging rooms had, for as long as anyone could remember, emptied their collected waste and nightsoil into these bunkers. Now they sat shoulder deep, until the carts of the midnight mechanics would come and haul the stuff away to country fields. This evening in the mist, however, the nightsoil men were not out clearing. Nor did the pits stink as awful as they might. Yet George still kept his coat cuff to his face. Most of the piles were deeper than he was tall.

They had reached a cul-de-sac. The way through the cesspools was across a series of sheeted tin roofs. If they didn't get up and over the cesspits now, Tattersall and the Peelers would be on them. Silas pulled himself up awkwardly, blocking out the pain that was pounding through his arm. On top, he waited for his brothers.

Arthur pushed George onto the roof. 'Stick yer bum on my shoulder. Reach yer hand up to Si.'

George did as he was told, and Silas pulled him up with his good arm. The other hung loosely at his side, a steady trail of blood running down to drip from his fingers.

'Me now.' Arthur held his hand up so that his brother could take it. Silas clasped his brother round the wrist then yanked him up. Arthur's feet scrabbled at the wall for better purchase.

A moment later the three of them were squatting on the metal roof. Silas looked over his shoulder down the alley. 'I think we finally lost 'em.'

'C'mon,' said Arthur, 'let's get across. And home.'

'I don't want to,' said George, dropping his sleeve from his mouth to cross his arms on his chest once more.

'You'll bloody do as you're told,' said Silas, looming over him. The youngest boy flinched.

'Just a hop across the roofs and we're done,' said Arthur, stepping between the two of them. He threw a glance at Silas. 'Don't spook him now,' he whispered. Silas stared hard at his brother and then turned away.

'I don't want to run across the roofs,' said George. 'They won't hold us...'

'Course they will,' Arthur said. 'We'll go one by one.'

'But there's all that... stuff... underneath.'

'And there's them dogs coming up behind us.' Silas's eyes flickered.

'It'll be alright, George. Just dash across and wait over there.' Arthur pointed to the haven of a low chimney on the other side, where the boys could gather. He looked down at George, but the lad still needed convincing. 'I'll go first then, deal?'

George hesitated, then nodded. Arthur needed no prompting. He dipped his shoulder, tensed his calves and set off quickly across the sheeted roofs. Behind him, Silas watched his dark figure glide across the roof. He could hear his brother's footfalls and, every now and then the vibrations of the metal sheets as they flexed and boomed beneath his weight.

'See, George,' he said. 'Safe as houses.'

The smallest boy nodded his head reluctantly. When he looked up, Arthur had made it to the chimneystack and was now crouching down in the shadows at its base.

It was a good fifty yards across the span. To the other side Arthur was beckoning.

'Go on, Georgie, you next,' Silas said.

The little boy stood and stared his brother in the face. 'It's *George*,' he said. 'I ain't little *Georgie* no more!'

'Alright,' said Silas. 'No need to get narkey.'

'You said *Honour Bright*,' George said.

'I'm sorry, alright?' said Silas.

'I hate your bloody stupid plan, Silas. I shoulda stayed at home with ma.'

'And how would that have worked out, George, when she asked you where we were? Think about it.'

'I hate your plan,' the younger boy repeated.

'Just run will you George, for Christ's sake!' Silas span his brother around by the shoulders and pushed him forwards.

George's first steps were cautious as he grew used to the flex of the tin beneath his feet. The roof panels were tarnished and, in places, slippery with mist. Every few steps he could see the gaps between the rickety panels and the shapeless mass of muck beneath him. Each footfall made the metal bend then rise a little, so the smell of muck wafted up in reeking clouds. As his stomach heaved, he lifted his sleeve once more to his mouth and ran on.

To the rear, Silas watched. Arthur was at the chimneystack, urging George on. The kid's arm was moving vigorously at his side like a miniature piston.

Above them, the moon disappeared behind a high bank of cloud and the whole scene darkened.

'Go on George,' Silas whispered. He'd thought about running across with him, but Arthur had been right – the tin sheets wouldn't bear more than one at a time. The moon reappeared. George was halfway over. Silas waited, crouched low to the gables, clutching his wounded shoulder, pressing hard to numb the pain. He'd wait until George was done, then go himself.

Once more the moon disappeared behind a heavy bank of cloud and Silas felt himself shrouded in darkness. It was as if all the streetlamps in London had suddenly been blown out with one godlike puff. 'Good lad,' he sighed. 'You done it.'

Above them the moon reappeared. The darkness lifted and the rooftops were cast in bright silver light. Silas looked across the roof towards Arthur, and Arthur looked back towards his brother. But George was no longer there.

Silas stood up, staring into the emptiness. 'George?'

Across the roof he saw Arthur stand and also heard him call George's name. Their voices travelled across the span of the roofs and collided with each other.

George had vanished. It was as if the moon had cast some charm and, in that dark window of time, magicked their brother away.

'George!' Silas called back, louder this time.

In the silence he threw himself forward, charging across the roof. His feet made booming noises on the metal, but he didn't care. He didn't care if their pursuers heard every clanging footfall and turned from the false trail the boys had laid. All he wanted was to reach that point from which his brother had mysteriously vanished.

It was all happening in a blur. Silas sprinted. Arthur ran towards him. The stink of the cesspools grew stronger. The sounds of scavenging vermin rose from beneath them. Under his feet, Silas could feel the metal changing in strength and thickness.

The two boys found themselves standing on either side of a great hole in the roof. Its jagged edges caught the moonlight.

They looked down into the rancid, decomposing depths. Ten feet there beneath them, they could see their brother's head and shoulders poking out of the muck. His head had lolled to one side and his eyes were closed.

Perhaps he had passed out with the shock, or banged his head in the fall? He didn't seem to be moving, but his body appeared to be sinking slowly, dragged down inch by inch into the repellent underworld.

The brothers threw themselves down on the tin and tried to reach their arms through the gap to grasp at George's shoulders. Neither of them could reach. Silas's own shoulder was screaming with pain. Their hands flapped around in the stinking air above George's sinking head. They grunted and strained and then lay still, exhausted. Without speaking, they looked at each other.

'Rope,' they said in unison.

'I'll get it,' said Silas. 'You watch him. There's some in the yard.' He knew it was still there, from the days when their father had carted skins to the tannery.

'Right.'

'Don't let him sink any further.'

'Right,' though what he was expected to do, Arthur didn't know.

'Won't be long.'

'Don't.'

Silas sprinted along the narrow bricks at the roof's edge, his arm jolting with every step. He jumped down into the deserted timberyard, turned into the main road and then ran down a familiar lane. It wasn't long before he found himself outside his own back gate. Tattersall and the Peelers had lost his scent he reckoned and, anyway, he only had one thing on his mind. Pulling out poor George.

Let them find me, he thought. There's nothing they can do. We're just out playing in the streets. Worst they can do is whip us for lying to ma, or getting stuck in the shit pits. It's not a crime.

The gate was still open, tilting gently on its hinges. He snuck inside the yard, shouldered up to the ground-floor window and peered inside. His mother was still asleep in her chair, the fire barely burning now. Her head was thrown back and her mouth was open. 'You're good boys,' she'd said to them, just before she'd relaxed back into her chair and fallen asleep. But Silas knew otherwise. He'd spun her a grand lie. All so they could go out and steal pure. 'What's all this for?' she'd said as they'd sat her down beside the stove, plied her with tea and stoked the fire, throwing on the last of the coal to make the parlour warm and sleepy. Now this. The little one was sunk up to his shoulders in a midden and it was all Silas's doing. He was a liar. And a thief. And now he'd gone and ripped his own arm open. How was he going to explain that to ma? He'd got little George in the shit. Exactly. He was going to get a beating for sure.

He turned away from the window and reached for the rope in the corner, terrified that his mother would wake and find him; terrified that he wouldn't get back to George on time; terrified that the man from the kennels had already found his sack of pure. It would all have been for nothing. It was all going to be discovered and traced back to him.

His hand slipped. A pail toppled from on high and rattled to the floor. Quickly, before his mother could wake – or Mrs. Kelly stick her head out of the upstairs window to shout 'Stop, thief! Wake up Mrs. Hunt!' – he grabbed the rope and ran, out of the gate, down the cobbled alley, through the arched terrace at the end of the close and back through his rat-run to where George had plunged through the roofing.

As he rounded the corner behind the middens one of the policemen was already waiting at the far end. Tattersall and the other Peeler must have gone on ahead – he knew the district as well as Silas. The man had headed him off with this sentry.

Silas scrambled up onto the dividing wall and ran across the beams of the decaying roof. The events of the night were snapping at him like Tattersall's dogs – all the climbing, the running, the gash to his arm, George tumbling through, the police, the Bull Terriers, Tattersall with his temper and his truncheon – it was all too much. His feet felt leaden. Behind his eyes he could feel a familiar mist descending. If only he could blank it all out.

Ahead of him Arthur was standing exactly where George had fallen through, silhouetted in the moonlight. Silas picked his way over, mindful not to go the same way as George. When he reached Arthur he threw down the rope and started issuing breathless instructions.

Arthur didn't move.

Silas shoved at him with his good hand, but still his brother stood stock-still, his face pallid, his eyes fixed in a forbidding stare.

'What is it?' asked Silas. 'I got the rope... let's bloody pull him out!' Silas stared down at his feet, through the ragged hole. But George wasn't there. 'Bloody hell! You got him out Arthur! By yourself!' He turned to look for George, sitting by the chimneystack perhaps. 'Where is he, Arthur?'

Silas lunged forward and threw his good arm around his brother's shoulders. Still Arthur stood petrified.

A beam of light from a policeman's lamp shone up into his eyes. The man's curt voice cut the silence. 'Alright sonny, game's over.' Constable Fletcher's eyes were two points of light in the darkness.

Silas looked beyond the shattered roof of the cesspool, into the dingy yard below. There was Tattersall with his dogs and one of the Peelers. Within a moment, constable Bunce, who had been standing sentry, joined them.

'You're really in the shit now, you little thief,' the kennel keeper sneered.

Silas felt his spirits crumble. He saw the gleam of the officers' buttons, their tall, hard hats, their truncheons swinging from their fists. He heard the subtle clink of the cuffs.

'Don't try running off again,' Fletcher said, 'or the dogs'll have you.' The Bull Terriers were stretching their leashes to breaking point.

'Come down quietly,' said Bunce. 'It's gone far enough.'

Beside the men lay a motionless shape. They had already found the sack of pure, Silas thought. Then he realized.

George.

He felt his stomach rise into his mouth and retched into the ragged hole where his brother's body had plummeted through.

When he had finished puking, he found himself standing in the yard. His head was spinning. There was George's ruined body beside him. He wanted to puke again, but there was nothing left. Bunce's truncheon hovered over his head.

'Stand still or I'll club you,' the policeman ordered. Silas stopped struggling. 'That's better. Now, hands behind backs.' Once again Silas complied. 'Clap the darbies on them, Fletcher.'

The subordinate officer handcuffed the boys.

'Where's home then? And no lying!' Bunce's voice was loud in the stillness of the yard. With each question it seemed to grow louder until Silas yielded, worn down by the thoughts in his clattering skull.

Fletcher had already placed George's body in a wheelbarrow commandeered from the yard.

'He's booked for kingdom come,' Tattersall jeered. 'Now, where is it?' His voice rattled in the back of his throat. 'Where the devil's what you stole from me! That's my livelihood that is!'

At first Silas stayed mute but, as the kennel man let his dogs draw closer, Arthur pleaded. 'Tell him, Silas, Christ sakes. Who cares about the bloody sack?'

Arthur's surrender hurt Silas almost as much as his wounded

arm. His head trembled on his neck in defiance. Then he too surrendered and told Tattersall where he'd stashed the stolen pure.

Bunce put his hands on their shoulders and pushed the boys forwards. He turned to Fletcher. 'Speed up with that barrow at the back!'

While the officer was occupied, Tattersall raised a fist and swung. Silas felt the crunch of the man's knuckles at the back of his head. A low moan escaped his lips. Bunce turned back to see the boy nursing himself.

'What?' said Tattersall.

Bunce eyed him suspiciously. 'We'll do it by the law, thank you, Tattersall.'

'Oh, to the letter!' the kennel man said. He turned, laughing, barreling away with his dogs leading, back to the waste ground to retrieve his pure.

Mary Hunt had once been a collector of pure. Since her husband William had died, she'd turned her hand to the work to support herself and her boys. She knew the business from William's work at the tannery. Each morning she'd take her basket and glove and go to gather the muck scattered along the streets. At first, she'd hated the work but, with time and from necessity, she'd come to bear it gratefully. Times had once been not so bad, with only a few collectors in the parish and a solid eightpence paid for every bucketful. 'I can do seven or eight buckets in a good week,' she told Silas. 'Three or four when it's bad. Which is why you got to go to school. God help you that you'll never have to do what I do.'

For a few months the tannery foreman had remained loyal and went on buying the pure from her. But once William's name had been forgotten at that place of employment and he'd been replaced by some other man, the tanner took her aside. 'We don't need your services anymore,' he'd said bluntly. The man had the same smell about him as her husband – part human, part animal, part street.

'What d'you mean, *don't need my services*?'

'I mean we've got our own reg'lars now. I can't afford to pay you all. Mine's a business, not a charity.' He tapped his yardstick against his leather apron.

'But I was one of your first!'

'There's too many of you in it now,' the tanner had said, 'since all the Irish…'

She looked into his plump, round face. His lips seemed even more gross than usual.

'It's not my post to keep you all employed,' he'd said. 'The quickest, most efficient pickers keep the work. Simple as that. Some of you have got to go. There ain't no helping it.'

'Then pay each of us a little less,' she'd said. 'Keep me on for something at least?'

'It ain't gonna happen.' He dismissed her with two shillings for her losses. She knew he was getting a cheaper load from the dog pound. And much more of it. The city was overrun by ten thousand muck-rakers and collectors of pure. What did such a man care for the fortunes of just one of them?

She spent the two shillings on a hawker's license and began selling flowers – primroses, violets, wallflowers, stocks. She started early and left the house before her boys went off to lessons – a Ragged School close to home, paid for by a Jewish benefactor who taught them arithmetic, handwriting, simple tool work. Both Silas and Arthur were passable readers. Silas could turn a sum.

'One day I'll be rich,' he'd told her, on more than one occasion.

'There you go, getting ideas in your head,' she'd said.

'I will be. One day. Just you watch. Sooner than you think.'

'Course you will, Silas. Just keep to your station and learn enough so you don't have to pick pure.'

Once they were at lessons, she made her way to her spot by the water pump, next to a washerwoman and a patterer, a broadsheet seller, whose lurid tales of crimes and passions kept her mildly entertained. What with the comings and goings of folks pumping water, the spot guaranteed her a reasonable trade.

'Roses, pinks, carnations,' she called over the clank of buckets and kettles, the slooshing of the spigot. There she sat in her dark print frock and blackened bonnet, a threadbare shawl around her shoulders, a pair of worn-out brogans on her feet. It was gentlemen mostly who took sprigs for their buttonholes, or posies for their wives, or mistresses. It wasn't her business to ask questions. The work brought her a shilling a day. Better paid than the pure. And at least the scent surrounding her days had turned from foul to sweet. She sat up evenings in her chair by the stove, making bouquets to sell in the morning.

Tonight she had fallen asleep before the job was done. But now she'd been awakened by some animal disturbing the buckets outside and her boys were missing. Finding the three of them gone, she raised an alarm with the neighbours.

They lived in the back of a two-up-two-down. The front was taken by a shopkeeper, Greaves, his wife whom she never saw much, and their daughter, Nellie. A young girl the same age as Arthur. Mary often saw them sitting on the wall together, passing an innocent moment, until his elder brother came to tease them and pulled his brother away to do whatever things her boys did together. She liked Nellie well enough and wondered whether the girl and Arthur would still have time for each other when it came to courting. Upstairs to the front lived an Irish labourer, his wife and three children – a noisy family, headed by a brute. Mr. Kelly. Mary avoided them. The family who lived to the first-floor rear were quieter – a mechanic, his wife and their children.

A band of these disgruntled folk had gathered in the alleyway behind the terrace, unhappy at being roused in the middle of the night, but perhaps there were burglars about. They stood gossiping amongst themselves. Mary hung back in her own yard, shifting pails from a corner and then moving them back. It was unlike her boys to sneak out of the house without her knowing.

It wasn't long before the police arrived with two of her sons in hand. Fletcher left the barrow outside the back gate and Bunce ushered the older boys through. George's body lay in the alleyway, draped in sackcloth taken from the midden yard. His head lolled on the slope of the barrow. His legs hung over the brim towards the handles.

'Holy Mary mother of Christ!' Mrs. Kelly hollered.

'Get back inside woman,' her husband said, clipping at his children's heads with a flick of his wrist.

'Show is over people,' constable Bunce announced.

The straggling neighbours went indoors, looking back to catch whatever morbid glimpse they might. Inside the yard, Mary stopped and looked at her two shuffling sons, their hands cuffed behind their backs. George was conspicuous in his absence. She looked from sons to policemen and back again. Her tears came quick on the heels of her anger.

'Where in God's name have you been?' she cried. 'Where's my Georgie?'

'Ma'am,' said constable Bunce, 'perhaps you'd like to step back inside...?' He pushed Arthur and Silas and they stumbled in under their mother's tearful gaze.

'Tell me what you've done!' she bawled. 'I've been nearly dead with worry.'

The boys stood in the moonlit yard not knowing where to look.

'What's that dre'ful look on your faces? Georgie! Where's George?'

'Ma'am,' said the officer again. 'This matter's best conducted inside the house.'

In those moments, Silas felt his whole world changing – his mother sobbing before him, their family diminished, his own fate uncertain. Surely he'd be flogged. Sent to reform prison. And what of Arthur? He could hear George's voice nagging at him, 'I hate your stupid plan. You said *Honour bright*.' He closed his eyes and tried to blank it out, but all he could picture was George's head sinking ever further into that putrid mass.

Fletcher brought George's body inside from the barrow. A heavy scent wafted off the child's corpse and filled the room. Mary moaned. Her knees gave way, the floor seemed to move beneath her feet and the very fabric of her dingy room began to cave in around her. And yet she found the strength to pull her little boy's clothes off, mired as they were in all kinds of offensive matter. She laid his naked body tenderly on the table. The officer bagged his clothes in a hessian sack. Mary fetched the kettle and poured its lukewarm water over her son's body, barely able to hold the vessel steady, her hands shaking as if palsied. She sponged down his face, his filthy hair, moaning beneath her breath with each stroke. She draped her dead son's body with her shawl.

Silas knew then that George would always be there in his mind exactly as he was now, laid out in this hateful little room. Naked. Reeking. Dead. He knew that his brother would forever haunt him with that distressed and sorrowful look in his eyes, the one he'd had just before Silas sent him running across the rooftops. He fought back his tears at what he himself might now be facing. A beating, sure. The clink, perhaps. It was his fault, but not entirely his. Yes, *he* had put his brother in the gravest danger. *He* had made the boy come along on their mission to steal Tattersall's pure. *He* had led the lad through the maze of streets, chased by the bobbies. By Tattersall and his dogs. And *he* had made him run across the decaying roof of the cesspools.

But it wasn't *he*, Silas, who had piled up all that filth in the first place. It wasn't *he* who had left there, in the heart of their district, all the crud and dung. He could do nothing about bringing George back to life, but he *could* do something about what had killed him. He swore to himself that when he was freed, after whatever punishment was coming his way, he'd clear up the muck and the shit. He'd cart the wretched nightsoil clean away. His wounded shoulder burned with a bright pain as he made himself these promises.

He looked again at George's body on the table and felt as though something of his brother was lifting itself from beneath the shroud. It floated across the room and entered him – a tiny glimmer of light, of warmth. A fragment of his soul perhaps; a simple glint of recognition that, from this dreadful accident, some small good might yet come. He sensed his own tears running down his cheeks and felt himself washed clean.

Meanwhile, Mary Hunt wept and, when she had finished weeping, her boys were marched out by the Law and taken into custody.

Overnight and into the following morning, blinds were drawn across Mary Hunt's window. She could afford neither black crape nor funeral mutes to stand at the threshold. What little money she did have would be needed for interment. The benevolence of the neighbours did not stretch to mutes or crape.

George's body rested on top of an old linen cloth gifted by her neighbour, Mrs. Grieves. Her son's face was the one peaceful thing in the room. Mary herself was frantic with useless activity. She sat tying wilted flowers into bundles then, hating their appearance, destroyed them, scattering the blooms across the floor.

By noon the parish cart had come to take the body away for the coroner. For the rest of that day, he lay on a cold and indifferent mortuary table in the back room of the police station. Above his head, a barred window set high in the wall shed miserly rays on his naked form. From the hour he had suffocated, to the hour when he should have been taking his morning slice of bread, his early cup of tea, his boyish muscles had begun to stiffen. By lunchtime his whole body had braced, his delicate mouth gone into a horrible rictus.

In the dim light of mid-afternoon, two men entered the room and began to inspect the body. Coroner and Medical Examiner. The coroner wore a cambric suit, a loose cravat, a tatty velvet cap on his head. His cheeks were framed with muttonchops. The man dabbed continuously at his forehead with a grubby handkerchief.

Behind him, the medical examiner swept ceremoniously across the room. He removed his grey flannel overcoat and hung it over the back of a chair, standing now in his chequered three-piece and bowler. Sunbeams breached the bars and caught his golden, jeweled tiepin with tiny glints. 'Shall we?'

The coroner shuffled forward and prodded at the body. 'What a way to go!'

'The boy's convulsions in the filth have speeded rigor mortis,' the medical examiner murmured.

'Indeed,' the coroner nodded. 'Pathological changes, if you please?'

The medical examiner looked askance at his colleague and, ignoring him, swept in front. He began to inspect the body, humming gently to himself. With gloved fingers he lifted the dead boy's left hand and inspected the fingers. 'Maceration at the finger pads,' he noted. 'Damage to the fingertips and tearing of the fingernails consistent with attempts to grasp objects while... submerged.'

The coroner began scribbling in his notebook.

'Material under the nails,' the medical examiner observed, before letting the arm drop. 'Pass me that handkerchief,' he requested.

The rag was passed, and the medical examiner wiped the fingers of his gloves where he had held the dead boy's hand. The handkerchief was passed back, and the coroner continued mopping his sweat. The medical examiner shifted his position to the corpse's head, where he peered between the parted lips and teeth.

'Foam in the windpipe, exuding from the mouth and nostrils...' he said.

'Mouth and nostrils,' echoed the coroner, scrawling at pace.

'Spasm of the larynx,' continued the examiner. 'Traces of...' he paused, '*matter*... in the windpipe, consistent with ante-mortem immersion.'

The coroner wiped his own mouth on his pocket rag and

coughed. The examiner turned owl-wise towards him, then proceeded. 'Skin abrasions over the prominent points of the face, anterior trunk and extremities. I note significant oedema.'

'Damn this light,' said the coroner, only half-listening. 'One can barely see to write! What was that?'

'Oedema,' the examiner pronounced impatiently.

The coroner cocked an inquisitive look.

'Swelling, Sir. Swelling!'

'Indeed,' muttered the coroner and scribbled again. 'Swelling.'

'Shoulder-girdle bruises, consistent with ruptured muscles in the submerged struggle,' the medical examiner dictated. 'Congested conjunctivae.'

'Your pardon?'

'The eyes, Sir. The eyes, deuce damn it!'

'Indeed,' said the coroner. 'Do proceed.'

'Lividity, most prominent on the head, neck and anterior chest, mottled and irregularly distributed.'

The medical examiner brushed his hands together and turned away from the body. 'All indications suggest that the victim was alive and conscious at the time of immersion, resulting in drowning... shall we say "suffocation"... caused by childish misadventure.'

'"Suffocation" it is, Sir.' The coroner wiped furiously at his forehead, as though trying to rub away the very taint of George Hunt's death.

The examiner then picked up his overcoat and slid his arms into the sleeves. 'Our work is done,' he declared with some satisfaction. 'Born in the shit. Raised in the shit. And to the shit they shall, inevitably, return,' he said disinterestedly. 'Shall we?'

The coroner held the door open and the officialdom of the parish departed.

George Hunt's body was carted through the rain to the workhouse chapel where it lay-in overnight. He had, at least, been cleaned and dressed in a rinsed shirt and shorts. Mary's neighbours had dropped loose coppers into a tin; she'd never been able to pay the fees of the Burial Club and so there was no pay-out against the demise of her son. Without the charity of parish and neighbours, who knew where George would have come to rest, or if he would have found a resting place at all. Most likely his body would have ended up on some surgeon's table, she thought, a student doctor's experiment. At least she'd been there to claim him as her own flesh and blood. She'd saved him the indignities of the dissection table, where so many other poor folks she'd heard of were going.

The following morning, rain unabated, the sexton appeared, an old, bearded man in stocking cap, neckerchief, waistcoat and gaiters. He lifted the rickety lid of the coffin so that the mother could see her son one last time. The coffin walls were flimsy, and the cover bore no nameplate. Instead, the sexton had chalked the boy's name on the lid in crude, misspelled lettering. *Gorge Hunt.*

Mary Hunt handed the man his burial fee. 'He looks so different. His face is cold.' She touched her dead son's cheek and shivered in her black cape and bonnet. The string beneath her chin chafed at her skin. She rubbed at it distractedly.

In silence the sexton nailed the coffin shut, each hammer blow registering in Mary's spine. She blenched, her muscles stiffening.

Lid secured, the sexton shouldered the box and carried it haltingly out through the rain to the municipal plot. Mary followed slowly behind, her bonnet barely keeping the raindrops from her face. When they reached the patch of disturbed soil, the sexton pulled away some heavy wooden sleepers to reveal the communal grave, before lowering the coffin on top; a teetering tower of boxes and bodies, as cramped now in death as they had been while living cheek-by-jowl in their crowded courts.

George's coffin lay in a deepening pool of muddy water. There was neither headstone, nor marker of any kind. Neither was there a priest to offer spiritual succour, nor words of earthly condolence. Mary stood beside the sexton. The man removed his stocking cap and began some rudimentary and bored intonation, leaning on his spade.

'God, Heavenly Father, maker of all, who knows our thoughts and our sins...'

His voice was indifferent, hurried. Mary would have preferred him to say nothing at all. She stared into the reflective sheen of his bald head and hated him. Then she hated herself for her grudging spirit. Before he had finished his prayer, the man's cap was back in place. *The Lord giveth, and the Lord taketh away*, she thought to herself.

As the sexton finished, Mary's thoughts wandered, struggling to recall the last time she had seen George alive. He must have been there in front of the fire with his brothers that night, before they'd... She tried to solace herself with a homely image but couldn't keep the tears from coming. She wiped them away with her sleeve as the sexton readied himself with his shovel.

The man began tipping soil into the hole. It rattled down on the vanishing lid of her boy's coffin, just as the rain rattled down on the pair of them. She shuddered with each and every one of the sexton's tumbling shovelfuls. The planks of the coffin looked as though they might give way with each load. In her hands she held a flimsy arrangement of leftover blooms from her basket. She couldn't afford to throw good ones into her son's grave. She kissed the makeshift posy and tossed it in. It disappeared beneath a heavy fall of earth.

'He's in his long home now,' Mary said sorrowfully. 'Wait for me in Heaven, won't you dear Georgie.'

During those nights and days of Mary Hunt's grief, officers Fletcher and Bunce had hurried Silas and Arthur to the station where they each spent their time alone in cold, bare lockups. Their time had passed in silence and unease. The wound on Silas's arm had begun to fester. In the neighbouring cell, he could hear

Arthur crying. In his own, his growing fever tipped him in and out of agitated dreams.

First it was visions of his mother, wailing uncontrollably. 'What's that dre'ful look on your faces? Georgie. George!' She wasn't old, he knew but, with dark hollows around her eyes, sunken cheeks and sallow skin, she looked more like a woman of fifty than the thirty years that had actually shaped her. There was something in all that pure she'd collected that had made her sick. She looked exhausted. She'd been suffering for a long time, got stomach cramps and the runs all the while. She'd told him she thought her eyes were going. The pure could do that to you. Make you blind. That was why he had wanted the pure: to sell it for money to pay for a doctor. He had done it for her.

Then it was visions of little George himself just... *vanishing*... mid-air, an absence in the moonlight, then falling, falling endlessly through the darkness behind Silas's eyes, landing dead with a thump, dead on the midden, dead in the wheelbarrow, dead on the parlour table.

Then came the visions of his father, William. Dead himself these several years. Visions of him with hands stained brown from tanner's oak; the wizened, wheezing form of a man poisoned by smoke, stinking lime, caustic fumes and endless labour. A man who'd lost his self-respect in groveling to the tannery foreman, just to keep his hateful job.

Within two days, the case was brought against the brothers at the Petty Sessions.

'Silas!' Arthur called as they emerged from their cells into daylight.

Silas looked at his brother. Arthur's face looked puffy and his skin so white it was almost blue. It felt as though they'd been separated at birth, now reunited.

'Where's ma?' said Arthur.

'Dunno.' A shutter had descended in Silas's mind, closing off all thought, all feeling, save for the smarting pain in his arm. He couldn't think straight. The infection and fever were making him delirious.

'P'raps she'll be in the courtroom?' Arthur's eyes were hopeful. 'What'll they do to us?'

Bunce's face leaned-in close across the station desk. 'Button it!' His moustache and beard jiggled on his rounded features.

The courtroom was in very poor condition: a wooden-paneled backroom in the basement of the magistrate's house, dilapidated, ill ventilated and smelling of mold. Silas could smell the trace of rot and decay drifting into the room from the sewers and conduits that lay beneath the house footings, and from the open runnels in the street below the window.

He looked up at the bench, a podium to one side of the room, where two desk lamps stood, one to each side, their silk shades yellowed and fraying. There sat the magistrates, the Reverend James Puddephatt and the Reverend Thomas Tyrwhitt, as their gold-lettered nameplates declared at the front of their desks. Tyrwhitt was an elderly man, with a lean face, a chiselled nose above a white moustache and a pair of glasses balanced across its bridge. Puddephatt was overweight and rosy, his white beard obscuring his bloated lips. The beard descended to the middle of his chest above his black robes, where it left a messy scribble of stray white hairs.

In a disorganised manner, the Clerk, Mr. Boakes, ushered in the two arresting officers. Boakes readjusted his courtroom wig, which had become trapped in the high collar of his jacket. As he walked back to bring in the sole witness, Tom Tattersall, the clerk's short-hemmed trousers climbed ever higher up his shins.

The brothers were made to stand behind a bar. Arthur looked to Silas in alarm, his eyes in search of their mother. Silas's mind was blank. He barely noticed his mother's absence. Instead, he vacantly watched Tattersall take off, put on, take off, his bowler hat. Bunce and Fletcher were standing like two bookends, one to either side of the witness stand, the one rounded and moustached, the other tall and clean-shaven. Mr. Boakes shuffled between the officers and Tattersall, before settling at his desk below the magistrates' podium. Each time he wished to address them, he had to turn his head and crook his neck like some strange bird.

'Recognizances of the defendants, Mr. Boakes?' boomed Puddephatt in a voice too big for the room.

'Messrs Arthur and Silas Hunt, milords,' said Boakes, twisting back and forth between defendants and judges. 'Some thirteen and fourteen years respectively. Approximately.'

'Well, are they or are they not?' said Puddephatt.

The clerk turned to Silas. 'What's your age, lad?'

Silas looked through the man as though he wasn't there.

'I asked you a question,' Mr. Boakes urged him.

Beside him, Arthur mumbled nervously. Silas eventually spoke. 'Like you said,' he said to the clerk.

Mr. Boakes turned back to the judge none the wiser. 'They don't seem to know for certain, milord.'

'Stand forward,' Tyrwhitt ordered the boys.

Silas felt pressure at his back from Fletcher's truncheon. Arthur stood with his arms behind his back, his head drooping forwards. Silas stood clutching his arm.

'Look up at your superiors,' said Tyrwhitt, 'so we may see the truth, or the lies, in your eyes, and you may see the probity and justice in ours.'

Silas lifted his head beside Arthur. His senses were so fevered it was as much as he could manage to stand still without swaying.

'Do we have an affidavit, Mr. Boakes?' said Tyrwhitt.

'No confession necessary, m'lud,' the clerk said, 'the offenders were caught red-handed.'

'And what depredations have the boys committed?' asked the Justice.

Mr. Boakes blinked.

'What are the Summary Offences and charges against the defendants, Mr. Boakes?'

'Larceny, milord.'

'Theft of *what*, exactly, Mr. Boakes?' asked Puddephatt.

'Theft of... pure... my Lord,' Mr. Boakes replied, craning from his court ledger towards the magistrates.

'Speak up man,' said Puddephatt, irritated.

'Pure, milord,' the Clerk repeated.

'Pure? Pure! Whatever won't these felons stoop to stealing!'

Silas watched the shades on the lamps tremble.

'Any previous convictions against the two, Mr. Boakes?' asked Tyrwhitt.

'None, your Honour.'

'None that we know of at least,' muttered Tattersall from his position below the bar. Silas turned to look at his adversary and felt a coldness down his spine.

'Sir,' Puddephatt addressed the man. 'However villainous they might be – and villainous they certainly are – they are not, at least, being tried for what they might have done in the past, but for what they have done in the here and now. Understood?'

Tattersall stood corrected. 'I didn't mean nothing by it, yer 'onour.'

'As well as not. Now, what is the evidence against them Mr. Boakes?' Puddephatt asked, stroking his beard.

'Please to hear the deposition of the plaintiff, milords,' said Boakes, gesturing to Tattersall.

Silas watched the kennel man step forward and sheepishly hold his purple bowler before him, a hand on either side of the rim. He had not shaved. It was the first time Silas had seen him since the chase. A charge of hatred flickered back and forth between them.

'Name, address, age and occupation?' asked Mr. Boakes.

'Tom Tattersall. Kennel keeper. Thirty-two years of age, your excellencies. Of Dog Kennel Lane.'

'What are the facts and details of the matter, man? Who, why, what, when, where and so forth?' asked Tyrwhitt. He pushed his glasses onto the bridge of his nose and leaned forward.

'That boy there,' said Tattersall, pointing aggressively towards Silas, 'the varmint who's clutchin' his arm...'

'There is no need to excoriate the boy now we have him in custody,' Tyrwhitt tutted.

'Your honour?' Tattersall shuffled dumbly in his boots.

'That the boy is a villain, Mr. Tattersall, goes without saying!'

'Of course, yer 'onour. Sorry, yer 'onour.' Tattersall dipped his head. 'Shall I...?'

'Yes! Go on man, go on!' Puddephatt rapped his knuckles on the desk.

'Well, your 'onours, he broke into my kennels and helped hisself to a sack of pure. Pure that I sell to the tanners for preservin' their leather. Pure, on which I make my very living...'

'What proof is there that it was *this* boy?' asked Tyrwhitt.

The dog handler dipped his hand into his pocket and pulled out a scrap of bloodied cloth. Silas felt sick to his core. 'He wounded hisself on my wires, my Lord. Here's what he left behind on the barbs.'

'The evidence seems to match the boy's coat exactly,' said Puddephatt, poking with the stick of his gavel at the scrap of cloth presented to him. 'It would certainly account for the wound on his arm. Tell me boy,' he directed at Silas, 'are you injured? Did you harm yourself in this heinous escapade?'

Silas stared up at the two judges but could barely make them out. His senses were spinning.

'Incontrovertibly!' said Tyrwhitt, turning the piece of cloth over and over.

'Boy...' thundered Puddephat, 'how did you maim yourself?'

Silas looked at his judge, again unsure of whether he should – whether he could – speak or not.

'Speak boy,' prompted the Clerk with a thin, reedy expression.

'Like he said, Sir,' Silas replied weakly.

'Well, there you have it,' said Tyrwhitt. 'We need waste no more time. The sprig has confessed. Have the stolen... goods... now been sequestered?'

'Yes, my Lord,' said Boakes. 'Retrieved, if not returned.'

'Meaning?' said Tyrwhitt.

'I went to c'llect it from where the rogues had hidden it, Sir,' Tattersall explained.

'So you are not out of pocket then?' Tyrwhitt asked.

'No, milord,' said Tattersall. 'Only out of time and on account of troublesome sukumstances...'

'Indeed,' said Tyrwhitt. 'Inconvenience and so forth.' He turned to his colleague and addressed him. 'The case seems cut and dried?'

'Cut and dried,' said Puddephatt. 'The deponent may step down.'

Tattersall looked to the magistrates, then to Boakes, to constables Fletcher and Bunce and then to the boys.

'Step down man,' Tyrwhitt said, waving his hand at Tattersall to shoo him from the stand. The kennel keeper stepped back and replaced his bowler. Puddephatt stared at him and the dog-handler removed it.

'Boys like yourselves was born to be hanged, you little wasterals,' Tattersall passed judgment.

Silas shook at the thought. Beside him he could feel Arthur trembling in his shoes, his lips moving silently.

'That would, in this case, seem a little severe,' said Puddephatt. 'Now, we move to sentence,' the Justice added.

'Milord...' said Boakes.

'What is it man? Speak.'

'There is the other matter.'

'What other matter, man?' said Puddephatt. 'Speak plainly, Sir. This is a court of Law, not a penny gaff for entertaining mysteries!'

'The death of the brother, Sir,' said Mr. Boakes.

'The brother looks perfectly alive to me!' Puddephatt boomed.

'No, Sir,' said Boakes. 'The dead boy. The little one. George Hunt, Sir. Was buried two days ago.' Silas winced. Arthur's quaking shoulder juddered against his own.

'There is *another* brother?' said Tyrwhitt. 'Will these people *never* stop breeding?'

'Yes, milord. Another brother. George Hunt, Sir. Deceased,' said the Clerk.

'The lad was corpsed that day,' Tattersall interjected.

'Silence man!' shouted Tyrwhitt. 'Dead or alive,' the magistrate demanded, 'what does any of this have to do with the case at hand?'

'He died on account of the theft, milord,' said the Clerk. 'If it pleases your Honours,' Boakes went on, 'the officer may explain.'

Silas watched as Bunce stepped forward. The policeman cleared his throat, wiped his brow and took out his notebook. Silas listened hazily as Bunce divulged the details of George's death. When the sergeant had finished, he stepped back to his position beside his colleague. The Justices looked to each other again.

'Is there any family?' Puddephatt asked.

'Yes, your honour,' said Bunce. 'Mother, Mary Hunt. Father is deceased.'

Silas's heart quickened at his mother's name.

'And where is Mrs. Hunt?' Puddephatt inquired. 'Not present to hear the fate of her progeny, eh?'

'Infirmary, your honour,' said Bunce. 'Took a grave chill in the rain at the young boy's funeral by all accounts.'

Silas let out a weak groan. Arthur's breath was rasping fast and fitfully.

'Silence boys!' Tyrwhitt exclaimed, gesturing as if to bat away a fly.

Puddephatt cleared his throat. He leaned forwards and addressed the boys. Silas stared into his eyes like he was staring into a drain. '*If* we were considering theft... and theft alone,' the Justice said, 'then this court might have shown you measured justice and meted you out your just deserts of a simple, yet merited, flogging...'

Once again Silas winced at the word.

'However...' the Justice went on, pointing his fat forefinger at the brothers, 'given the circumstances of this death by misadventure of your poor brother, a death for which you both must take an equal share of the blame, and for which you shall always carry the burden of guilt, let alone the effect this escapade has probably had on your luckless mother's health… the sentence for theft alone cannot suffice.'

Silas looked to Arthur, adrift on the Justice's speech. Over his shoulder he could see Tattersall looking bewildered and, to his side, the Clerk, also seemingly lost to the meaning of Puddephatt's ruling.

'It is the condign judgment of this court, therefore,' the Justice growled, 'that both of you shall learn the harder lesson for such gross turpitude. You may have abandoned decent Christian ways, and education may have failed you for the ignorant guttersnipes you have so plainly become, but there are other means to make you useful to society and turn you from your ways. Poor you may remain, immoral you shall not!'

Silas stood impassively. Beside him Arthur was shaking at the impending verdict.

'Twenty stripes with the birch…' Puddephatt left a weighty pause. Silas could hear Arthur's heels clacking against the boards in fright, but the verdict barely registered on his own face. 'And…' the judge continued, 'one month's hard labour in the Bridewell.'

The wind huffed from Arthur's chest.

'No sniveling there, boy!' Tyrwhitt shouted. 'Your new home,' he concluded, 'shall be the house of correction. May it serve *us* well in remedying your rampant ways. And may it serve *you* well as you consider the righteousness of ours. The case is closed. Officers, remove the prisoners.'

The walls of correction stood in a tall, grey pentagram, a tower looming at each corner, a grey shadow cast to the pavements beneath, where a few grey figures in their freedom hurried past those inside who had lost their own. Through the gatehouse, with its imposing pillars, its heavy arch dated and adorned with wreaths and overhung with a barely-flaming gas lamp; through the gatehouse with its huge wooden doors studded with great rounds of iron; through the little wicket doorway set in the bottom corner of that daunting entrance; through these defences, the walls of the inner courtyard declared themselves, as the horse-drawn prison van rattled up and delivered Silas and Arthur Hunt to their reckoning.

Inside, yet more grey. The walls of each wing were arranged in a star that spread out from a central point, from where the watchman could sit in his tower with a perfect view and take in every action and deed, each whispered word, simply by swivelling himself around in an arc on his seat.

This all-encompassing grey star was surely the only star to grace these acres, for no object in the sky ever shone favourably on those ill-favoured boys inside. All that came down on their heads was rain and snow and the heavy weight of the Law. No human sound could penetrate those walls to remind them of their former lives. Nor birdsong, or barking dogs, or whinnying horses at the dray or carriage. No babble of water hurrying by in a stream. No chatter of wind in the trees. Just silent greyness without and within, and one long, grey, silent month looming in the minds of Silas and Arthur Hunt.

On admission, Silas was giddy with infection. His wound was weeping. His fever had taken hold of his mind. They sent him straight away to the hospital wing where he passed his first hours imprisoned in delirium.

For Arthur, the arrival was blunter. No sooner was he through the wicket gate, than he found himself in the governor's office, hurriedly strapped by the wrists face-down across the flogging pony, his back and buttocks bared, a guard to each side of him, a gag in his mouth and twenty stripes across the naked skin of his back, his rump, his legs, each crack of the birch delivered with jurisdictive zeal by the unflinching hand of the Governor, Mr. Hardonby.

'With five extra for good measure,' the man added.

No sooner had this been done than his clothes were pulled back up and Arthur was bundled upright. 'I trust that makes you feel a *touch* more contrite now, boy?' Hardonby's smug amusement rattled in Arthur's drumming ears. 'You ruffians may lack what we might call *natural intelligence*,' the Governor said, 'but a little discipline will polish you up and maybe even make you worth a little bit to someone. Possibly.' Arthur stood wiping his tears, his whole body shaking. 'Oh, take the snivelling child away,' the Governor said. 'Process him.'

In a high corner of the prison, locked in a ward and strapped to a bed, Silas would have to wait for this punishment but, for now, the hospital ward was terrifying enough. There was a boy in the bed next to him whose face was pitted with pox and who looked like some grotesque, warty toad. Next to this boy was another whose legs were bandy and twisted like some strange insect from the back of a bush. In his hallucinations, Silas saw the toad's slobbery mouth crunching down on the limbs of the brittle little insect.

The whole place smelled to him of whitewash and something foreign. It stung his nostrils and eyes. As he swam in and out of awareness, he heard the nurse speaking to the Medical Officer – 'Yes Mr. Tait, Sir. Certainly Mr. Tait, Sir' – and watched her bustle about her business under the stern eye of her superior.

Through the clouds of his dreams, he saw the doctor wash his hands in some dark liquid from a bottle, before coming at him with a poultice. He struggled to free himself from the pain but couldn't move – his arms and legs were strapped to the bunk with coarse webbing. It cut into his skin through the sheets. His head swam. He watched the doctor treating the wound on his arm. 'Carbolic!' the medical man snapped through his beard to the nurse, who duly supplied him with the astringent. 'Iodine,' he rumbled again. Silas recoiled at the bite of the compounds. 'Bind that poultice, sister.'

The nurse stepped forward. Silas looked up at her face encircled by a white bonnet. He searched in her eyes for something kind and, as he searched, her features shifted into those of the mother he missed so badly. 'Ma?' he whispered weakly. 'I didn't mean it, ma...'

The woman's voice grated back at him. 'I certainly aren't your ma.'

The image of Mary's face dissolved. He watched the vision peel away like a pretty mask pared off a street entertainer.

'You won't be seeing her again in a hurry neither,' the nurse added. But Silas had already passed out into troubled dreams.

His dreams came and went with his fever over several days. Mostly they were of ravening dogs. Of Tattersall and policemen and prison cells. Of judges and trembling lampshades. But his first night was more unsettled. He was lying strapped in his bed, staring at the standard lamp that stood in the corner of the sick bay. Carved from dark mahogany, with three feet curling underneath itself like a tripod of snakes, the gas lamp stood about the height of a boy. At its apex there was a lantern shade of coloured glass that looked like the turban of an oriental genie he had seen on music hall posters pasted up on city walls. Within the glass, the gas wick burned diffusely, casting a weak yellow light across the ward. Next to him, the toad-boy's face twisted itself in ugly, darkened grimaces. In the wider shadows cast by the lamp, the insect-boy's legs seemed to crawl up the wall in murky shapes. Silas stared hard at the lamp itself until, the more he stared, the stranger it became to him: the lantern on top seemed to transform into a human head; the stem of the lamp into a thin, frail body; the sinuous feet of the lamp into legs and pint-sized boots, until there, in front of him, stood the figure of his brother George, alive once again, his light poll of hair, his familiar features and smile radiating from the buttery glow of the lamp.

'Is that really you, George?' Silas whispered.

The ghostly boy in shabby linen jacket, grubby vest and knee-length shorts, pulled at his ill-matched stockings. 'Course it's me Silas. Don't you know it?'

'But how did you...? I thought you were...?'

'I am,' said the boy, floating towards the sickbed. 'Dead, Silas. Dead.'

Silas scrunched his eyes tight, struggling to shake himself free of his restraints. But he could do no more than wriggle beneath his sheets and soon lay motionless.

'Don't worry yourself,' said George. 'Don't worry, Silas. You're fine. But look at me.'

Silas opened his eyes slowly and saw that the spirit of his brother was still there, hovering at the foot of his bed.

'I told you we shouldn't be out stealing pure,' said George. 'I told you we shouldn't run over the rooftops. I told you it was all bad down there. You said *Honour bright*, remember?'

'I'm sorry,' cried Silas. 'I'm sorry, George. I'm gonna make it good for you. You watch me, George. I'm gonna do away with all that muck. I'm gonna do it for you, George. All for you.'

'I don't like it,' said George. 'The smell, the stench, the rottenness. I don't like it. It lingers on me, Silas. Clean it up, can't you?' the voice implored, 'clean me, clean me...'

'Yes!' Silas cried, echoing his brother. 'Clean me, clean me!'

Within moments, the nurse was standing beside his bed, a small bottle of liquid in her hand, a few drops placed upon his lips. 'Oh, I'll clean you, you rascal,' she reproved him. 'Don't you dare wake up the others!'

The bitter drops made their way from the nurse's pipette, between Silas's lips, across his tongue and trickled down his throat. He choked them back and, almost immediately, began to feel their soothing effect. Slowly, the figure of his brother faded back into the shape of the lamp and then the lampshade too began to fade into the blackness of sleep.

When he awoke, the wound on his arm was still irritated, but it felt to him that something had begun to shift within him. His arm festered for a few more days, through poultice changes and more carbolic acid and then, with their combined effects and some inner will of his own, Silas Hunt at last began to recover.

While Silas lay dreaming of George in the infirmary, Arthur was learning what a month in reform was actually going to mean. The prison was packed with boys, a nursery bed of crime. Each wore the uniform of their shame, their number sewn onto the breast pocket of their jacket. Everywhere he looked he saw nothing but a sea of cropped heads. His own had been shaved no sooner had they finished flogging him. 'Rid you of them bloody lice and fleas,' the barber had laughed at him as his scissors snickered. After he was shorn, he had been made to stand naked in front of a man who doused him with a bucket of freezing water. It stung to high heaven on the welts of his flogging. These humiliations happened to everyone, he presumed, although he doubted whether any of the boys in here had seen a bucket of water since. Everywhere he turned he smelt nothing but sweat and the stench of unwashed bodies. Yet the most oppressive thing of all was not the smell. It was the brooding silence of the place.

The silence, he soon found out, was imposed: a boy could earn himself another flogging from Hardonby for talking out of line. So it was that all their talking was done in whispers. At night. And mostly in code. A language he didn't understand at first at all. 'Swercs, tou kool...' he heard them whisper in back-slang, when one of the warders patrolled the yard. Or else he heard the remnants of a jargon these boys had learned while travelling with Romanies. 'Vada the parni,' they said looking glumly through the barred windows at the rain. Food, whenever it was slopped up was 'Numgare'. *Oni duey tray quarto* they counted themselves to sleep at night.

Arthur didn't know how he was going to last a month – if he thought his *head* was spinning, then his *feet* were spinning faster. He had been put straight away to walking the treadmill. Its cylinder was kept revolving by stepping up onto boards, as though it was some kind of flour mill, and the boys were nothing but human water turning the paddles. Except there was no purpose to this. No flour to be milled. 'Just grinding the wind,' his neighbor whispered the first time he found himself on the wheel. A slight boy, younger than himself. George's age, or thereabouts.

To their side, a Screw stood watching closely, listening for chatter, tightening the lever for greater resistance whenever he heard a whisper. By the time he had finished his first stint on the wheel, Arthur was exhausted. They stepped down from the mill dejectedly. While the guard was distracted with some commotion at the end of the line, they took their chance to pass a few words.

'What you so lemoncholy about then?' His neighbour's lower lip hung open beneath his heavy eyelids.

'What?' said Arthur.

'What you moping about?' repeated the boy. After each phrase he licked around his lips as though they were coated in something sweet.

'I ain't moping,' said Arthur.

'Oh, it's nuffink is it? They'll have us pickin' oakum next, you watch.'

'Oakum?' Arthur whispered back.

'Old ropes. Buckets of thread. "Tow" they call it. Christ, you're greener than goose shit you are!' Carelessly the boy scratched at his scalp and inspected beneath his fingernails, flicking away some matter.

Arthur looked away in disgust. 'What's it for, oakum?'

'Stuffing cracks on board of ships. Stops 'em sinking.'

'Sounds terrible.'

'T'ain't so bad. T'ain't so bad in 'ere neither. You'll get used to it.'

Arthur couldn't imagine how that might be true. He looked at his companion's puppy-fat cheeks, his heavy eyes, his hanging lip. All he could think about was George. His hideous death. How much he missed him. How much he missed his mother. Was she better? Was she even allowed to come and visit them?

To their side, the Screw returned to their end of the line and shouted. 'Alright, shut your gabbing.' He swished a stick in front of their faces. Arthur dropped his head and shuffled away from the mill.

'Awright,' the boy said boldly.

The guard edged forward, cane in hand. 'Don't even think of chaffing me, or you'll have Mr. Woods here to think about.' Again, he let the stick cut an arc before the boy's face. 'Step away from the treadmill, boy.'

Silently, the lad did as he was told, his tongue still going round his lips like a cow's.

Treadmill. Oakum. Exercise yard. Oakum. Such was the pattern of Arthur's first few days, lonely and disoriented until, at last, he saw his brother come down one morning from the fever ward. Arthur was sitting in the oakum room amid a field of hunched shoulders, each boy busily unpicking old rope and dropping the tow into their bucket. He looked up and saw Silas being led in by a Screw. He thought his brother looked better. Almost his old self. His dark hair had been shorn, just like his own, but his eyes were bright again. It looked as though his arm had healed, although he must have been bearing that other pain – the aftermath of Hardonby's flogging.

There was no chance to talk of it now, however. Their eyes simply found each other out across the room and acknowledged their presence with the slightest of nods. It was only a flick of the head and the eyes, but it was the first sign of warmth either boy had felt since that night. Arthur puffed his cheeks and blew out in relief, turning back to his oakum. Perhaps three more weeks in here might be bearable.

No sooner had this feeling begun to warm him, however, than it was crushed. 'Stone breaking. In the yard. Now. Down tools. All stand!' The Screw's whistle blew. The silence following it pressed down heavily on their shoulders. They put down their oakum in unison, stood up silently and filed out into the yard. 'Two hours of road cobbles'll sort you lot out,' the Screw laughed as they passed beneath his panoptical eye.

That night, Arthur and Silas found each other again. Perhaps

Mr. Hardonby was not as sadistic as his flogging had made them believe – Silas has been given a neighbouring cot in the same bunkroom. They sat on straw-filled sacks and chewed slices of black bread in the shadows. The Screw had left the bunkroom to inspect the other wing. In his absence, a hum of chatter struck up.

'Once a day, they make us trudge the courtyard. In circles,' Arthur said, as though recounting the treats of an outing. 'You got to hold this rope and keep your distance from the boy in front.'

Silas nodded his head.

'There's schooling too. An hour of reading and writing and adding numbers. I only done it once though.'

Again, Silas nodded. 'That's good,' he said, lost elsewhere in thought.

'Most of the boys are in for worse than us. Some's got two years. Two years, imagine it! Far as I can tell, they're all thieves and villains.'

'When did you start talking like a judge?' said Silas.

'I ain't judging no one,' said Arthur. 'Who can blame 'em? Outside of here they ain't got nuffen to live on but their wits.'

'And when did you start speaking like one of them?' Silas added.

The boy with the hanging lip was stationed in the cot beside them. He leaned over. Silas looked down at him. The boy was small like George, he thought, but with expressionless eyes. 'At least in 'ere there's clothes and bed and food,' the lip-licker said.

Silas supposed he was little more than six or seven. 'There might be bed,' he replied, 'but you've got to share it with bugs.'

'You don't wanna mind that,' said the boy. 'Just pick 'em off and crack 'em with your fingernail. "Pop" they go and don't taste half bad.'

The three of them laughed quietly.

'You get used to the bed,' said Arthur. 'Just like you get used to oatmeal and oakum. Even the treadmill.'

'Egsackly!' the young boy agreed. 'It ain't so awful. You'll even get used to the gypsy boys' chaffing.' He paused and picked at his scalp. 'What beak d'you get then?'

'What?' said Silas.

'What judge?'

'Don't know their names.' Silas's face was sullen.

'How long d'they quod you for?'

Silas stared back. 'He always talk this much, Arthur?'

The neighbour went on. 'Sent me down for a drag. Three month.'

'I couldn't last that long,' said Arthur and then, without thinking, 'I miss ma, Silas. When we gonna see her?'

'You don't *have* to go that long,' said Silas. 'Just a month. We'll see her when we're out.'

'I miss George too.'

'Who's George?' The boy leaned further over and leant on Silas's bunk.

'Mind yer own business.' Silas pushed the boy's hands off his bedding.

'Only askin'! What was up with you when they put you in the hospital then? Influenzy was it?'

'He hurt his arm,' said Arthur, pulling himself together.

'Fever.' Silas stared at his brother.

'D'they give yer a dose of Mother's Blessing when you was up there?'

Silas stared at the boy, annoyed by all his questions. Annoyed by his drooling lip. Annoyed by his habit of picking at his head.

'That lord-num kills the pain like no one's business.'

The persistent pangs had, by now, gone from Silas's arm and there was little there by way of a reminder that it had ever happened, save for an angry, scabbed scar.

'What they put you in steel for then?' the young boy asked.

'You're all questions you are, ain'tcha?'

The boy shrugged.

'Stealing,' Silas said, 'if you must know.'

'Stealin' what?' the boy asked.

'Pure,' said Silas.

The boy raised an eyebrow and laughed softly. 'You're kiddin'?'

Silas fixed him with a stare. 'It's not funny.'

'Alright, I didn't mean nothink by it.'

'Nothing bad done by it,' said Arthur.

After a moment the boy spoke again. 'What, so you went out stealin' shit and got fluttered?'

Silas ignored the question. He paused. 'What you in for then?'

'Damage to property,' the boy whispered, 'but I been done for stealin' bread, two weeks. Pickpocketin', three weeks. Vagrancy, three months. Unlawful lodgin', two months. Burglary, six months. I got nabbed by the police for garden robbin', takin' turnips off a costermonger's cart. Two months for that. I bin flogged with the cat for joov-nile link-wency.'

In the darkness Silas flashed Arthur a look. How could a boy so young have got himself into so much trouble?

'Alright, silence there!' The night warden's voice came burling across the room as he returned from his rounds. The hum of chatter died. A beam from his night-light sought out any boy who dared to talk. Looming shadows morphed on the walls like threatening figures in dark alleys. 'Stop your talking. Now! Or you'll find yourselves in the lock-up after a nice long chat with Mr. Woods.' They heard the swish of his stick through the air.

The boys bit their lips. No one wanted that – three long days and nights in solitary, with irons on your hands and no bunk, just the cold stone floor and nothing to eat and drink but bread and water. They dropped their heads onto their chaff sacks. The young boy turned away. The warder's beam passed over their heads like the tracking beam of a lighthouse at the river's mouth. The room returned to silence. Eventually they listened to the warder leave his post again, to go and check on the other dormitory.

'Silas?' whispered Arthur when he was sure the Screw had gone. Silence. 'Silas. Good night.'

Throughout the night and the nights of the weeks that followed, Silas wondered on George's ghostly visit. Whether or not he saw his ghost again, as he had done that first night in the fever ward, he couldn't be sure, but moments of clarity came upon him as though they were such a visitation. Images of George's body sinking in the mire. Of George's spirit rising through the heavens. Of George's casket buried deep in the grave. Of George's soul ascendant to the Lord. He thought of his short, unhappy life and of how he now no longer suffered its ills. Of how little George was free of all this. He thought of George in happy times, counting on the abacus at school, so proud of himself to remember his numbers and how he would run back home to tell their mother simple sums, or tell her how to spell his name. And then those pleasant memories fell through the roof and he thought of George no longer around to enjoy those things. Of his life adding up to nothing. Away with all that rots, he thought. Away with all that festers and decays. With stinks and swamps and cesspools full of shit.

They were woken early in the mornings by the watchman. Before work began, they ate bread and milk. Soured. At lunch they ate a small porringer of gruel and cabbage. Sometimes, once a week, there was some unidentifiable meat for supper. 'The meat in 'ere's so bad,' the lip-licker said, 'it might as well be bow-wow mutton,' and he'd been right. Both times they were served meat, it smelled rotten. Just once during their month, there were potatoes. Along with the soured milk, there were soured tempers. Bouts of testiness and defiance. Mostly, however, the days went by in a mundane blur of oakum picking. Rock breaking. Walking on the treadmill.

Silas and Arthur kept their heads down and their record cards clean, working in silence, the hard fibres of oakum chafing at their hands, a whole three pounds of it to unravel each day, from an eight o'clock rise to a six o'clock supper. If they could just endure it a little longer, they'd earned their right to leave and go home to their mother.

Inside, there were endless offers for how to make a living when they were released. 'I been done for thievin' handkerchiefs,' a boy would say. 'Can show you how if you like. You know, for a price, when you get out...' But Silas had promised himself. He wasn't going to be like the head-scratcher, in and out of prison his whole life. He'd do his month, get out and go to work. Little George wouldn't have died for nothing.

The month was up. The boy with the drooping lip told them what was coming. 'They'll give yer a shilling. And new clothes. You can sell 'em if you want. The whole world unnerstands prison garb. Flog 'em and get some browns in yer pocket instead.'

'That right?' Silas dismissed him.

'What you gonna do for tin when you get out then?' The boy shrugged his shoulders. 'You got to grub yerself somehow. Where you gonna live?'

'We're going home,' said Silas.

'I can't wait to see ma again, Silas.'

'Home!' the boy scoffed. 'Course you are...'"I can't wait to see ma"!'

Silas squared up to him and the lad dodged to one side. 'Alright, no harm!' His tongue went around his chops.

'I want to go to back to school,' said Arthur.

'Well lah-di-dah,' said the prison fly.

Silas pushed his face towards him and the boy quietened. 'D'you ever mind yer own business?'

'Only askin',' he said.

'Once I've done my 'prenticeship I won't have to deal with little twerps like you...'

'Prenticeship?' scoffed the lips. 'In what?'

'We're gonna be nightmen,' said Silas.

'Shovelin' shit don't take no prenticeship!'

'Neither does being locked up.'

On the morning of their release, the boy's account was proved correct. They nodded him a passing goodbye and walked out of the mess hall to the governor's office. Leaning on the flogging pony, Mr. Hardonby twitched his cane and gave them a stern speech about morals and hard work and not being sent back, his cane cutting brisk arcs before them. When he was done, he dismissed them peremptorily.

One of the Screws took them to the gate, where they received a coin from the turnkey. Out in the street, everything looked familiar, yet with a strange and harsh new light. They hardly recognised themselves, in black cloth trousers and jackets, black cotton neckerchiefs and dark caps.

'Where you going then?' the turnkey asked brusquely. Silas considered the man. He looked as though he took a mean pleasure in his job.

'Home,' he said. 'Back to our ma.'

The turnkey stared at them and laughed. The boys looked at each other and shrugged. 'They haven't told you yet, have they?' the turnkey said.

'Told us what?' said Silas.

'You don't know?'

'Know what?' said Arthur.

'She's done gone under the sod, your muvver. Just like your little bruvver before her. An' it's all on account of your doin',' he said. 'You're all on yer own, boys. All on yer tod.'

Silas heard the man's words and felt them echo in his head, around the empty quad. He looked into the turnkey's cold eyes, at the cold bricks of the prison wall. He could feel the air pricking at his shoulders. Within his chest a great heave began to rise. He turned to Arthur, as if staring into a miserable mirror. Arthur too was choking back the feeling, but Silas could feel an overwhelming rage welling inside him.

'You bloody liar!' he hollered, lunging at the man.

'Silas!' Arthur grabbed his sleeve and pulled his brother back.

The turnkey laughed and spat on the ground. 'Whoah! Big brave boy,' he mocked. 'Just you try it you little tyke.' He grabbed the baton from his belt and thrust it in Silas's face. The boy stopped short of its swinging arc. 'You'll be back in here faster than you can cry "mummy"...'

Silas stood shaking, his lips huffing out hot bursts of breath. 'Liar!' he shouted again.

'Go look for yourselves. You'll find out soon enough.' The turnkey began to close the gate. 'Be seein' you in a matter of months boys, no doubt,' he laughed. 'We'll keep your beds nice and warm for you...'

Silas listened to the heavy clunk of the deadbolt on the prison door as it slid back into place and felt the cold shilling in his pocket. He felt his anger subsiding. Beside him, he could see the tears on his brother's face. If he didn't collect himself, they'd both be sunk.

'C'mon, Arth,' he said, putting his arm about his brother's shoulder. 'Don't let him upset you. He ain't nothing but a filthy liar.'

Hours later, after picking their uncertain way home across the city, Silas and Arthur sat on the kerbside outside the place that had once been their home. There seemed to be a strange woman living in their room. 'I told you boys,' the woman said, pushing them back to the gateway with small thrusts of her broom, 'I don't know nothing about it.' She was heavily built, in a black dress, with a white, dimity apron tied at her waist. Her sleeves were rolled up to reveal two raw forearms.

'Where's our ma?' Arthur's voice was verging on hysterical.

Silas put his hand against his brother's back and ushered him out into the alley by the gate. 'It'll be alright, Arth,' he said. 'Just wait. I'll do the talking.' He watched Arthur sink down by the wall where, only a month before, George's broken body had lain in the wheelbarrow. He stepped back inside the yard where the stranger was still busying herself, moving dust from one pile to another.

'You still 'ere?' The woman raised her voice.

'We just want to know where our ma is?'

'I'm sorry sonny,' she said, 'but what they told you is true. Go to the workhouse. I dunno. I can't help you. I'm sorry.'

Above them, at the first floor, a window suddenly shot open. Silas recognised the red hair and flushed features of Mrs. Kelly. 'Didn't you hear the woman?' she shouted down. 'You in't welcome round here no more, boy! Not after what you rascals done. Your poor mother! Lord have mercy on her soul! An' that poor little brother of yours! God rest their souls, the pair of 'em. You ought to be ashamed of yourselves. Now git goin'. Go on. Away with ye! D'ye hear me, before I call the Law...'

They had never stood in good relation to the Kellys, but in that moment Silas hated the woman more than ever. Everything pointed to the same fact. The turnkey had been right. Their mother, like George, was gone. He felt the realisation settle on him like a heavy murk of fog on the river. 'What's happened to her?' he heard himself ask breathily.

Upstairs, Mrs. Kelly leaned further from the window. 'Never you mind what happened to her! You're nuthin but a pair of common murd'rers! You're lucky they din't hang yous! If you don't get goin' by the count of three, I'll be down there meself to see you off and I don't mind callin' the Peelers neither. Now, git goin', d'ye hear me?'

Downstairs, the woman with the broom looked at him despondently. 'Do as she says, sonny. We don't want any trouble. Your mother's gone. You gotta get used to it.'

'It wasn't my fault!' Silas suddenly shouted. 'It wasn't my fault!'

'That's it!' Mrs. Kelly cried from above. 'I'm comin' down, right now! If I ever find you round here again, so help me god, I swear I'll have the coppers on you murd'rin' little thieves!'

Silas watched Mrs. Kelly's head withdraw through the window. Already he could hear her heavy feet beating across the floorboards. He knew she meant it and didn't want trouble –

he'd seen the way she and her husband beat their own children and a disturbance now would only mean a quick return to the cells.

He span on his heels and nipped through the gate.

'Don't come back,' the broom said. 'Your mother's gone. This is my place now.'

Outside in the alleyway, Arthur was still crouched at the foot of the wall, his head in his hands. 'C'mon, Arth,' Silas said. 'We gotta go. Quickly.' He pulled Arthur up by his sleeve and they ran to the end of the street, turning the corner before Mrs. Kelly made it downstairs. At the end of the block they turned another corner. There they stood face to face. Silas put his hands on his brother's shoulders.

'She's gone, Arth. She's really gone.' He looked down into his brother's eyes. Like his own, Arthur's were slick with tears. He sniffed away his grief. 'We're on our own now, Arth. It's up to us.'

'Where'll we go, Si?'

'I dunno. I'll work it out.' He knew now that he had to take charge. They were on their own. But a sluggish blankness was settling on his mind. Whatever anger he'd been feeling was suddenly quelled. Anger towards Mrs. Kelly. Anger at their mother's death. Anger at the turnkey and Mr. Hardonby. The judges. The whole shitty world. It was as if a door had closed and shut his feelings off. He felt strangely calm.

Up the street a young girl was walking towards them. She approached but stood some four or five paces distant. 'Arthur?' the girl said.

Arthur turned his head, rubbing the tears from his eyes. 'Nellie?' He exhaled a puff of air, something between a cry and a laugh.

'I didn't think we'd see you again, Arthur,' she said, 'not after... what happened.' Her hair hung in braids to either side of her face. She was wearing a dark cotton dress and a pair of heavy black boots. 'You look different,' she said.

'They beat us in prison.' Arthur hugged his own shoulders.

'We're out now. This is what they give you.' He lifted the lapels of his jacket to show the girl his release garb.

Nellie held her skirts nervously at either side and twisted her hips. The hem twirled around her ankles.

'D'you know what happened?' Silas interrupted.

Nellie nodded. 'The night of the funeral. Your brother. George...'

'Yes?' Arthur had contained himself by now. 'What?'

'She got taken ill. They said it was the shock. The cold and the rain.'

'And?' Silas said coldly.

'My ma found her slumped on the flagstones. Couple of days later. In front of the fire. It wasn't lit.'

Silas considered his mother's cold, lonely death.

'We got her carried to the workhouse 'ospital.' Nellie looked down at her boots. Her braids dangled forwards. 'I don't know how long it took. Sorry. That's where she...' she paused, 'passed away.'

Arthur smiled weakly at the girl. 'Thanks, Nellie.'

They measured each other in the cold light. 'You better get going,' the girl said. 'I heard Mrs. Kelly shoutin'.'

'She's always bloody shoutin'!' Silas looked over his brother's shoulder to see if the woman had followed them. She was probably standing at the gateway, arms crossed, huffing and puffing to no one in particular. The three of them laughed unconvincingly.

'Where'll you go?' said Nellie.

'I dunno.' Arthur smiled wanly.

'Look after yourselves,' the girl said. 'Be seein' you. Don't forget me.' Then she was gone.

Arthur turned to his brother, a new emptiness spreading in his chest. 'Where we gonna sleep tonight then, Si? I'm cold.'

'I dunno, Arthur, but it ain't gonna be on this street, nor any other.' Silas looked resolute. The afternoon was drawing on and soon dusk would be settling.

'Where then? They only gave us a couple of shillings.'

'It'll keep us in food and lodgings for a few days.'

'I don't want to stay in no doss houses, Si. They're no better'n prison.'

'Don't be daft, Arthur! I don't want to sleep in no doorway!' Momentarily the two boys seemed to stand each other off. 'Look, we'll sell off this prison garb and get something for it, just like Lip Licker said. Once we've got some new trousers and a jacket we can pass anywhere. Thre'pence'll get us a shared cot somewhere. It'll be just like the old days Arthur. Back at home abed together.'

'I s'pose so,' Arthur agreed. His brother seemed to have a plan in mind.

'C'mon then,' said Silas, 'let's get it sorted.'

They wandered the back lanes and traded their release clothes with a seamstress – she would get her money back returning the cloth to the gaol – and out they stepped in some hand-me down jackets and shorts.

'I feel funny,' Arthur said.

'We'll get used to 'em,' said Silas. 'Better'n being recognised as a release boy, right?'

Shortly after, they found a doss house to overnight in, near to where their family had lived until recently. They paid their pennies up front. The landlord sat at his desk, a chicken bone in one hand, a toothpick in the other. His cracked smile revealed a maw of black and missing teeth.

'Shared cots at the back,' he belched at them, pointing in the direction of some figures dossed down at the rear.

As they walked to a low-slung bed by the back wall, Silas could feel the gazes of the huddled faces falling on them: out-of-luck gamblers with drink-soaked eyes, lushes who'd taken a skin full as they tumbled from the music halls.

Arthur shuddered. 'I hate it Si, it stinks as bad as the clink.'

Silas sniffed the stale sweat and bad feet, the damp clothes and bad air that seemed to hang beneath the rafters.

'You'll get used to it, my love.' The voice was a woman's as she stepped out of the shadows. She grabbed at Arthur's sleeve and pulled him close under her arm. She looked like a gaudy streetwalker, Silas thought, back from working the streets in what had once been a fine silk and satin dress. Now she looked little more than a sideshow clown, her cheeks painted-up, her scalp itching beneath a frowzy wig. As she took the hairpiece off to scratch, he saw she'd had her own locks shorn.

'Sold 'em to the wig maker, love, since you're wonderin',' she said. 'Easiest two shillings I ever made.'

Arthur shrugged her arm off and hurried to their shared bunk. Within minutes he was falling asleep.

The woman sidled over to Silas. 'When it was last swept out's anyone's guess,' she drawled. He wondered if she'd ever raised a broom herself. He thought of the strange woman living in their house in place of their mother and felt the blankness spreading behind his eyes. Out in the hallway, the night pails stood ridden with flies.

'Someone'll empty them come morning,' the woman said. 'Til then, hold yer nose.'

The smells that came from the bunkhouse kitchen were just as bad as the ones that drifted around the doss room, Silas thought. The kitchen was set to one end of the hall and, for all its brick and plaster, looked more like a campfire in a barnyard than a place to cook proper food. The walls were crumbling and hung with pots and pans and dirty utensils. For a penny deposit, a boy could borrow a fork and spoon for the length of his stay and reclaim the coin when he left. 'There ain't no knives,' the landlord had said just earlier. 'Knife can be a dangerous thing in a place like this.'

A man's gruff voice suddenly came from behind the woman. 'Oi, get some shut eye won't you. We got an early start!'

Silas looked at the man and steeled himself. Before he knew it, he heard himself butting in.

'Early start, sir? With what, if you don't mind me asking?'

The man leaned across from his own bunk and stared him

down. One of his eyes wandered wildly to the side. 'Mind yer own business, *if you don't mind* me sayin',' he said.

'It's only that..." Silas went on.

'Only what?'

'Only that, if you got some work that needs helping with, well, me an' him,' he nodded back towards Arthur asleep on his bunk, 'we're willing. And able.'

'Are you now?' said the man. 'Well there's nuffink, alright? G'night.'

The woman looked at Silas and seemed to catch something in his eyes. 'Aw c'mon Malachi,' she said to the man, 'the boy looks alright. We could do with a hand tomorrow morning, couldn't we?'

The man brooded, puffed his lips, then wiped his mouth on his sleeve. 'S'pose so,' he said. 'You wanna come earn a penny or two in the morning then boy, or what?'

Silas pondered the offer, though he knew that he would take it, whatever. 'What we gonna be doing?' he asked.

'Never you mind that. You want it, or no?'

'Yes.'

'Then come with us after breakfast... if you can call it that.... you like gruel, dontcha?' The man let out a laugh and tugged at his woman's arm. 'Now, *if you don't mind*, I got to catch up on some sleep.'

That night, Arthur slept solidly, though Silas barely slept. He kept himself awake the whole night through with worry, and with the snoring of the drunks and the din of traffic outside the broken windows. He had landed them with somewhere to sleep, and now he couldn't manage to. It also seemed that he had landed them with some work in the morning, but what they might find themselves doing was anyone's guess. He remembered the thousand petty crimes and dodges that the prison boys had tempted them with. 'I ain't going to be like that,' he had promised himself and

Arthur. They would turn their hands to earning money at whatever came their way.

The next day, before Arthur knew what was happening, Malachi commandeered them and bundled them down to the market. There they called out the prices for a man, a costermonger with a stall of garden vegetables. They carried and collected his bushel baskets as they had done a long time ago, for pocket money, before all of this. By the end of the day they held thre'pence between them. Malachi seemed pleased and pointed the brothers to his associates: a cutler who needed his grindstone turning, a chandler who mended pots and pans. One day of work turned into another.

'See,' Silas said to his brother. 'Once you're in it, you win it. Work leads to work. We're back on our uppers, bruv.' And it seemed true. Mending pots and pans led to a day's work at a pie house, and a day with the pieman led to another driving pigs and sheep to slaughter for a butcher. Each day yielded them a palmful of pennies. They worked as hostlers, holding horses at cab ranks, loosening their cruppers to let them rest. Watering them. They loitered at the livery stables, and earned the odd penny carrying bags and cases at coach and railway stations. One week they cleaned shoes outside the station. Another they ran errands or cut tall grass for donkey feed. For their own food, they ate skilly gruel at the casual wards, or took food in payment for the work they had done. Once, they turned over the piles left by Malachi and the other costermen and fed themselves on bruised apples and shot beets.

'Get yourself some soup at a kitchen if you can bear to queue,' a boy had told them. 'There's hundreds of lads there every day.'

In this way the weeks and months went past in a stream of disparate jobs. Not once did they beg or steal, nor turn their hand to prison tricks. Neither did they turn themselves in to the workhouse, nor let themselves fall into slumps over their mother, over George. Survival buried their feelings deep down in their hurt souls. Silas had no time for feeling.

'There's nothing wrong in taking charity,' Arthur would complain when he was feeling tired and beaten, but Silas would have none of it.

'I made a promise to George,' he'd say, 'and that's the end of it, Arth.'

'And what about me, Si?'

Silas considered his brother. 'You an' I are in this together,' he said. 'And I *ain't* going back in gaol.'

Such work brought them enough money for food and lodging. Sometimes there was a sixpence left over. They shared their bed, a penny each for the night, under the stern governance of severe landladies, sleeping with what little money they had stashed in a purse they'd found on the riverbank. It slept with them under the pillow. Once a week in places like these, a missionary or priest called round to read the lodgers tracts and scriptures for their spiritual advancement. Close to midnight most nights an officer would come to the bunkrooms. Then the swearing and cussing would stop, and the last candles put out. For breakfast there was sometimes half a loaf and a cup of tea for a penny more. Supper came each night in the form of boiled potatoes for two further pennies. In this way the money spent itself and the days and nights passed in lodgings stuffed with thirty or more beds.

They began to feel a little better here than they had done in prison, or the bedding wards, but there were seldom any clean sheets and, depending on when washday fell, the bedclothes might be either white, or black with the previous occupant's filth. There was barely room enough between the beds to walk. The other lodging boys were ne'er-do-wells of whom Silas asked no questions. They spent their evenings playing cards, dominoes, pushing ha'pennies, drinking and cussing. 'You'll be coming out with us to lighten a few pockets then?' they taunted. But each time, Silas thought of the treadmill, of the friction of the oakum, of Mr. Hardonby's birch cane and the flogging pony.

Towards the year's end, their lot improved by their own efforts. As they saved the odd shilling, they grew stronger inside and out. They bought themselves some better clothes – long trousers, boots, and jackets. They no longer needed the company of scoundrel boys in lodging houses and found themselves talking instead to diligent men and women at the work stands. Those who had fallen on hardship through no fault of their own. Whose circumstances had been blighted by fickle changes in their dealings, by a slap of dull trade, or bad weather, or market forces that no one could have foreseen. Out of work mechanics and tradesmen. Builders, paviers, and shipwrights, forced to spend their days in indigence, their best clothes and belongings held over at the pawnshop.

Each morning they would turn up at the casual hiring stands with these willing workmen, waiting for whatever work might come their way. They listened to the foreman and looked at the advertisement cards pinned up on the boards. There were notices from businesses across the city.

One morning, a particular card caught Silas's eye: a print of a cart, a horse, two men carrying a bucket yoked across their shoulders and, underneath, the legend: *John Pearce, Nightman & Rubbish Carter, near the Dog & Chickens Inn, London*. He looked to see if he was being watched and pulled the card away from its pin. Quickly he pocketed it. 'This is it, George,' he whispered under his breath.

Behind him, Arthur was listening to the foreman call out the details of day jobs. A doctor who needed a boy for deliveries. The telegraph office who wanted a lad to carry dispatches. The newspaper office in need of delivery boys, or any one of the hundred small businesses who might have need of a running porter to carry their wares across town.

The foreman turned to Arthur; the ticket in his hand was for a porter running errands for a lodging house in the vicinity – the *Belle Maison* – owned by a Frenchman.

'We'll take it,' Arthur said, pulling his brother away with the foreman's ticket firmly in his hand.

'The name is Monsieur *Belle-Maison*,' the Frenchman said to them as they arrived to collect the packages. 'But you Londoners manage to make it Belmerson every time. I am happy with this. I have to be... how could I not?'

Mr. Belmerson was a slight man, but with shaggy and luxuriant whiskers. His hair was oiled and his complexion dark, his features fine. A wiry lip, a sculpted nose and cheekbones that could cut open an envelope. He seemed to maintain a gentlemanly appearance, dressed elegantly in high-waisted trousers and a dress shirt, a chain across his waistcoat. His boots were polished and guarded by gaiters. His collar stood upright. His cravat was scrupulously pleated, and his tiepin gleamed. To each side of him hung a hand with clean, clipped nails.

Once the boys had collected the packages, the Frenchman gave his terms. 'I will pay you your shilling when you bring back the receipts from your delivery. Understood?'

'Yes, Sir.' Silas looked to Arthur. They both knew what to ask.

'You got any beds, Sir?' Silas tossed his brow.

Mr. Belmerson looked them up and down doubtfully. 'I only take in boys who have the wages,' he said. 'This is no common lodging den. *La Belle Maison* is a house for decent boys. If you do not know the dif-fer-ence,' he said, inflecting the word heavily, 'then you do not deserve to be 'ere.'

'Certainly, Sir,' said Silas. 'We're just in between lodgings.' He thrust his hands down into his pockets and rocked his shoulders.

'So, you are the running porters then?' Mr. Belmerson said, considering the nails of his right hand.

'Not exactly.' Silas looked to the ceiling. 'This is extra work, to earn a shilling.' His eyes descended and fixed Mr. Belmerson in a confident stare.

'What is your perfession then?' Mr. Belmerson asked, now considering the nails of his left hand. His speech was more London than Paris, as though he had made extra sure to mimic the tongues of his new home.

'Why you asking?' said Silas. He turned his shoulders so that he was standing half-on to both Belmerson and Arthur. Behind him he could see his brother shuffling from foot to foot.

'I am asking, *mon brave*, because I am *le boss* and you are not staying 'ere unless you 'ave the work and some tin. *Ca va*?'

The brothers shrugged. The idea of a profession was foreign to them.

'Are you in funds?' asked the Frenchman.

George's face flashed into Silas's mind. 'We're nightsoil boys,' he said. Beside him, he felt Arthur catch his breath.

The Frenchman recoiled a little at the explanation but didn't seem to think it so unlikely. 'Where is your tin then?'

Silas dipped his fingers into his jacket pocket and pulled out their little purse with its stash of saved shillings. He tipped one out on the table in front of him. With the purse came the calling card he'd picked up at the casual stand.

Belmerson took it and held it lightly at the corner. 'John Pearce. Nightman and Rubbish Carter,' he read. 'This man is your boss?'

'Yes.' Silas pressed the toe of his boot down hard on his brother's foot. Arthur glanced at him sideways.

Belmerson handed the card back and eyed the boys. He pointed his finger at Arthur's smaller frame. 'There is not much... *avoirdupois* on you for work like that, *non*?'

Silas took the man's gist. 'We work hard.'

'A few shillings won't keep you here for very long,' Mr. Belmerson said. 'Where are your wages? From your nightsoil...'

'We're paid tomorrow,' Silas lied. 'It being Saturday and all.'

Mr. Belmerson looked them up and down and seemed convinced. 'It's fourpence a night. Two shillings the week,' he said. 'You're lucky because I am usually full. It just so 'appens that, since this week we 'ave room for two more. With the shilling I pay you today, you 'ave enough to stay the week.' He took Silas's coin and pocketed it. 'Deal?'

'Deal,' said Silas. He gave his brother a relieved smile. Arthur raised his brows and sharpened his eyes.

They went with Belmerson through a reception room that gave off an air of struggling refinement – a mis-matched suite of coburg chairs and sofas, the mullioned windows curtained in heavy drapes, a dilapidated chandelier dangling from the ceiling, and a mantelpiece, sacristy to a row of cheap porcelain figures. It was, nonetheless, the plushest room Silas had ever seen. Beside him, Arthur was casting around his gaze. They passed through to the kitchen. Two boys were kneeling in front of the stove, busy with kindling, matches and scraps of paper. The stove was bulky and sooty, with a blackened firebox to one side, a hot plate balanced above and a heavy oven door to the other. Beside it stood a rusted andiron, filled with kindling and, alongside in a battered crate, a pile of coal and a pail of yesterday's ashes. 'When it is done,' Mr. Belmerson addressed them, 'put the urn on the grate. Hot water. Tea. Coffee.'

'Yes sir, Mr. Belmerson, sir,' the fire makers said in unison. One of them was striking impatiently at a match and putting it to the kindling with no result.

'Here, give me that,' his companion butted in. The match flared. The paper caught. The kindling slowly glowed. Within a few moments the urn began to rattle on the hot plate.

Silas watched them with a tilt of his head and thought of the times he had done the same in his mother's room. Their home hadn't been much; nothing more than a back-to-back two-up-two-down. But it had kept them all under one roof: his mother's chair, a couple of stools, two beds, a single for his mother in the corner behind a curtain and, to the other side of the room, a double, the old marital bed, that he'd shared with his brothers.

Belmerson went to the dial on the wall and turned it. The gaslight over the kitchen table flared, casting light on the sink and water faucet, the deal tables, the plate rack, and the cooking utensils on the block. Tin coffee pots and crockery glittered softly in the gaslight. The floorboards were bare wood and, above them, clothes hung drying on racks raised high with rope and pulleys.

On the wall behind the door, an array of coats dangled neatly from a row of wooden pegs.

'What do you cook?' asked Silas.

'Breakfast is coffee, eggs if we have them. Bacon. Sometimes a piece of dried fish.'

'And dinner?'

'Well haven't you got all the questions, *mon brave*,' said Mr. Belmerson.

'We get hungry,' said Arthur.

'Steak and onions, pork and mutton, kidneys, sausages, potatoes,' said the Frenchman. 'All the finest English *viands* my young *connoisseur*. All the finest *viands*. It all depends on what we have in.'

'And what about sleeping?' said Silas.

'Fourpence a night, as I said, or two shillings a week if you want to stay, how you say, for the duration. You'll have the cover and the bedding. The earth closet is outside. Everyone uses.'

Silas thought of their old home. The privy had stood at the far end of the street. One outhouse shared by a whole terrace.

Mr. Belmerson stopped himself suddenly and studied the two boys. 'You are the nightsoil boys, *non*?' he said after a considerable pause. 'You work for a clearer?'

Arthur went to answer, but Silas pulled his arm back and spoke over him. 'Yes, Sir. Good money. A man with a cart and horse and us two boys.' Again, he pulled the mechanic's card from his pocket and showed it to Belmerson. The Frenchman held it by the corner and tapped it against his palm.

'Don't we Arthur?' Silas cocked his head.

'So we do, sir,' Arthur agreed.

'Well, you bring him here soon, this week, why don't you,' said Mr. Belmerson. 'I don't want to waste my *monnai*, but that closet, by anyone's account, has not been cleaned for at least the decade and I do not want the authorities coming 'ere and closing me down on account of too much *merde*, if you get my drift. Perhaps we can come to some sort of agreement on the terms?'

'I'll see what we can arrange with our boss, sir.' Silas took back his card. Surprise and satisfaction were bubbling up inside him like the gas in Belmerson's lantern.

'You do that *mon brave*,' the Frenchman said. Their business, it seemed, had concluded.

Out in the street, Arthur scratched his head.

'What the hell d'you tell him that for, Silas? How we gonna get a nightman to come and clean his closet out?'

Silas pushed the calling card under Arthur's nose.

'Stop it. What you doing?' Arthur batted his brother's arm away.

'This, my friend, is our ticket into business.' He held the card triumphantly above his head and laughed. 'Our ticket onwards and up.'

'Jesus Christ!' the younger brother cussed.

'No,' said Silas. 'John Pearce.'

Their first night at the *Belle Maison*, the brothers played cards with the other lodgers. The oldest of them, Harley, a tall lad with dark hair hidden beneath a black cap, took the Ace of Clubs from the pack and set it aside, leaving one ace unpartnered. 'You know Old Maid?' he nodded to Silas.

'Course.'

Harley's stained white collar jutted from his jacket. He worked as a boot blacker. Silas recognized him as one of the boys lighting the fire grate. 'The odd-one-out's the Old Maid,' he said. 'Whoever holds it at the end's the loser.'

There were fourteen boys in the Frenchman's house, Arthur and Silas included. Stable boys and lads who worked for tailors and glovers. A furrier's and a cobbler's boy. A couple of the quieter, cleaner ones held clerks' apprenticeships.

'You two new'uns can play as one,' Harley said. 'There's too many to play at once. The rest of you'll have to take turns.' He snapped his fingers at the younger boys who stepped aside to make space.

The players leant in while the younger ones stood on benches to look over the players' shoulders. A boy called Pegler deftly flipped the cards across the table to each player, reciting their names in a chant as he did so. Peck, Kimber, Barret, Kipps...

'What's your names?' he said reaching the brothers.

'Hunt,' said Silas.

'What, both of you?'

'We're brothers,' said Arthur.

'Hey! I got more cards than him,' one boy complained.

'Shut up Peckers!' Pegler jabbed his cards at the whining boy's face. The onlookers laughed. It looked to Silas as though Peck might also have been a boot blacker.

'It's not fair,' the boy complained again.

'It don't matter who's got more, dimwit.' Pegler slapped his palm against his forehead. 'Everyone get rid of your pairs now.'

The players looked at their hands and discarded the pairs. Silas held the cards, Arthur dipped in to remove the sets. Peck sat smiling at a much-diminished hand. Pegler began play. He offered his hand face down to the boy on his left. 'Choose one, Hayloft,' he said.

'It's Haylot,' the boy replied indignantly.

'That's what I said, Hayloft.' Pegler laughed. The name chimed with the boy's thatch of straw hair. Resentfully Hayloft selected a card and added it to his hand.

'Any new pairs?'

He searched through his hand, matched a new pair of Jacks, and discarded them face up. The onlookers whispered. Then he offered his hand to the boy on his left. So the game went around the circle.

One boy shuffled his hand before offering it on. 'That's cheating, ain't it?' Peck complained again.

'No it ain't. Fair play to him Peckers,' said Pegler. Again the circle laughed.

They went around the ring taking cards, discarding pairs, until everyone but one had discarded all their cards.

'Kipps! Kipps has the Old Maid!' they chorused. Silas and Arthur smiled at each other. At last, this long year down the line, here was a small pleasure. Something that felt like friendship, and a home.

The nights that followed, they played at shove ha'penny and hunt the slipper. Pitch-and-toss. One night they danced and sang, ballads and halfpenny songs – 'The Bonny Blue Jacket', 'Farewell Fanny Frail', 'Have You Seen My Missus?' – whatever songs they knew or had picked up from listening to others at the windows of public houses.

Mr. Belmerson appeared in the dormitory doorway. 'Quiet now boys,' he said firmly, but affably. Harley was standing on his bunk impersonating an exotic dancer, his hands cupped at his chest, a pout on his lips.

'*Tres belle*, I'm sure, Monsieur Harley,' Belmerson said stepping into the room and ushering the boys to bed. 'But it's time to quieten down. You have the work in the morning, *non*?'

Grudgingly the boys consented. Kipps and Peck and the young ones scurried to their beds. Silas and Arthur pulled their feet up onto their bunks and buried themselves under their blankets. Belmerson turned the gas tap off at the wall and the room subsided into darkness, just the glow from a candle or two on bedside tables around the dormitory. '*Bonne nuit*,' the Frenchman said. He closed the door behind him.

A boy's soft whisper filled the candle-lit room. 'I got a book,' he said. It was Woodroffe, one of the clerk's apprentices. He held a hymnal left by some visiting missionary. His soft voice settled into the shadows of the room with one of the printed verses: '*A few more years shall roll*,' he read, '*A few more seasons come. And we shall be with those that rest, asleep within the tomb.*'

'Bloody hell Woody!' Harley whispered. 'Can't you find something a bit more cheerful?'

In the low-lit warmth of his bunk, Silas thought of his mother and brother George laid within their own graves.

'Sorry,' said Woodroffe. 'It was the first one I opened on.'

'Well, find us another!'

Silas listened to the pages rustling as Woodroffe flicked through the hymnal. Again the boy's soft voice came with the pulse of a verse. '*Every morning the red sun, Rises warm and bright. But the evening cometh on, And the dark cold night. There's a bright land far away, Where 'tis never-ending day...*'

Silas relaxed back into the darkness. At last, he and Arthur had escaped the company of the oakum room and the padding kens. Now they were in with boys who shared their shred of ambition. Perhaps the chance would come to make a never-ending day of that pledge to George's spirit.

That weekend, Silas and Arthur went in search of John Pearce, the nightman's card in hand. They had run a Saturday morning of errands from the work-stand and now, in the late afternoon, with enough coins in their hand to pay Mr. Belmerson's rent, they made their way through the streets, past conjurers turning the first of their evening tricks, thimble-riggers conning the crowd. A troupe of jugglers, fire-eaters, and tumblers. A man with a monkey in a scarlet and gold-frogged jacket and a little stiff cap like a miniature doorman. A hurdy-gurdy player. 'Hot p'taters for sale,' a hawker called across his stall, a hand-pushed cart on wheels that soon moved on when no one stopped to buy from him.

They found the *Dog & Chickens* easily and looked around for signs of the nightman's dwellings. They walked down one side of the street away from the alehouse, a road given over to shops of every conceivable kind: milliners, dressmakers, furriers, cheap seamstresses, artificial flower makers, weavers, carpet shops with patterned rugs in carmine and cobalt from hotter lands. To the other side of the street was a watchmakers, a stationers, a rag and bone, a pawn and dolly shop – the black-faced doll in its window whispering to potential customers 'You'll get good money here for your unwanted wares.'

'Where is it?' said Arthur.

'Keep looking. We'll find him.'

Eventually they came to a commonplace shop front at the far corner of the street, its bow-fronted windows catching sparks of light from the newly lit streetlamps. Above the doorway hung a painted sign: *John Pearce, Nightman & Rubbish Carter.*

'Got him!' Silas's face wore a broad smile.

'You knock, Si,' Arthur said sheepishly.

Silas pushed past him and banged on the door. It echoed coldly in the hallway to the other side. A moment later, the door was opened by a woman dressed in a cotton gown whose pattern had faded with wear. Around her shoulders hung a woollen shawl that she, or some previous owner, had patched up. Her tawny stockings hung loosely around her shins. She was carrying a newborn wrapped in a scruffy blanket. As she looked at the brothers her eyes narrowed.

'And what may be *your* pleasure at this hour?'

'We've got a job for Mr. Pearce,' said Silas.

'Mister Pearce indeed!'

A voice came down the entrance hall from deep inside the house. 'Let me nuss the babby, won't you Hilda. It's no use you doin' it while there's folks botherin' at the door. Give 'im 'ere, or the babe won't get no nourishment. Hilda!'

The woman at the door turned. 'Alright! Alright ma! They're just leaving.'

'We've got a job for the nightman,' Silas repeated urgently.

The woman turned back to him. 'A clearance?'

'Yes.'

'Where?'

'Nearby. Belmerson's lodging house. The *Belle Maison*.'

'Lah-di-dah,' the woman said. 'Well he ain't here.'

'Where is he then?' Silas's voice was impatient.

'That information lives in annuvver 'ouse,' the woman said sharply.

'Sorry ma'am,' he said. 'Where to find him, please? It is urgent.'

The woman eyed them cautiously. 'Well ain't you the little charmer,' she said. 'Ma'am indeed!'

Silas nodded politely.

'Upstairs at *The Dog*,' the woman said.

'Thank you ma'am,' he said. The woman smiled as they turned to leave.

'You watch yourselves up there,' she warned them.

Hesitating, Silas turned back to the woman. 'Excuse me ma'am,' he said. 'How'll we know him?'

The woman looked down and laughed, the baby kicking at her shoulder. 'Oh you'll know him alright,' she said. 'Savoy hat, whiskers, and the smell. Go for the smell...' Her voice trailed off in disgust.

'Thank you, ma'am.' Silas turned and tugged his brother's arm.

They walked back towards the *Dog*. Outside the door, the air span with the smell of drink and smoke and other stranger, exotic aromas creeping from beneath the doors of neighbouring dens.

'We ain't supposed to go in there.' Arthur's voice wavered.

'You're always the same, Arthur. Shouldn't do this and shouldn't do that.' He weighed each half of the phrase in his upturned palms.

'Well look where it got us when you went stealin' pure!'

'It isn't the same!' Silas snapped angrily. His brother stared back, and Silas recomposed himself. 'We aren't going to steal anything, Arth. It's a public house, not a dog yard. We shouldn't be going in, but we are. That's it.' He pushed through the door and stepped inside.

Arthur needn't have worried – inside the taproom, no one paid them the slightest attention. By the dim light of gas lamps and candles, drunks sat discussing the merits of their ales and brandies. A card sharp was working the room with tricks and sleights of hand. He had a jug and a glass on the table and, between tricks, swilled ale from the former into the latter, emptying the glass at his lips then hammering his palm on the table.

'Which of you jennermen wants to hear a little song and dance?' the trickster asked. 'Look at the face on this one,' he said, pointing out a glum man with puckered cheeks. The card sharp pulled at the man's weathered shooting jacket. 'Give him a drop of summink short, won't you barman? Looks like he hasn't had a drink since yesty morning.' The crowd laughed and the subject of the joke forced a smile onto his lips. 'Blue ruin to keep 'is spirits up. Just the ticket.'

Silas looked around, but there was no Savoy hat and no unusual smell that the woman had mentioned, only the stale odours of beer and sawdust, unwashed clothes, and the reeking exhaust of cut-rate cigars and tobacco. Through the smoke they peered into the parlour, divided off from the taproom by the wooden bar, occupied by the landlord and his wife. Around them, men were pouring rum down their gullets, the spirits soured with lemon or sweetened with sugar; their teeth rotten from the latter, their brains rotten from the rum.

'She said he'd be upstairs,' said Arthur.

'Let's go look then.'

While the drinkers' attention was fixed on the performer, the boys slipped through and made their way up a long flight of narrow stairs to the rear of the inn. Silas groped forward into the shadows, his brother at his heels. When they reached the top of the flight, the figure of a huge man appeared out of the recess. He was sitting on a low bench that barred a closed door.

'You boys ain't comin' in 'ere,' he scoffed, a coarse rattle in his throat. He turned his head and spat heavily into a pot, wiping his lip. His coat was frayed and had faded to a nondescript shade of dusk where once it had been jet. There were buttons missing and patches on the elbows. The collar of the coat had, one time, belonged to another and had since been stitched roughly on. His waistcoat was similarly mismatched.

'We got a message for the nightman,' Silas said.

'Didn't you hear me?' the man barked, fiddling with the handkerchief knotted round his neck. 'Go on, sod off!'

'John Pearce,' said Silas. 'The nightman? We got a message for him. From his wife.'

The doorman stopped and pondered. 'From his wife?' He looked puzzled. 'About the infant?'

'Yes,' Silas lied. 'About the baby. It's urgent.'

The doorman's deliberations seemed written into the lines of his brow. 'Alright,' he said. 'But be quick. I'll give yer a minute or two and nuffink more, you got it? You,' he jabbed a finger at Arthur, 'you wait here.'

'Silas?' Arthur's hands shot up.

'It's ok,' Silas said. 'I'll just be a minute.'

'That's egsakly what you'll be,' said the doorman. He turned the handle and let Silas through, then turned and leered at Arthur. 'You sit pretty,' he said. 'I'm timin' him.'

Arthur slunk back to the top of the staircase and sat down, out of the doorman's reach.

Silas's eyes adjusted to the darkness. There was no natural light in the attic, just a dim glow from gas lamps and candles. The cramped space was taken up by a wide enclosure, a rat ring surrounded by benches and tables. Around the perimeter a crowd of men were leaning in. The kinds of gamblers, drunks and fences whom Silas had encountered in a string of tawdry doss houses across the year. He looked into the face of one and saw a strange look in the man's corrupted features – a hankering for blood. Beside him a sporting tradesman was leaning over the palisade shouting at another – a mechanic still in greasy work clothes. Silas's eye was caught by a gentleman who seemed out of place with his neighbours, sharing only his desire to win money on the lives of savaged rats – he was shouting just as stridently as the others and his face was as swollen with liquor.

A man stepped into the ring with a basket of rats held high; a master of ceremonies of sorts. He was dressed in a frock coat that appeared to be on loan from the distant past. 'Gentlemen!' he shouted. 'Your last two wagers tonight. Plucked from haystacks and barnyards, from riverbanks and pass-tor-ral streams, here we have... fat brown country rats to fight your city dogs in the sporting ring.' Above the rumble of men's voices came the high-pitched squealing of a hundred terrified creatures fighting with each other inside their cage.

'All rats die,' a flashy gentleman replied. 'Sewer rats, warehouse rats, country rats. Rats from the Thames's ditches. It makes no difference.'

'A pound says the dog kills thirty in five minutes,' said the man's companion, a well-dressed swell in a bib, high collar, and waistcoat. He looked as out-of-place as Silas was feeling.

'Well, thank you Sir,' said the master of ceremonies. 'I'll be more than happy to take your money from you.'

With that, the rat catcher tipped out his cage of country rats and, at the man's announcement, the last dog of the night was let in with them.

When he heard the animal bark, Silas saw the dogs from Tattersall's yard flitting across his mind. A pang of pain shot through his shoulder. As it spread he heard, above the noise of dogs and jeering men, his brother George's voice. 'I don't like it, Silas. I hate your stupid plan.'

He stopped and looked around him, as if he might catch sight of his lost brother. 'It's for you George,' he muttered and pressed on, trying to blank out the brutish animal noises of the ring. He looked for the Savoy hat of John Pearce, as the woman had told him, but nothing caught his eye. Then, to the far side of the room, like the slow realisation of a face in a nightmare, he saw the one hat that he had never wished to see again. A bowler hat of shabby purple felt. Beneath it, through the huddle of bodies and distorted faces, Silas caught the bullish countenance of Tom Tattersall. For a moment, the world seemed to stand still. The sounds and voices died to a blur and the lights around him faded, leaving only that man's face lit up, as though by a lamp in the night. It was as if they were back in the streets once more, in those dirty alleyways behind the middens. Silas shuddered. 'Keep calm,' he said to himself. His thoughts flurried. He hasn't seen you yet. And he won't. He's got his eyes set on the dog. The rats. Not you.

The short, thickset legs of his adversary were stamping the ground as the man shouted encouragement at the dog, a wiry little rat terrier, white for the most part, with a black patch over its rump and another over the eye. Tattersall seemed blind to everything but the destruction of the vermin. Each clack of his boot heel on the ground was, to Silas, a slow drumbeat measuring out his journey through that crowd. In his temples he could feel the blood beating as loud as the man's boots. He tucked down low and made his way through the crush. As he went, the dog also went about his business, shaking the rats senseless then cracking their spines at the shoulder. In less than a minute it had killed twenty, chasing them round the enclosure. As its teeth went in, the crowd cheered louder and louder still when one put up a fight, drawing a line of blood at the dog's muzzle.

Through the din, Silas could hear Tattersall's voice above the others, screaming encouragement at the beast. 'Go on you little beauty! Go on!'

Soon enough the dead rats lay in a cluster and the rat catcher pushed them aside with his boot. The remaining live rats cut about until the dog pinned them down and severed their spines.

Silas reached the far side of the room and turned his back on Tattersall. He drew a breath and looked to his side. There, in the corner, he saw it – the brown Savoy hat, hovering just above the crowd. Beneath it stood his quarry.

The man wore a torn brown jacket and a drab waistcoat. Round his neck hung a plaid handkerchief. His boots were caked in muck beyond the calf. The man's wife had been right about the smell – even above the stink of rats and dogs, Silas caught the trace of outhouses and cesspools. Standing close to the man, he almost gagged. Above him, the Savoy hat rocked back and forth on its owner's head as he shouted at the dog to finish its bloody work.

Silas tugged the man's sleeve. He wanted this over now as quickly as possible. Slowly the face beneath the Savoy turned down to look at him.

'What is it?' the man said. 'The dog's still fighting!' His voice was deep. Irritated. But his face was not as Silas had been expecting – he'd imagined hard, filthy features but, beneath the Savoy, the man's brow was broad, and his eyes were widely set, making a moon of his face, framed by brown locks to each side and, beneath those, a giant W of sideburns and moustache, descending from the ears to the jowls, that zigzagged back up in a peak to his nose.

'What is it?' the man said again, his whiskers moving animatedly.

'Mr. Pearce? John Pearce?'

'P'raps. Why? Who's asking, boy?' Distractedly the sideburns and Savoy turned away.

'I got a job for you, Mr. Pearce. Quickly, if it please you Sir.'

'Can't it wait til the fight's over?'

'It's the last fight, Sir. I heard the man say it. Dog's done his business now.'

'Has he indeed? It's a hundred rat match, boy. That takes time.'

'Can't we step outside? It's a paying job.' Silas cast his eyes to and fro to check on Tattersall's position. To his relief the bully hadn't moved or noticed him.

At the prospect of earnings, the wide face of John Pearce turned back. 'A job?' he said. 'A clearance?'

'Yes, Sir.'

'Paying... proper money?'

'Yes, Sir.'

'Well, this night's paid me nothing,' Pearce complained. 'Who is it asking?'

'Me, Sir. Silas Hunt. On behalf of Mr. Belmerson. The lodging house.'

For a moment John Pearce considered the boy's proposition. 'Belmerson?' he said. 'The Frenchman?'

'Yes, Sir. You know him?'

'Cleaned him out before, must be, what, ten year ago? Prompt payer. Decent feller.'

'Well, he needs you again now. Quickly, please.'

'Then let's talk business and step outside. And stop calling me Sir, won't you?'

They backed out through the crowd and left the attic. Silas knew he'd dodged a beating if Tattersall had seen him. He left the dog handler back beside the pit. Outside, Arthur was cowering on the top step, away from the massive doorman on his tiny stool.

'Let's go,' Silas said, and Arthur led the way, two steps at a time.

In the street, the pubs and eateries were turning out their customers, the dregs and lees of London. The obscurity of night had fallen and was giving itself over to a troupe of beggars and shallow coves who turned all the tricks they knew, slatternly women, high-flyer genteel beggars. A crippled youth on crutches. He must have fallen beneath the wheels of some omnibus or hackney carriage as he ran alongside it, Silas thought. He'd seen that happen before, with the lad carted off to the wards.

A down-on-his-luck swell in once fashionable weekend best, his collars, satin scarf and jewellery now worse for wear, fell from an eatery to take a turn around the lanes. Behind him, an upper-class madame in whalebone crinolines tumbled through the doorway of her chambers. Those who had lodgings were sinking back to them – a meal, if they were lucky. Tea and sugar if they'd earned some money that day and hadn't used it up in the tavern or had won wagers inside at the dog pit.

In an entranceway, Silas saw a figure fallen to the ground without hope of getting back up again – an elderly man whose hair was turning white and whose cheekbones looked like the carcass of a chicken. His clothes were washed-out canvas. His eyes looked alert to some danger or threat. Next to him lay a wizened child. There was nothing of him but bone.

'The Frenchman, Belmerson, you said?' John Pearce ushered the boys past the doorway. Some moments later they stood outside his own shop front. Above them, the nightman's signage squeaked back and forth.

'Yes,' Silas replied. 'You said you'd done him before?' He peered beyond the nightman to see if Tattersall might also now have left *The Dog*.

'I did.'

'You know where he is then?'

'Yes,' said Pearce. 'I'll remember.'

'When can you do it?'

'You pulled me away from the dogs,' the nightman grumbled. 'It'd better be proper money.'

'It is,' said Silas. 'The going rate.' He had no idea what a nightman might charge, but hoped his pitch was convincing.

'Good,' said Pearce.

'He said it's getting... urgent,' Silas said. His fear of Tattersall fading, he was now imagining some cut of the profits.

'I can't do it any time soon,' the nightman said.

Silas's spirits dropped. Beside him, Arthur whispered. 'What?'

'My boys are out of commission,' the man said.

'What's that mean?' said Arthur.

John Pearce stopped to think and looked down at the boys' disheartened faces. He sniffed, making his whiskers move in a downy wave. 'It means, my boy,' he said, directing his eyes at Arthur, 'that if he wants it doing soon, then you two are going to have to help me.'

Silas's eyes brightened. 'Help you?'

'We don't know how,' said Arthur.

'We'll do it,' Silas said, elbowing his brother. Arthur winced and nursed his ribs. 'I said we'll do it,' Silas repeated. John Pearce seemed unmindful of the altercation.

In front of them, a man hurried past in a billycock hat and heavy boots, a woman on each arm. One wore a straw bonnet trimmed with frowzy flowers, the other a ribboned cap with lappets hanging down the side of her face. 'I'll 'ave you buy me a nice fur tippet when it gets cold,' she screeched, 'to keep me bloody shoulders warm.' They passed by in drunken laughter. John Pearce continued.

'My team's all sick,' he said, 'laid off work. Who knows if they'll be coming back. And then what for me?'

'What's wrong with 'em?' asked Silas.

'Cholera p'raps, or something like it.' He spat on the ground and wiped his whiskers. 'Whatever it is,' he went on, 'no one knows.'

'How d'you get it?' said Silas.

'Different ways, people say.'

'From...' Silas hesitated, 'shit?'

'No boy!' Pearce laughed. 'Not from shit! I'm a nightman. I ain't never gonna catch cholera! I'm up to me neck in it all night and ain't never been sick. Not once.'

'Then what?' said Silas.

'Smells. Stench. Clouds of vapours. Some folks say it's a cree-tur, an insect, a thing what gets inside you...'

Silas grimaced.

'Others say it's some 'lectrical disturbance.'

'What's 'lectrical?' said Arthur.

'Lectricity boy. Lightnin'!'

'So how'd your men get it?' Silas asked. 'Struck in a storm?'

The nightman laughed. 'It's probly just summink they ate,' he said. 'Anyway, I ain't got time to natter on about health and what-not. Here's the bottom line. I'll do the job, but I need two boys –

one to carry, one to empty.' He grabbed a hold of Arthur's arm and squeezed it. 'There ain't a lot of meat on you boy, is there?'

Arthur pulled his arm away and shrugged. 'I'm strong enough.'

'I suppose you'll do,' the nightman said. 'Look, I'll give you sixpence,' and, before they had time to reply, 'between you.'

'A shilling,' Silas countered.

The nightman's eyes widened. 'A right proper bargainer you are!' He paused. 'I s'pose it was you what brought me the work. Ninepence then. And don't go getting no ideas in your head about nothing more.'

'Done.'

'Tomorrow then,' said Pearce. 'Wait up late. I'll bring the cart and horse,' and, turning to his domestic threshold, Silas watched the Savoy hat disappear behind its bolted door.

As the moon announced midnight, while all the respectable parts of the city were asleep dreaming lives of health and wealth and happiness, where no one starved and none were poor, where filth and illness and disease were just wild imaginings, John Pearce pulled up outside the *Belle Maison* in his night cart.

His Savoy hat had been replaced by a fantail nightman's hat, whose drapes covered his neck and shoulders. The night mechanic tethered his horse to the sooty post of a gas lamp and began to gather his equipage. He hoisted down two lanterns from the driver's perch and lit their oily wicks with a match. These he placed on the pavement in front of the house and turned to pick two buckets from the back of the cart behind the nightsoil hopper. He clasped the buckets in one large hand and slung across his shoulders the two ropes he had gathered from a hitch post on the side of his waggon. He grasped a short ladder slung onto hooks at the side of his cart and hung it over his arm. Laden down in this way, he approached the door to knock, when it suddenly opened before him.

There stood Silas and Arthur, the elder with his eyes alight, the younger with his eyelids drooping. The other boys were all asleep, despite the best efforts of Harley and Pegler to stay awake until the nightman came. Peck, Kipps and the younger ones were already long strangers to wakefulness.

'Lads,' the midnight mechanic greeted them curtly.

'Sir.'

The nightman scowled back, his whiskers wriggling.

'Mr. Pearce,' they corrected themselves.

'John'll do,' he said. 'Where's this shithole then?'

'Out back. There's a side alley.' Silas indicated a wooden gate beneath a bricked archway.

'Grab a lamp,' the nightman said.

The boys picked up the lanterns and made their stumbling way down the narrow passage, Silas in front with one lamp, Arthur behind with the other. John Pearce was sandwiched between them, laden with buckets, ropes, and ladder. When they reached the courtyard, he explained how the job would go. 'I'll be holeman. You,' he tapped Silas on the shoulder, 'you look strongest. You'll be ropeman.'

'What's that mean?'

'It means sore hands, boy.' John Pearce laughed.

'What?' said Silas.

'Oh, don't you worry. I'll give you some gloves. Your delicate little fingers'll be fine.'

Silas dipped a hand into one of the buckets and pulled out a pair of leather gauntlets.

'I'll fill the buckets,' the nightman said, 'you haul 'em up.'

'Right.' Silas slid his fingers into the mucky pouches of the gloves.

'What do I do?' said Arthur from behind. 'I'm strong.'

'You better be. You're tubman and cartman all rolled into one.'

Arthur absently looked at the nightman.

'*He*'ll hand you the buckets.' John Pearce pointed at Silas.

'*You*,' he pointed at Arthur, '*you* carry 'em back down the alley and throw the muck on the honeycart. Then you bring the bucket back. Got it? The next one'll be waiting, filled, so you'll have to be fast. No slouching.'

'What's the honeycart?' said Arthur.

'The next door neighbour's front room, of course.' The nightman watched the confusion spread on Arthur's face. 'It's the *cart* boy, the bloody cart! What else d'you think? The cart that smells like honey.'

Mr. Belmerson was waiting for them by the back door. He ushered the nightman over to the outhouse. Belmerson was wearing a nightcap and a faded silken gown, a pair of house slippers on his feet, his whiskers suspended in a net hammock slung from ear to ear. 'I think you have been 'ere before, Monsieur Pearce, many years ago?' the Frenchman said sleepily.

'Got to be ten years if it's a day.'

'But tonight you have your protégés!' He gestured to the boys. 'They tell me good things about you, Monsieur Pearce.'

The nightman looked bemusedly at Belmerson and then to the boys. He paused. 'Best team in the city,' he replied. 'Best prices too.'

'So I hear,' said Belmerson. 'Here. A gratuity.' He offered the nightman a small bottle of gin, which Pearce took gratefully.

'We'll need that when the smell gets strong,' he said turning to the boys. He slid the bottle into the pocket of his overcoat and adjusted the protective tails of his hat.

'I'll let you get on with your business then,' said Belmerson. 'I trust you'll be as quiet as you can?'

'Church mice,' said the nightman.

'In that case I will go back to the sleeping,' said the Frenchman. 'Monsieur Pearce, your payment "up front" as you say?'

'If it's all the same to you, certainly.'

'No need to disturb me any further,' Belmerson said, handing the nightman his money. 'It is correct?'

John Pearce counted it carefully into his pocket. 'With thanks,' he said.

'No, no. Thank *you*, as you Englishmen say.' The Frenchman laughed and disappeared through the back door.

As they stood alone in the dim back yard before the outhouse, John Pearce pulled up his thigh-length boots. 'Bring those lamps over here, boy,' he said to Silas in a heavy whisper.

The new ropeman took the lantern from his brother and brought it over with his own, a bobbing light in each hand, setting them on the ground to either side of the outhouse.

'Next, floorboards,' Pearce said bluntly. Silas watched him wriggle a finger and then another into a slot between two of the wide boards in the outhouse floor and, with a heave, begin to lift the board. The wood gave easily, its rotten nail holes releasing their grip in a shower of damp, mouldy fragments. Followed by a second board. In a few moments, Pearce had lifted enough to be able to bucket out the contents and, when the time came, to climb down into the mire.

The light from the lamps crawled across the floor and dipped its head into the fissure. Like a tentative creature it seemed to teeter there at the brink, competing for space with the thick cloud of vapours that had begun to push upwards and outwards. Silas shielded his mouth and nose with his sleeve. The stench was like nothing he had smelled before, except that night when George... The scar on his arm ached. He felt himself dizzy at the smell, the memory, then pulled himself together. He looked down into the depths.

The cesspool was filled with nightsoil three or four feet deep, with a liquid skim that was soaking up the internal walls. The back wall had nearly collapsed, Silas noted, so that what had appeared as a stable place to sit and do his daily business now, on close inspection, was nothing of the sort. The outhouse was crumbling into the very earth. Unlucky the boy who might be sitting there when the wall finally decided it was time to give way. Poor, poor George, he thought.

'Let's crack on then, shall we?' said the nightman. 'Shouldn't take more'n a few hours. You like the look of that?'

Arthur grimaced.

'Get used to it boy! You're gonna be well acquainted with it by the time the night's out.'

Pearce hitched a rope onto a wooden pail and handed the end to Silas. Then he lay himself down and, huffing gently, reached an arm down into the cesspool, lowering the bucket until it reached the surface of the muck. With broad sweeps he began to scoop up the contents of the cesspit, bucketing the filth and tugging on the rope when he was ready for Silas to haul it out.

Silas pulled on the rope and saw the first bucket come back from the underworld into the night air. His muscles burned. His scarred shoulder stung. He unhitched the rope from the bucket's handle and, turning his face away in disgust from the stench, handed it on to his brother, the tub man.

'Quickly Arth,' he said. Arthur turned on his heels. Already John Pearce had begun to fill the second bucket. It was going to be quick and tiring work, Silas had no doubt.

When enough of the ordure had been taken out in this manner and he could no longer reach down to the pile beneath them, John Pearce called back for the ladder, which Silas fetched and lowered down into the pit. The holeman then climbed down into the cesspool, steadied at the top by his ropeman.

'Hand me a lantern.' Pearce's voice came up from the depths.

Silas reached for a lamp and handed it down. A warm waft hit him in the face as he lent over. He reeled backwards, catching his breath.

The nightman was now down there alone, deep in the hole beneath the ground, filling the tubs for Silas to haul. With every heave on the line, he heard it rasp against the outhouse boards. The scraping sound made its way into his mind and, there, transformed itself once more into a quiet, insistent voice. 'Clean me, Silas, clean me...'

He hauled the buckets as fast as Pearce was filling them.

Behind him, Arthur ran to and fro like a machine, trying to keep up with the speed of the clearance. In this way their labour was discharged.

By the time the job was finished, the light was hinging between night and morning. The three of them stood beside the honeycart at the front of the *Belle Maison*, watching the last of the nocturnal prowlers complete their rounds. Steam rose gently from the barrels on the back of the cart.

John Pearce was quietly sipping on gin and, between swallows from the bottle, checking the tack and bridle on his horse. As he leaned in to check each fastening, the exhausted brothers watched the indistinct shapes lying beneath the porches along the street. From these recesses, dark figures were waking, fossicking for scraps of food that might have been left lying in the street overnight. It wasn't so long past that Silas knew what that felt like.

In silence, they watched the six a.m. traders begin their preparations, carting their baskets of watercress and flowers, of fruit and vegetables hoisted onto their heads. Little knots of twos and threes had begun to stop at the coffee stalls to the far end of the street, to buy a cup to warm their blood. The simplest of these stalls was nothing but a man with a coffee can yoked to his shoulders, balanced at the yoke's other end by a brazier. The brothers watched the watercress and flower girls pay him for a coffee, or perhaps a warm gin and milk to fortify themselves against the coming hours.

To the other end of the street, the more up-market coffee stalls were also now being laid out with tablecloths and cups and, at these, a growing trickle of workmen stopped on their way to factory and yard. The coffee shop proper and the morning bakery, with their gas lamps sparking in the windows, raised their shutters and opened their doors and, at these, a few respectable clerks and office workers began to stop, punctuating their morning march into the city from the suburbs. Thus the customers divided themselves according to their means. The noises of the day began to mount into their usual din. The bray of a donkey pulling a cart.

The rattle of pushcarts and barrows. The whinny of a horse bridled at the dray, the carriage, the honey cart.

'All done,' said John Pearce, quieting his horse once the tack had been secured. He beckoned the boys towards him. 'Here,' he said, handing them their money. 'Black hands for white dough,' he laughed. He swiped a palm towards Arthur's brow, which the boy wearily dodged. Silas looked at the coins in his hand. They were bright against the filth.

'You know what?' said John Pearce with a rhetorical flourish, 'I think I might just need your help again. Never seen two young'uns work so hard as you two!'

Between them, the brothers smiled.

'There's thousands of cesspools 'cross this city,' the man went on, 'and most are much fuller than what we've just done. There's muck everywhere boys. We're sitting on a bloody great puddle of it, just waiting to be turned into gold and, while my lads are sick in bed, I can't be sitting idle. Man's got to make his own cash. And there's money underground for digging it out and money for selling it too.'

'Keep us on?' said Arthur, looking less enthusiastic than he might.

'Sure. Why not?' said Pearce. 'You'll do. You done a good enough job tonight. You want to work, don't you boy? Can't do it meself. Got to keep the business going.'

'Anything!' Silas's enthusiasm was immediate. 'We'll do it. We're *can-work* lads,' he said. 'You won't catch us shirking.' He pulled a scowl at Arthur, who nodded wearily.

'Good lads!' said the nightman. 'Sounds like a deal then.' He spat on his hand and extended it towards Silas. 'Go on,' he said. 'Shake it, before it's dry. Be too late then.'

Silas took the nightman's hand in his own. In seconds, the agreement was sealed. 'You too,' said the nightman, spitting again and thrusting his filthy hand towards Arthur.

'Take it,' Silas ordered. Arthur placed his small hand in the nightman's encompassing fist.

'There, it's done,' John Pearce said when the handshakes were over. 'If you prove yourselves good,' he added, 'you never know, I might just take it on me to bind you boys as 'prentices.'

The suggestion was more than Silas could have hoped for. 'Prentices?' he said. 'In this? It's all I've dreamed about...'

The nightman laughed and shook his head. 'Then you've had pretty worthless dreams, boy!'

'Don't matter,' said Silas. 'A dream's a dream. You serious?'

'We'll see.'

'You hear that, Arth?' Silas said, slapping the horse on its rump. A small cloud of dust puffed up from the creature's hide, but otherwise she stood unflustered by such an everyday occurrence. 'Prentices!' Beside him his brother was almost asleep on his feet. 'He's glad for it,' Silas said.

'Sure he is,' said Pearce.

'Where we taking it all then?' Silas asked.

'Market gardens. Farms outside London. Two quid a ton. I got my contacts.'

'We'll have enough brass to buy ourselves a cart and horse, Arth!'

'Whoah!' said the nightman. 'Let's not go running before we can walk... you'll be putting me out of business next!'

'Gotta be room for a couple more nightmen in town?' said Silas.

'There's twenty teams across the city,' said Pearce, 'all taking a share of it.'

'And there's still muck everywhere.'

John Pearce reflected on the boy's shrewdness. 'Suppose there is,' he said. 'If you're willing to scrape it up, I guess you're welcome to take it. Come on. Let's get this stuff on the road. We got some money to make.'

That day they slept for hours. Later, they scrubbed the stink from their hair and skin. Silas thought it might never come off, but an hour with a scrubbing brush left him passably clean, if not red from scalp to toe. If he was going to keep the city clean by carting off its waste, then sure as hell he was going to keep himself clean too. Thoroughly. When they looked at him, he promised himself, they wouldn't know what he did for money. Everyone was going to think him a gent.

Come evening, they paid Mr. Belmerson what they owed in rent and took what remained of their earnings for a walk across the park in search of entertainment. They had earned themselves a little pleasure. Silas couldn't stop talking about the promise of his dream.

'But it's bloody awful work,' said Arthur. 'The smell... my muscles!'

'What muscles?' Silas laughed. 'Look Arth, it's work! Regular. And you'll grow to like it. I promised George, you know that.'

'I know!' said Arthur resignedly. 'Like you'd ever let me forget...'

Behind them a gentleman and lady passed by on their mounts, kicking up the cinders of the ring, the man astride, the woman turned to side-saddle.

'So, what are we gonna earn from digging all this nightsoil then?' said Arthur.

'I dunno. Ten shillings a week? Twenty? Depends how many holes you clear.'

'You think we'll get all that, just from carting crap?'

'You heard what John Pearce said.' Silas was already making the calculations in his head. 'There's thousands of cesspits across town and every one of them's full to overflowing, just like Belmerson's. You gotta earn twice as much as any other mucker in this god-forsaken place. Think about it, Arth. Thousands of cesspits. That's thousands of shillings. Work it out. Just sitting there for us to take it...'

'But we'd only get a tiny part of it,' Arthur reasoned.

'Don't matter. It's a bloody gold mine. Mr. Pearce said so.'

A nurse with a child in a pram walked past. Hearing the boy

curse, she hurried on. Silas pulled his lip to one side and raised an eyebrow behind her back. His brother's face at last broke into a smile.

'Whatever it is, you got to dig for it, Si... and it certainly ain't gold.'

'But it *is* a load of money for what comes naturally...' Silas opened his hands towards his brother. 'Then there's selling it. You heard Pearce. On to gardens and farms out beyond. Two quid a ton he said. Think about that. Half a ton in every pit in London...'

'Take off what it costs to get it there...'

'Listen to you, Mr. Bloody-Problem-Finder. Don't you wanna work or something?'

'I do,' said Arthur, 'it's just...'

'Just what?' Silas stopped walking and turned to his brother. 'Listen, Arth. It can't be much to cart it out. We'll be making a mint for digging it and even more selling it. Split it between us, you and me. Minus costs. We'll be clearing hundreds a year before long. I bet the bloody Guv'nor of the Bank of England don't even earn that. And to think, all I wanted to do was sell pure!'

As the church bells tolled the evening hour, they found a house of entertainments and paid their penny, going into the makeshift theatre at the back. Benches stood arranged in front of a stage and, above these on a mezzanine, the semblance of a balcony. On stage, a woman was singing lewd songs at the piano while a line of women with loose teeth and thinning hair raised their dresses and kicked their legs. When they'd finished, the stage was taken by a raconteur telling stories of murder and ghosts.

'You want to hear 'bout Daniel Good?'

The audience cheered in approval.

'Daniel Good bashed his wife's head in,' the storyteller warmed to his theme. 'Or Hannah Brown? Legs and arms and body parts strewn all over the city. Eliza Grimwood, another sorry moll... another crime that's never been unscrambled.'

The songs and tales went on. Those entertainers who didn't

meet the crowd's approval were showered in sprays of fruit peelings and beer.

'When we're rich we'll go to a posh theatre,' Silas said. 'One with boxes, where rich gents and ladies sit. And galleries. Real dramas. Farcicles. Proper music. None of this filth.'

'Yes, when we're rich,' Arthur replied wearily.

'John Pearce said we'd soon be in business.'

'John Pearce this. John Pearce that,' Arthur complained.

'So-rry,' Silas drawled. 'Just looking out for us.'

Above them, in the gas-lit gallery, the drunks were stamping their feet, swigging from beer bottles stashed in their pockets. Their wives screeched and threw peanut shells. The cries of their babies interrupted the show.

As they walked out onto the dark street, a light rain was just beginning to fall.

'D'you ever think about that night, Arthur?' Silas suddenly asked. 'You never talk about it.' Arthur remained silent. 'But you must though, right?'

'Not much,' Arthur said.

'We couldn't have picked a worse night. It was mizzling out.'

'Like tonight.'

'I remember Ma coming home. Taking off her bonnet. We made tea. Ate bread.'

'I made tea,' Arthur corrected him.

'What does it matter who made it?'

'Always the same dark loaf,' said Arthur. 'Like a flipping boulder.'

'Two slices and a cup at breakfast. Same again at supper.'

'Herring on Sunday…'

'If you were lucky!'

They looked at each other and laughed.

'You remember her trying to find out what we were up to, Arth? And we all just sat there and lied…'

'We couldn't tell her, Si.'

'Doesn't stop me feeling bad about it though, does it?'

They turned a corner and bought a sandwich and a hot potato from a street vendor; an oyster pie from another.

'Remember that pie you had last month?' Silas said.

'I ain't buying from him again if I see him. Just full of shortenings. Disgusting.'

'Probably kitty meat.'

'Leave off it, Si, you're putting me off.'

They walked on, oblivious to the drizzle. There, at the crossroads, they passed a vendor of broadsheets and ballads touting his tales; his penny and halfpenny romances, filled with tales of thwarted love and murder, crimes of passion. Beside him, a crookbacked washerwoman, in black dress and bonnet, a smutty white pinafore and crocheted shawl, cranked the wrought iron handle on a public pump, to let water flow into her crack-rimmed bucket.

'Hoi, Joe!' she called to her neighbour. 'You wanna get them papers of yours inside. Looks like there's a deluge coming!'

The patterer considered the skies from his patch of pavement. 'Ever watchful, Martha!' he replied, lowering the tip of his pole to fetch down his broadsheets. The long sheaves of newsprint fluttered there like the prayer flags of the East. He began to roll them into a tube to stash them beneath the lapel of his overcoat, plashed up the back with dried smatterings of sludge. He pulled down his stovepipe hat against the coming rain.

'You sold much today then?' the washerwoman asked.

'Enough,' the man said.

'You'll eat tonight at least.' The washerwoman hefted her bucket on to her hip and turned away to her own four walls.

And if the brothers had stopped to listen, as well they might on any other dry evening, then it would have been *this* patterer's story that they would have heard. And if they had not been so enthused at the reversal of their fortunes, the success of their first clearance, the money in their pockets and the promise of further work and, who knew, maybe an apprenticeship and peace at last for George's spirit... then certainly they would have stopped to listen to whatever lurid story it was that this patterer was selling. But they didn't stop. Instead, they walked on together in anticipation of what might yet come their way. And they were happy to let the patterer's words fall on the ears of other passersby.

'Read about it 'ere!' the man called, like a fire-and-brimstone preacher, hoping for one last sale before the full weight of rain arrived. 'The blameless little rascal, Georgie Hunt, drowned in a cesspool while his two wicked brothers was out thieving...'

The crier's words echoed off the sooty facades of the buildings and dispersed themselves into the night air to mingle with the raindrops in the clouds; words dissolving into nothingness before they even had a chance to catch up with the disappearing backs of Silas and Arthur Hunt.

A woman in a velvet skirt with satin stomacher approached the patterer and held out a coin. With a flourish he tore a broadsheet off his roll and pressed it on his customer. Her hair was red and her white skin was closely freckled, yet she blushed still redder with the thrill of her purchase.

'Don't you let your 'usband catch you reading that one, ma'am!' the patterer joked, pocketing their coins. 'Wouldn't want my own missus reading stuff like that...'

'Poor little mite,' the freckles said as she hurried off with her companion. 'Drowned in a cesspool! How perfectly horrid!'

'I heard the mother died of fright and grief,' her friend replied. 'We must read it!'

She fiddled with her plaid shawl to secure it round her neck with the one hand and, with the other, clutched at the straw bonnet that was perched on the back of her head like a small halo.

'Both the brothers flogged,' said the freckles.

'Both of them imprisoned,' said the halo.

'No wonder the poor woman died,' said the first. 'Boys these days!'

'They had it coming to them,' said the halo.

'They're probably deported,' said the freckles.

'Best thing for them, boys like that...'

# Two

*Twenty years later, London, circa 1859*

IT WAS the kind of Saturday morning that she had grown used to: homely and quiet, spent together. After a fashion. Nellie Hunt, the dynamo that ran at the heart of this small domestic sphere, was polishing the tabletop and preparing lunch. She wore her best, her only, weekend dress, soft grey muslin, round at the collar with a pink neck cord and a pink lace trim to the skirt. Around her middle she had tied a white apron that grew progressively grubbier as she ticked off her list of morning chores. Her plain grey stockings ended in a pair of black slip-on shoes that moved her from room to room in a habitual domestic dance. She wore her hair as she had always done, in two long braids that framed her face. Her husband, Arthur, had liked it that way when they had sat together as children on the neighbourhood wall. And, according to his occasional fleeting compliments nowadays, he liked it that way still. Already she had burnished the grate and set the fire. Beside the hearth, Arthur was now warming himself as he read his weekend paper.

The years had ushered Arthur Hunt kindly through his twenties. He was well fed, but not corpulent. He was strong, but not muscle-bound. His face still held some of its boyishness, although he had grown into the figure of a man in control of his own fortunes. In control of everything bar his appearance, Nellie thought – his hair was scruffy, his whiskers patchy and unkempt. Stand him next to his brother, Silas, she considered, and you'd never even know they were brothers. Where Silas was fussy, her husband was dishevelled. Where Silas was scrupulous, Arthur was unpredictable. Both brothers worked industriously, yet Arthur was the one who liked his rest. When the weekend came, she practically had to prise him from his armchair.

On the hearthrug slept their cat, a small black rag-doll creature with a diamond of white at its forehead. Nellie had called him Scrap, on account of his size, but Arthur and Silas had given the tomcat the moniker 'Crap', perhaps because of their own bitter-sweet business in the cesspits of London, but certainly because the creature was always leaving his mess on the garden path. Scrap, or Crap, his name and habits were a source of amused dispute amongst the three of them.

From the kitchen table Nellie took up a double-sided earthenware pot and, in one side, piled potatoes with a respectable joint of beef on top. On the other side she poured a stream of pudding batter, carefully replacing the lid. Deeply she inhaled the steaming aromas.

'I'm just taking lunch down the cook shop, Arthur,' she called, pulling a shawl around her narrow shoulders.

Her husband shifted in his chair by the fire and grunted in accord, watching his wife's figure slip off through the back door. The cook-shop stood at the corner of their street. She would be back before he'd had time to turn the page. Then she'd get on with making pudding. In three hours she'd be back to the cook shop to bring the pot roast back to their familial table.

From his chair, Arthur considered his good luck. Saturday for other working men was another half-day's graft but, for the midnight mechanics who made their living clearing the middens and outhouses of the capital, their work was done while the city was asleep. London's other workingmen wouldn't finish their jobs until one o'clock today. Then they'd collect their pay, release their best suits from the pawnbrokers and wear them all weekend. But for Arthur and Silas Hunt, Saturdays were as good as a holiday, and built on a different routine. Arthur would pass his morning warm by the fire, while Silas would soon be up and heading to the washhouse.

Upstairs Silas was readying himself for his own weekend. First would come the customary highlight of his week: a trip to the municipal baths. He'd carry his clean suit down there in a bundle and, once he'd rid himself of every trace of muck, he'd walk out as smart as a Lord. Clearing cesspools was his and Arthur's bread and butter, but bathing every weekend was Silas's holy manna. He couldn't abide to be seen dirty. To be seen marked by the filth that supported him. It was unthinkable.

After bathing, he'd come home for lunch. Their workmates would join them. And they were welcome, these fellows who made their team, so long as Joseph White hadn't been drinking. That chap among them was a melancholy soak, and Silas wondered how long it would be before his patience snapped and he'd have to let him go. On a good day, White's habits might mar his efforts at work; on a bad day they revealed the malcontent inside him. Their cartman, Henry Shrimpton, was his opposite. A joker whose spirits were often high for no other reason than his own eccentricity. If occasion demanded, he'd be happy to take a drink; a swallow from the bottle after clearing the midden. The last of their workmen was Gamble. Harry. A reformed drinker who had, just last year, signed the pledge. On which he'd kept his word. His view of the world was simple; his judgements he reserved for himself.

Soberly then they would all sit down in their best clothes to dine on Nellie's fare – a chair set by in memory of brother George as always – to eat the roasted joint, potatoes, cabbage, peas, a steamed pudding, or a fruit tart, depending on what Nellie had left in the pantry. Bread and celery to finish. The whole thing washed down with a glass of beer for those who would, and all undertaken with the proper forms and observances of carving and serving, of cutlery chinking the platters, and weekend conversation.

Silas was proud of the spread he was able to share. *Hunt Brothers* had made good money from London's waste these twenty years past.

'We'll have to be on famine for the coming week,' Arthur would laugh dryly, satisfied with what they'd made of themselves.

'Days of feast and famine are over, mate,' Silas would reply, although he knew that downturns in business could take anyone by surprise. If only they could stave off that prospect. If only they were not proud, or foolhardy in making decisions, they'd forestall any knocks to their fortunes. And all of this good luck thanks to the man who had first set them up in the trade, John Pearce, *god rest his bones*, and thanks to the cesspools beneath the city's buildings whose muck they had turned into gold. Silas had made good his oath. And who'd have thought it? A better living than they could have hoped for and all of it made on what folks leave behind.

Silas padded downstairs and found his brother reclining by the fire, a newspaper draping his lap. 'Nellie at the cook shop?' he asked.

'I nearly finished the papers,' Arthur replied, clutching up the paper and ignoring his brother's question.

'And what you going to do for the rest of the weekend then?'

'Loaf.' Arthur cocked him a sideways glance. 'Where you off to anyway?'

'Buckingham Palace.' Silas swung his parcel of clothes beneath his brother's nose. 'Queen's doing hot baths for sixpence.'

'Very funny.' Arthur licked his finger and turned a page. 'Take my washing with you, won't you? I'll give you the penny.' But in the pause, Silas had already departed.

Outside, the weekend air was warm. Theirs was an agreeable terrace, Silas thought. Nice little part of town. You could live here in comfort; ply a decent trade. Even hail an omnibus. He watched the vehicle turn the end of the street but, when it reached him, it was already overburdened with human freight. The ladies were seated inside while, on top, two rows of men sat back-to-back in chimney hats. He squeezed himself aboard beside the driver.

'Mr. Hunt,' the driver acknowledged him.

'Potts. How do?' Of all the drivers who worked his route, Silas admired Potts the most. His livery was always pristine: top hat and spotted cravat, dark green pea coat and shining calf-length boots. He liked a man who made an effort.

'Mustn't grumble.' Potts turned his attention back to the road.

Behind them, the conductor stood on the footplate, halfway up the back of the omnibus. Each time he smacked his riding whip onto the roof, narrowly missing the nearest passenger on the knifeboard, Potts would pull the omnibus to a graceful halt.

By now the city was on its way to work: the rich riding into office on horseback; the middle classes on the omnibus, in a hackney, or a brougham. Clerks from the suburbs were walking in along the pavements in steady streams of charcoal suits. On the river steamers, businessmen and professionals were making their way from the well-to-do districts in the west. From the east, artisans and skilled tradesmen were steamed upstream and dumped on the landing stages beside the great bridges, where the tollbooth men lightened them of a penny. Silas inhaled a self-satisfied breath.

He alighted at the public baths, slipped a modest tip in Potts's hand, and climbed down the steps of the bus.

'Thank you, sir.' The driver raised a gloved finger in Silas's direction then pressed it to the brim of his hat.

'You're welcome.' Silas touched his cap to the driver and, delaying his pleasure no longer, walked up to his temple of cleanliness.

To the outside, the bathhouse was characteristic of the row in which it stood: narrow courses of plain red brick interleaved between layers of yellow limestone, with blackened stone cornices and greying pillars at the entrance, all overhung with a carved portico.

He mounted the steps at a lick and went inside. The counter stood to the near side of the vestibule, staffed by a clean, thin youth, who sat behind an ornate iron grill. He was scribbling on a pad of loose-leaf paper. Silas coughed and the youth looked up, flipping up the grating to poke his capped face through the gap.

'G'mornin' Sir,' he said. 'The usual today is it, Mr. Hunt?'

'First class hot bath and towels, Johnson.'

'Certainly, Mr. Hunt. That'll be sixpence please.' The doorboy took the coin and turned to open the armoire behind him, retrieving two clean towels, monogrammed with the bathhouse's initials. He handed them over to Silas then stepped out from behind his desk, keys jangling.

Silas followed him to his usual washroom. Johnson looked smart enough, he supposed, in his blue uniform, its shoulders capped with tasseled epaulettes. The boy's pillbox cap slipped a little from side to side with each step.

The men's baths were to one end of the building, the women's to the other. To each side there was a plunge pool built for common use, one for men, one for women, filled with tepid water, though Silas never used these. Why, he reasoned, would he share some other person's dirty water once he had steamed himself clean in his own bathtub? He had been as good as immersed in muck all week and had no desire to wallow in the dirt from other people's bodies.

He turned the porcelain knob on the cubicle door and let himself into his sanctum. Reaching behind, he fastened the latch and listened to Johnson outside, opening the spigot to release hot water through the pipes. The floor of the bathroom was laid with slate that disappeared under the divider between his bathtub and the next man's. The washbasin stood to one side, beside which lay a pat of soap, a brush and comb. Above the basin hung a looking glass.

Silas peered into it and spoke softly to himself. 'Time to get clean.'

He looked to the tub, judged it to have been scrubbed satisfactorily and pushed the plug into the base of the cold enamel. He turned the hot tap and let himself be enveloped by steam.

Stepping from his everyday clothes, he hung them on a brass peg on the dividing wall, unraveled his package of clean clothes and laid them out on the bench – moleskin trousers, black coat and waistcoat, white shirt and necktie, a sporting cap to tilt on his head. Soon he'd be spruced up for his girl. One had to always be impeccably turned out for Flora Street, he reminded himself.

He ran a finger over the two towels beside the sink. 'Everything... perfect.'

For a moment he stood naked in the cubicle, inspecting himself in the mirror. His neck, his arms, his chest, were thick with muscle and without blemish, save for his shoulder where the red welt of the old scar still cut a jagged course across his arm, linking his past to his present, tying him still to little brother George. He ran a finger along the scar's length and sighed. Instantly the mirror clouded.

Twenty years as hole-man on their team had bulked his frame into a mannish shape. He could stand his ground against anyone but, as he'd aged, his height had leveled off and Arthur had caught up with him in stature, leaving them now standing shoulder to shoulder. Yet while his brother's hair was dusty brown and unkempt, Silas wore a thick head of dark hair, cut close at the sides, and carefully slicked back on top. His chin was well defined, and his five-o-clock shadow came quickly. It set off his eyes, which had remained keen, despite the hardships he had seen.

There was room enough in the cubicle to extend his arms out to the sides and he stretched out the aches of his week's labour, shaking loose his fingertips. The walls were high, but there was no ceiling, so that the building's ventilation could siphon the steam away. In the apex of the roof a row of skylights gave ample light. Often he had lain here, lounging back and dreaming upwards and upwards out through the casements into the distant blue.

He closed off the taps and stepped into his bath. He wasn't a religious man, but this was as good as a weekly baptism. At first he just lay there, relaxing in peaceful stillness. Then he began his fastidious routine, scrubbing at his face and hands with the bar of bathhouse soap, lathering his torso with its thatch of dark hair. Once he'd rinsed off the suds and the grime, he reached out for the pocket of his jacket, hanging by the side of the bath, and retrieved a small implement with which he dug beneath his fingernails, trimming them down with the clipper itself. He then turned his attention to his toes. These small sacraments completed, he placed the clipper back on the bench and let himself soak in the steaming water.

Some time later – he never knew how long, for here his time was whiled away in relaxed thoughts of nothing – Silas lifted himself from the tub, patted himself dry and left the towels to one side for the service boy. 'All part of the service, Mr. Hunt,' he could hear the youth saying in his chirpy, boyish voice.

His clean clothes lay there on the bench like a steam-rollered figure, but soon he fleshed them out, brushed his hair, applied lacquer and pulled on his cap. Every Saturday he did this and every Saturday it felt the same. It was like he was a new man, reborn on the weekend, cleansed of the guilt of his past, and of all the stink and filth that paid his, Arthur's and Nellie's way in the world. Away with all that rots and festers, he thought.

He stepped out of the bathhouse, his old clothes bundled up beneath his arm. Deeply he breathed in the cool air of the street and turned his stride towards home.

Outside in the street, the market was heaving. As far as he could see, heavily laden stalls lined the roadside. Costermongers in frock coats and cloth caps gabbled to each other in back-slang, touting their fruit and veg from barrow and truck. Market butchers in smocks and bloodied aprons skinned rabbits and plucked poultry, laying the meat out on tables piled with trotters. Flushed fishwives were chopping haddock and herring and shucking oysters on trestle carts, crying out for juicy whelks a penny a pint, and London's pinkest shrimps and plumpest winkles. He nodded to the grocers he knew, with their piles of cheeses, bacon, eggs, and listened to the hardware salesmen striking deals over tools and household goods: cutlery from the North, plated wares and kitchen goods, pots and pans and copper kettles. Their canny eyes shone like the coloured jars in the windows of the Chemist shops behind them. And, for those who couldn't afford the chemist's preparations, well, he thought, there were always the quacks and the mountebanks; those purveyors of remedies and ointments, embrocations, salves and pastes, magic potions and miracle cures.

'If only there was a *miracle cure* to secure me my girl once and for all,' he said to himself, 'life would be just about perfect.'

His girl. Flora Street. The daughter of the brewer to whom John Pearce had introduced them when they'd first joined him in business all those years ago. Pearce had called on the brewer, Joshua Street, for his used-up hops to mix with the nightsoil, with added bone meal and shredded rags, to make his own brand of manure. Now John Pearce was gone they no longer did that mixing themselves – their middleman, John Grundy, took care of all that business – but Silas had kept himself in with the brewer, in the hope of winning his daughter. Hope for Saturdays like this when he might step out to meet her. The prepossessing Flora Street. The girl, for Silas, unlike any other.

In his limited experience, most of the girls who would put up with a midnight mechanic were coarse mannered. But Flora, like Nellie, was fair and decent. Her skin and teeth were good; he liked that in a woman. In private she would kiss him and hold him close, but in public she maintained propriety, offering him her hand, which he would brush decorously with his lips like a demonstrative lover in a music hall show. But, most importantly for Silas, her clothes were clean and in decent repair. She was a strong-headed girl, passably schooled and knew where she was headed; what she wanted from life. She was like him – make a plan and set about it. What was more, she didn't object to his trade, so long as it brought in good money. And it had certainly been doing that. Flora Street knew where her bread was buttered.

But in his mind, there were two nagging problems with Flora. Firstly, her line of rival suitors. She seemed to be forever surrounded by other men. Men who would snatch her away in an inkling if he wasn't wary. Sometimes he felt she was playing them all off against each other, for her own secret pleasure. 'I can't be visiting with you this evening,' she'd say, matter-of-factly. 'I've made other arrangements.'

'And what "other arrangements" would those be, Flora, that you can't see me?' he'd ask, trying to maintain an even expression.

'That's for me to know and for you not to bother yourself with...'

'But I am bothered, Flora, which is why I'm asking.'

'Well, mind your own, Silas Hunt,' she'd say. 'I'm not askin' after you all of the time, am I?'

'So, you won't say who, then?' He found it fiendishly hard to remain composed when she was baiting him with such vague details.

'A woman's business is none but her own,' she'd say, touching a finger to her lips. 'Now stop asking all these overbearing questions, or I'll be making my own way home.'

Once she'd uttered such words she was as good as sovereign. It ate at him. He'd wanted an independent girl, and now he had one. But it was he, wasn't it, who held all the prospects? *He* was the one with his own, successful business. *He* could give her what she wanted. Couldn't she see that? Why did she have to go off promenading with other chaps as well; was she testing him?

Which raised the second problem. Flora had told him, flatly, that she'd never marry a man whose house wasn't fitted with a new water closet. 'Everyone has one these days, Silas,' she told him. 'You're living in the dark ages.'

It infuriated him. No way in a lifetime was he putting one of those things into any house of his own. It was those things that were putting nightmen across the city out of business. Flushing it all away. There was a time when a nightman could earn his wages clearing the muck, then earn a second wage by selling it on to the market gardeners as manure. Now the WC manufacturers, the sewer contractors and sanitationists were piling on more and more pressure. Not to mention the guano importers, bringing that bird's muck from southern seas in vast old cargo ships. How could he compete with importers like them for manure? That guano was becoming the gold standard for fertilizing fields.

Between them – the sanitationists and the importers – they were putting the squeeze tight on his business.

No, he'd never side with the enemy, but how to win his girl without a water closet? He didn't know which way to turn. He'd go to the park to meet Flora and, before he knew it, they'd be arguing about what comforts to put in a house. Just this time last week he had been waiting at the park gates, freshly bathed and newly dressed in moleskins, white shirt, jacket and tilted cap, when he'd seen her coming towards him. She was wearing a lace bonnet over her auburn hair, with a ribbon that hung down the back in a coloured cascade and another tied beneath her chin to keep the bonnet in place. He admired that she made efforts in her appearance. Her gown was dark blue, on top of which she wore a checked apron and an old pelisse whose furred collar matched her hair. She was everything he could desire in a woman. They had greeted each other affectionately – he took her hand and kissed her fingers lingeringly; they smelled of powder – and then they'd taken the main path through the park. Halfway along the path, a keeper of a Happy Family was stationed with his hawk and jackdaw, his rabbit and monkey and tortoise. The man was petting his wards kindly, dropping each creature a tidbit of food in their cages.

'How lovely!' Flora said. Her voice sounded like water in a fountain. Like garden birds. Like call-it-what-you-will beautiful, Silas thought.

'Penny to feed 'em, miss.'

Silas put his hand into his pocket, pulling out a coin. 'Go on,' he said.

She smiled at him with anticipation. He cherished her smile and would happily have spent all his earnings to see it more often. He hated the thought of her shedding its sunshine on others.

When she'd finished feeding the animals – half an apple for the monkey, the tortoise; a handful of seeds for the birds – he linked his arm through Flora's, breathing in her scent and, when he thought no passers-by were looking, he stole a secret nuzzle at her neck. In this way they strolled along, flirting in idle chatter.

'I've done just about every job a feller can do,' he said. 'Except that one... Happy Families.' He thought back to those years of scraping by. Years of which he had told Flora next to nothing. She knew very little of his past and he liked it that way. What would she think if she knew that he and Arthur had spent a month inside as boys? That he was responsible for his own brother's death?

'I dare say you have,' she said.

'Never much liked caged animals myself,' he said. They walked on. 'And you?'

'I think they're adorable.' She placed a hand to either side of her face and adjusted her bonnet. 'Straight?'

'Yes,' he said, checking for her. 'I didn't mean that though,' he smiled, 'I meant you; what have you done?' He knew almost as little of her past as she did of his.

'Oh,' she said. 'Workwise?' A light laugh skittered away from her lips like a squirrel from its hole. 'Oh, everything!' she said, 'Stepping, dress making, kitchen girl. I've minded babies too, but didn't much like that.'

'Whose steps d'you clean round here then?'

'Whose haven't I?' she laughed again. 'Luckily, I got myself some learning. Night school. Sunday school. Bible class.'

'I haven't much read the Bible,' he admitted. 'Some folks don't know where they'd be without it.... I don't know where I'd be without shovelling sh...'

'That's no way to talk to your girl, Silas Hunt!'

They came to a halt under a plane tree beside the lake. He tried to take her hand then, but she pulled it away.

'If you read your Bible, Mr. Shoveller,' she criticised, 'you'd know not to cuss and swear in the presence of a lady.'

'I didn't cuss,' he protested. 'I just...'

'I don't want to hear it, Silas.' She turned away and walked on briskly.

He stood under the tree and watched her go, then quickened his pace to catch her. He often seemed to be hurrying behind her, playing catch up. Not that he was slow. Rather that she was so self-possessed.

'Where was I?' she started again.

'Your schooling,' he said apologetically.

'I was a Saturday girl for a while, but they tried to make me their slavey. Pay wasn't much. At least I had quarters. *And* they gave me a nice cotton gown.'

'I'm sure you looked perfect.'

She rose to his flattery with a smile, but soon batted it away. 'Perfect as a serving girl can be – scrubbing floors, carting coals, emptying the grate and blacking the guards!'

'Still, all those... skills,' he said, 'you'll make someone a good wife one day.'

'Perhaps I will,' she said. 'I got my mind on a nice house in the suburbs. Two servants. With steps down to the street, iron railings, a boot scraper, and quarters for the butler in the basement.'

She had high standards, he thought. He hoped to be the one to fulfil them.

'A hallway with tiles,' she went on, 'and two reception rooms – a lounge and a dining room – separated off by folding doors. Drawing room and study upstairs. A piano. China hounds beside the fire, plants and pots, and a bird in a cage. A linnet or a little skylark, so I can hear it sing.'

'You've got it all worked out, haven't you? You'll be a right lady.'

'Three bedrooms on the top floor, for me and... my husband. A little nursery in the attic and the maid's quarters. I want a four-poster with chintz curtains and a bedroom big enough to lay on a bathtub of water and lounge there in front of the fire.'

'Now that *is* a picture,' he said, touching her cheek.

'Neatly furnished,' she went on, 'modern. A bathroom and a water closet...'

Silas felt himself flinch. The scar on his shoulder itched and shot a nerve the length of his arm. Surely she must have noticed him stalling for time?

'Shouldn't cost us more than forty pound a year,' he mumbled awkwardly.

'You're joking?' she said.

'I'm doing well enough.'

'Really?' she said.

'I put my profits in a savings bank. I live in a comfortable home. What more could a girl ask for?'

She looked at him inquisitively.

'I'm no millionaire...' he said quickly. Her inquisitive look faded. 'But I've money enough to live on...'

They stood looking at one another. How should he progress from here? Was this the moment to drop to one knee? But she wouldn't, would she, not without the flush? And anyway, he didn't have a ring.

'I got a small union pension and some savings and some interest on the savings,' he pushed on, accounting for himself.

Was she working out her prospects with him, as opposed to one of her other fellers? Couldn't she see that his profits were the only way of getting her that... how had she just put it... *nice house in the suburbs*?

'Well, aren't you just the catch, Silas Hunt,' she smiled, offering him her hand. He took it and pressed his lips against her skin, enjoying a kiss that was long enough to test decorum. 'Now,' she said, turning back for the Happy Family. 'I'd like to see that little monkey again.'

The Hunt's street was home to every stripe of workingman and family: labourers, artisans, commercial types. A handful of civil servants. To the far end stood a grocers and a bakers and, to the near, a hardware store, a doctor's offices. On the corner stood the cookshop, where Nellie took their weekend meals for slow roasting. Beyond the cookshop, a public house and, beyond this, row on row of terraced houses much like their own.

Returning from his weekend bath, Silas rounded the corner. There on the bend stood the street orderly. Silas tipped the man his cap and walked past.

'Looking sharp this morning, Mr. Hunt.' The orderly was dressed in a fustian coat with wide collars and a broad-brimmed hat. He ran his hand around its sateen band and pulled up his trousers. They were patched at the knees, Silas noted, above a pair of sturdy shoes.

'A morning bath does a man the world of good.' Silas nodded and strode past, down to the end of his street. Behind him, the orderly began sweeping, pushing small piles of dust into his pan with a long-handled broom before tipping it into his barrow. As Silas approached his gate, he could hear the man calling out to a carter or driver to keep their carriage moving on.

Silas stood outside his house. A nice enough home he reckoned – a lifetime away from the early years of their raising – of red brick and slate roof, with a porch over the front door and a carved stone lintel bridging the two facing windows on the upper floor: a bedroom for Arthur and his wife, another for himself. Once Flora had married him, they would need two houses: one for his own family, and one for his brother's. And room for all those – some of those – comforts that Flora required. And so long as there was muck in the ground, he could earn enough money to save for a lease on a second place.

Fronting the house stood a low brick wall set back from the pavement, mounted with simple railings. The tomcat, Scrap, was sitting there guarding his domain. Silas reached out a hand and scratched the creature between the ears. It arched its back and pressed its spine hard against his hand, letting its body slink through its master's grip to the very tip of its tail.

'Hullo little one. Got an itch to scratch?' The cat turned and butted his head gently against Silas's palm. These small satisfactions completed, the tomcat then flicked his head and, for little reason Silas could see, raised a claw and a hiss, jumping down behind the adjoining low wooden fence recently blackened with creosote.

'Suit yourself, Crap.'

The creature slunk across the back yard to where the outhouse stood, built above the midden shared by the whole terrace. If you want a cesspool anywhere, he often repeated to his neighbours, make sure it's in the midnight mechanic's garden.

Silas watched the cat disappear beneath the wooden arch at the rear of their yard. Here they kept their carthorses stabled and dry in the outhouse, a pair of mares, Queen Bee and Bumble, drivers of the honeycart. And there it stood, that much maligned vehicle, on the cobbles in the corner, with her six stout barrels.

There was also a small patch to the very rear for cabbages and chickens and, perhaps if they ever got around to housing one, a pig. Nellie was good with the cabbages and, no doubting it, they had the best manure any gardener could ask for.

He let himself through the gate and up the garden path, side-stepping a small deposit the cat had left on the encaustic. The front door was on the latch, and he let himself in, hanging his coat and cap on the hallstand.

Out in the back room, Nellie had decorated for their Saturday lunch, with greenery in a jardinière pot on a stand and flowers on the windowsill. When they first moved in here, Silas had hung a picture above the fireplace – 'The Angel's Whisper' – an artist's rendition of a forsaken mother leaning over her dying child, the family dog in the foreground, a choir of angels singing in the back. It could have been Mary Hunt and brother George. A pair of small porcelain statues stood below it on the mantelpiece. Here were his household gods. He leaned forward and straightened a second picture: the family of bucolic peasants were tilted upright in front of their sunny country cottage. Roses round the doorway. A clean stream gurgling through their garden.

Arthur was still in his chair by the fire, where Silas had left him before his trip to the baths, his feet extended in front of the grate. Silas kicked Arthur's foot on the hearth rug and picked up one of the pieces from the mantle – a Staffordshire spaniel with drooping black ears and a shaggy white coat spotted in grey.

'Wake up, sleepy. Finished that newspaper yet?'

He blew on the base of the statue and set it back down again. Back in the day, when they'd still lived with their mother, they had owned little of nothing: most of her things had been sold when their father died, or else she'd pawned them, or taken them to the dolly-shop for less than a penny. Now they owned things.

'What?' Arthur protested.

Nellie breezed into the room. 'Don't you go criticising my dusting, Silas Hunt!' she said light-heartedly, setting crockery on the table. Scrap followed her in from the kitchen, having completed his circuit of the house.

'I wouldn't dream of it,' said Silas. 'Everything looks perfect Nellie, as usual. Are we set ready for lunch?'

'Will be in a moment.' She adjusted her white cotton bonnet. 'If you'll give me a chance.' At her feet the cat was winding himself about her legs. 'Shoo, Scrap, before I step on you.'

Arthur leant forward in his chair and batted at the animal with his paper. 'Crap, out!'

'Arthur!' Nellie reprimanded him.

The cat satisfied himself with his unsettling effect on household harmony and disappeared once more through the doorway.

'Boys coming, Arth?'

'Believe so.'

'And you've set a place for George?'

Nellie flashed a look towards her husband.

'Don't we *always*?' Arthur said.

'So we do,' said his wife. She returned to the scullery to collect a further set of crockery.

It had been on a Saturday morning much like this, some decade ago, that John Pearce had passed away. The man had built up his modest empire on the nightsoil of the parish and had seen Silas and Arthur good for many years. From that first clearance of theirs at the *Belle Maison* they had come to work for him, casually at first while Pearce's men were laid off sick. And then, two of those men passed on with cholera, and the nightman found himself without a team and took the boys on proper. As they came into age and experience themselves, he apprenticed them and, finally, took them on full time. As the years passed, Pearce himself grew less fit for the rigours of scraping out cesspools. He made the brothers partners in his business. The calling card was changed to *Pearce & Hunt*, although that was the only thing that ever seemed to change much about John Pearce. Even when his wife left him. The boys hadn't been working with him for long when the woman upped and left with a travelling salesman who stole her away in his van, taking the child away with her also.

'Can't stand the bloody stink no more,' she had given as her parting shot.

'Two less mouths to drain the purse,' was all he'd had to say. The woman was never heard of, nor spoken of, again. Her betrayal had hardened Pearce's eyes a little in his moony face, but otherwise he seemed untouched by it.

'Work keeps comin' in fast, boys,' he reasoned to them. 'All them cesspools won't clear themselves. Ain't no time for sitting round and moping.' His W of moustache wobbled agitatedly around his jowls and lips, a little greyer now than when they had first met that night in the *Dog*.

There followed years of plentiful work for the Hunt brothers. Wages and decent lodgings. Clothes from the haberdashers; no longer from the tally shop. New shoes, rather than hand-me-ons. After some brief courting, Arthur had gone back and got himself in with Nellie and, by their early twenties, they were married. While Arthur was out courting, John Pearce had sat up with Silas and taught him all the ins and outs of their trade – keeping books, managing orders, keeping tabs on contracts and sub-contractors. The young man learned fast, tallying their income and outgoings on an abacus. He learned to shuffle the beads and tally the columns fast. The muck he could have done without, yes, but it paid their way. It was also his way of atoning. For George. For Mary. Muck you could wash off, but duties and promises such as those were with you for life.

And then John Pearce had suddenly gone and died on them one night after a week of clearances. They had finished a Friday night job out in a detached villa in the suburbs.

'They got their own little well!' Silas had noted, for drawing fresh, clean water. 'Not like our old place, right Arth?' It was, in truth, a long shot from the grots in the slums where they had grown up, with their rickety balconies overhanging the waterways, where drinking water stirred sluggishly, mixed with the muck that fell from above.

'Remember mother had to get the water from a barrel in the yard?'

Arthur had laughed, as though time had softened those privations. Those days had been hard, but he still harboured a fondness for what he had known. But out here in the suburbs life was far from hard: water was laid on and piped in, not only to the kitchen, but to the upstairs rooms as well.

'You watch though,' Pearce had said. 'Soon they'll be having a WC fitted and then they won't be calling on us no more to come and clean their cesspool. Everything's changing boys.'

A room in a tenement in the city cost three shillings a week, Silas recalled. And that with a bog house to share with the whole court and alley. Who knows how much they paid to live out here? Could be anything these days.

They'd finished the clearance and taken their wages from the owner. An hour later, the honeycart trundled back into the yard behind John Pearce's dwellings. 'See you boys for lunch tomorrow then,' the boss had said. It was the man's custom to give them lunch on the weekend; a custom they'd since taken up with their own men.

'And wages,' Arthur said.

'Alright, alright! Don't be getting greedy on me boy! Noon tomorrow. Lunch *and* wages.'

'You want us to unload?' Silas asked.

'No,' Pearce said. 'It's late. It can wait til later. I'll deal with the nag. You lads go home. Get some sleep. You earned it.' He nodded his head and tipped the brim of his Savoy.

'Til tomorrow then.' The brothers took the short walk back to their lodgings.

The following morning there had been a light rime of frost on the ground. When they came around for early lunch and wages the cart was still standing in the back yard and the horse had not been untethered. The creature's head was drooping. Her mane and tail were crusted. The barrels of nightsoil on the back of the honeycart were letting loose a noisome cloud.

'Hey girl.' Silas patted the animal's flank. 'She's freezing, Arth.'

'Don't look like she's been fed neither.'

'Nip in the shed and fetch out her nosebag and water.' Silas stood nuzzling the animal while his brother fetched her feed.

'It's coming girl,' he said, blowing at her nostrils. The horse's head lifted.

Soon enough she was champing happily on her feed and dipping her muzzle in the bucket of water.

'What's he up to?' Arthur asked. 'Ain't like him not to take care of her.'

His horse wasn't the only thing the nightman hadn't attended to. The back door to the house was also still ajar.

'Boss? You in?' Silas's voice echoed from the cold walls of the back parlour. They went through the hallway. The house was cold and dark.

'He still asleep, Si?'

'Dunno, mate. Look upstairs.'

Silas watched Arthur take the stairs two at a time before turning into the back room. He stood in the doorway and stopped, his hand still touching the porcelain knob.

'Arthur...'

Upstairs he could hear his brother's feet on the boards. 'He ain't up here, Si.'

'You better come down here, bruv.'

John Pearce was sitting in his Windsor chair beside the table. He was still dressed as he had been the night before when Silas and Arthur had left him.

Arthur pushed into the room behind Silas. He stopped at his brother's shoulder. In front of them, the nightman was sitting in his jacket, waistcoat and corduroys, his brown Savoy hat. One of his legs was thrown forwards, the other was crooked back at the knee. His right arm hung loosely over the arm of the chair, while his left hand was lifted to his neck, its fingers caught in the knot of his plaid neckerchief. His head was thrown back and his mouth lay open.

'Sweet Jesus, is he...?' Arthur blurted.

Silas stepped forward to the brass oil lamp, still glowing dimly on the table. He leaned over the chimney and blew. Slowly the flame died and the yellow glow in the shade subsided to unlit white glass.

'He didn't even get to take his hat off. I ain't seen a body, Arth, not since...' Silas thought of George's body lying on the ground by the middens but couldn't bring himself to speak his name.

'This ain't our fault, Si.'

Silas twisted his head and stared at his brother. 'The man's dead, Arthur. We got to do something.'

'What?'

'Well, I don't know, do I? *Something*.'

He reached out and lifted his boss's arm by its sleeve. He unhooked the fingers of his other hand from his necktie. Already the man's limbs had stiffened a little and it took some effort to cross his hands in his lap. In silence, Silas put a hand beneath the dead man's knee and crooked it up to match the other.

'Tip his head forward, Arth.'

'I don't wanna touch him.' Arthur took a step backwards towards the door. 'What happened to him, Si?'

'Poor old duffer,' Silas said. 'Must have been in his sleep.'

'That's how I wanna go when it comes.' Arthur wiped his eyes.

Standing beside the chair, Silas pushed the back of the nightman's head so that it weighed forwards on to his chest. With his hat shading his face, he looked as though he might have just been sleeping. Silas crossed himself. 'We gotta tell someone, Arthur.'

'Who?'

'I dunno. Someone. Peelers?'

'S'long as no one thinks it was us...'

'He died in his sleep you eejit, even I can see that.'

'An' what happens to us then, Si? What about us?'

Silas looked up at his brother and fixed him with a stare. 'I guess it's just you and me now, Arthur.'

The coroner had announced congestion of the heart. The probate lawyer had announced the terms of John Pearce's will.

'This being the last will and Testament of John Pearce...' the executor read aloud, a well-appointed man named Hawker who'd overseen affairs for the business in the latter years of its success, '... the testator, hereby revokes all previous wills and codicils and being of sound mind and judgement...'

Hawker was dressed in light cotton trousers and a long black cape that draped to the floor. His delicate hands took freedom through the vents in his cape, one clutching at a set of pince-nez, which he waved with emphatic flourishes, the other waving a sheaf of papers previously retrieved from the drawer of John Pearce's desk.

'...nominates two beneficiaries: one Silas Hunt and one Arthur Hunt,' Mr. Hawker Esquire continued, nodding to the brothers as they sat in his office, 'as legatees, to equally divide the moiety and manage his estate and affairs, receiving the value of his property and share of business, between them and no others.'

'What does that mean?' Arthur asked of the legalities.

'It means,' the notary said, 'that you and your brother are the official legatees of Mr. Pearce's will.'

'Begging your pardon?' said Silas.

'You need to have that signage changed above your door, Sirs. It all comes to you, Mr. Hunt. And your younger brother...'

So it was that Mr. Hawker turned a dark morning into a red-letter day. For the first month or two, the brothers had moved into Pearce's old dwelling, just down from the *Dog*, with its bow-fronted windows and signage squeaking over the doorway. *Hunt Brothers.* With their boss's death, the income from the business now only needed to support the two of them. Enough left over to take out a lease on a house and premises of their own.

Now they had not only turned that business into the leading nightsoil outfit in the parish, but they tendered out work to other nightsoil teams as well. Their empire – if that was not too grand a word to put upon it, Silas thought – had brought them to a position of security. A quiet house in a decent neighbourhood. A stableyard for Queen Bee and Bumble and the honeycart. An income that was easy enough to live on for any working family. If not better. An honest trade selling nightsoil on to farmers and market gardeners.

Silas's promise to George and to himself had finally come good. *Hunt Brothers* made a fine enough living in nightsoil, he reflected. But what's more, it was a necessary service; a service without which this city would sink further into its own mire. It held a certain nobility, he felt, a way he could feel good about himself.

Their weeknights were hard, no doubting that. Tough, malodourous work. But the money was good, and their weekends were restful. Once he'd bathed and scrubbed the filth away, Silas was his own man. When the abacus and paperwork was done, he was free to do just about anything he pleased.

In the afternoons he would attend to letters and business papers, dealing with all advices on removals and carting, just as John had shown him. There were accounts to keep of warehousing. Of the orders for rags and bones and leftover hops to mix with the nightsoil for making proper manures. After each clearance, they rode the honeycart back to the yard and spread the nightsoil out there on the ground. Mixed with hops brought on the cheap from the brewery. Mixed with ground up bones from the knacker's yard or bought cheaply from bone-grubbers. Finished off with shredded rags bought for pennies from scavengers and finders. There they would leave it to dry and shovel it up, bag it in sacks and sell it to the middleman, Grundy, who sold it on himself to market gardens.

Arthur would book the jobs in and record them in a ledger. After he was married, Nellie shared their house and kept the books and attended to invoices and payments. There were records to keep of sub-contracts to other teams. The Mills outfit from just across the parish boundary. The Reynolds team from further to the north. The Barnett Boys from southern districts. O'Brien the giant nightman, who never could fit himself through the entrance to a cesspool, but who could carry buckets at a faster rate than any man in the city and unload his honeycart single-handed. Men like these who kept the city clean and kept the market gardeners in muck. Gardeners who, in their turn, kept the city fed and the costermen in work selling vegetables. They all needed paying. They all needed managing. Silas and Arthur were brokering the nightsoil business for the entire northwest of the city, so it seemed.

So it had gone on. Good work and equally good money. Better than doing anything else they'd ever known. And then there was the Union – their association of nightmen and clearers. No, they couldn't ever go on strike if things got tough but, if you were laid off with illness or disease, then the Union would see you right. If you were infirm or injured in a working accident. Unemployed. Then your subs came back to you tenfold. And money paid in now, meant money paid out later as a pension. Nothing grand. But enough to see you good in later years if you managed to put a little bit by as well. A nightman earned good money. Twice or three times as much as any other working man. Silas and Arthur had learned to be prudent with theirs. Some savings here, some small investment there. Another team sub-contracted to pick up the work that they were too busy to do themselves. They even passed on the manure mixing and hopping to Grundy.

Yes, there were the stirrers and the Union busters, "The Family" as they liked to call themselves, those clots of shady businessmen, surly thugs and would-be politicos, with vested interests and fingers in the pies of sundry crime across the district. They wanted the streets run their way. They wanted a cut of your business. Silas and Arthur had had their share of hostile dealings with such heavies. No one ever knew their names. They were just a bunch of mindless lackeys, Silas thought; the kinds of faceless men who went about by shadows only, nothing more than a gang of petty criminals – coves who went in for stripping roofs of their lead at night, or breaking into untenanted houses to rip out the fixtures and fittings. They took extortion money from traders and, when they saw something to be gained from a racket on a business, or stirring up some local politics, they were never far from the centre of the trouble. Silas had often seen such rabble leaning on the windowsills of their Union meetings, waiting to stir things up with the decent men inside. Sometimes they came in and made trouble with a disaffected speech or made threats. But they were nothing more than a bunch of nobblers and cowards; bad boys who threatened to do you harm if you stepped on their toes. An introduction to O'Brien the giant was usually enough to see them off.

'We aren't ever paying them anything,' Silas promised himself. 'Give them cash to keep 'em off your back and you'll be paying out protection money for evermore.'

This small menace aside, the business dealings of *Hunt Brothers* were equable and made a tidy profit. And when work was done, then there were good times with Arthur and his wife. And good times courting Flora. Silas would walk her around the park and take in the music at the bandstand.

'I like the silver instruments,' she'd tell him, pointing to the cornets and tubas and horns, and he would take her hand and smell its scented back, kissing her fingers. Or else she might ask him to take her shopping along the more expensive pavements. 'Let's go look in the winders,' she'd ask excitedly. He could afford to do that now. She could look through the panes and dream up a fine outfit.

'That one's nice,' she'd say, hopefully lingering on the pavement outside a haberdashery. 'This old one of mine's getting awful threadbare,' and there would be some loose thread of cotton at her hem that she would suddenly find, fingering it distractedly until Silas took her inside to buy a new blouse, a scarf, a pair of lisle-thread stockings.

In such leisure his girl was kept satisfied, his rival suitors kept at bay, for a while at least. So their weekend afternoons passed in unwedded harmony – he'd get to asking that question when she dropped her other admirers.

And once their afternoon was done, he would walk her home to her father, drop her off and head back home himself for evening tea – bread and butter, cups of tea and small talk with Arthur and Nellie. An early evening settled by the fire with his own newspaper, before the night's entertainment, when he and Arthur would head off to the music hall to see some operatic melodrama, or a burlesque in a dancing hop, with a bottle in their bag and a basket packed by Nellie, full of small provisions.

'When we were boys, d'you remember Arth, I said we'd come to a posh theatre? A theatre with boxes where gentlemen and ladies sit. With real dramas, not penny shows? Well, we're those gentlemen now.'

Arthur considered his brother's scrubbed face and slicked back hair, his fresh cut nails and clean pressed suit of clothes. 'Well, you certainly look the part,' he nodded.

But that was all bygone now, *the good old days* as they liked to call them. John Pearce's final words out in the suburbs that night had been right on the money. 'Everything's changing boys.' Now there were indeed water closets going into every new home and, since the hot and stinking summer of fifty-eight, new sewers had been going down right across the city. It was like a form of mania. Everyone wanted in, or so it seemed: diggers, brickies, construction workers. Planners and engineers. The Board of Works was more like a religious order than a public service. And since Parliament itself had been stunk out by the river and closed down that summer, you couldn't turn anywhere for talk of sewers, nor for sight of them springing up.

It wasn't the end of their trade, but it had started to make a serious dent on their profits. This past year had seen their income fall; contracted clearances cut by half; their future prospects unpredictable. Flush systems everywhere, even going into old houses. Connecting sewers and branch-works all over the city. They had had to sell one of their horses – Bumble had been retired to a market farm out in the country. They'd started to eat into their savings. Silas feared their business was on the brink of recession.

Tonight was Friday night, the Union meeting. One of many in recent weeks. As darkness descended on the streets, gentle sparks ricocheted from the head brass of horses pulling private carriages and phaetons. The last of the day's donkey carts were trudging wearily over crusted paving setts and cobbles, where the city's street waterers were still dousing the ground to wash away the dust and dirt into the secret subterranea of the city; down there where the old Fleet river and the Effra, the Wallbrook and the Neckinger made their hidden way, bricked in beneath the feet of passers-by.

The waterer sat on a simple seat raised above the cistern, which sat itself between two massive iron-rimmed wheels. He lightly held the reins of his horse – a scrawny dappled mare. At intervals he flipped the reins on the mare's rump. 'On girl,' he shouted routinely, twisting himself beneath his broad-brimmed hat to check that the spray was issuing evenly. Small fountains of water curved into the air, refracting lamplight in a gentle line of rainbows.

Above the drain, a waist-high sandwich board stood on the pavement beside the steps of a redbrick building. The placard bore an advertisement in thick black lettering: *Tonight – General Meeting of the Union of Nightmen and Clearers.* Above it rose a sooty porch, beneath which a half-open doorway gave entrance to a meeting hall. Animated talk was spilling from the doorway into the street.

A small group of heavy-coated workmen advanced on the doorway. 'After you,' a small man said to a giant almost twice his size. The giant stepped through, only to find himself hindered by a table set across the entrance, where two Union stewards sat in their weekend best peering over the protective wall of a ledger and a caddie for fees.

'Dues gentlemen,' the first steward said, jiggling the whiskers on his upper lip like a hound on the scent. His companion licked the tip of his finger and opened the leather bindings of the ledger.

'O'Brien,' the giant man said, not that he could be mistaken for anyone else. He rooted disgruntledly in his pocket for his payment. Behind him his companions muttered and delved into their own pockets.

The keeper of the fee tin coughed. 'It may come back to you one day, O'Brien, either in money or in kind. This union... *your* union...' he corrected himself, 'has already looked after several men in need this year...'

'I know, I know,' O'Brien said, his deep voice rattling the tin.

'Seven shillings a week pension,' the second steward said, his badge of *Treasurer* winking proudly at his lapel. 'Twelve pounds to the wife if you die. Burial costs. Support of the family...'

The giant leaned down from his considerable height, level with the Treasurer's face. 'I wasn't planning on it,' he said. Behind him his companions laughed.

Timidly the Treasurer took payment and lodged a record in the ledger.

'You're welcome, gentlemen,' the second steward said, and the newcomers were ushered through.

Inside the meeting hall, Silas was readying himself to take the podium. The room smelt of floor wax, musty working clothes and outhouses. Smells to which the men inside were all inured. The evening's programme had already seen spokesmen for disgruntled workers and industrial agitators addressing their sense of injustice in exaggerated and preposterous language.

'The bosses? The masters?' they had ranted. 'They aren't on your side! They don't want nothing from you 'cept your undivided labour. Your sweat!'

What they were doing here, Silas didn't know. Simply haranguing the meeting and stirring trouble.

'And once they've wrung it from you, they'll toss you away on the refuse heap and move on to their next money-making venture. Resist the tyranny of the engineers and sanitationists! Hit them where it hurts!'

He hated their cant. It would do nothing but see a man out of work, or in trouble with the law. And yet they had also heard more moderate voices, speaking of compromise, discussion, change.

'Don't listen to the trouble-makers,' the liberals made their case. 'They'll stir things up against anybody if they think there's some personal advancement in it. Don't listen to them. Listen to your Union.'

Silas considered the current speaker. He was of the latter stripe and was now drawing his address to a close. Boisterous hecklers were barracking the man, calling out coarsely and stamping their feet on the echoing floorboards. Some of the shady coves from The Family were here, intimidating those they thought they'd be able to bully.

'Who let the troublemakers in?' Silas whispered to Arthur,

flicking his head back towards them. Beside him, Arthur frowned and raised a finger to his lips.

On stage the speaker was finishing his delivery. He stepped down and took his seat amongst his fellows, apparently thankful that his trial by public speaking was over. His partners patted him on the back, although their faces betrayed the shared conviction of the congregation: his speech had not gone quite as well as he might have hoped. The Secretary of the Union then shuffled onstage. Silas shook his head. The man's jacket was a tawdry item of moth-eared moleskin, fastened below the lapels where his waistcoat buttons popped and protruded at the belly. To be seen with your clothes mussed like that, Silas thought, unkempt and dishevelled in public. It was unthinkable. The Secretary clasped his hands to either side of the lectern and leaned forwards.

'Our next speaker is Silas Hunt. Mr. Hunt please.' A round of applause ruffled the air.

Silas brushed his jacket down and stepped up to the lectern. He had scrubbed up for his speech, though he knew well enough not to dress too showily for such a meeting. Cleanliness may have been his eccentricity, he knew, but at meetings like this they needed unity. These men might lose faith if they thought he bore airs and graces.

The edges of the lectern were waxy beneath his palms. He raised a hand and smoothed it down across his lips to the tip of his chin. An idle thought crossed his mind, about the pleasures of the next day's bath and shave. The promise of a stroll and stolen kisses with Flora.

He knew well what he wanted to say this evening, and had rehearsed it many times over the last few days, standing in front of his bedroom mirror. The matter, for him, was simple. Three things were to blame. Water closets. Sewers. And penguins. Water closets fitted in every new house in the city. Water closets that were, quite literally, flushing their income away. Sewers that took their nightsoil out to sea, irretrievably, no longer there for selling on to market gardeners to spread upon their fields. And penguins.

Penguins whose shit – their guano – was even now being shipped into the nation on great transporter ships at huge expense from the distant shores of Africa and Peru and sold at even greater profits to those self-same market gardeners and farmers.

*Hunt Brothers* had started to feel the squeeze from all sides. And the more they were squeezed, the less they could clear. And the less they could clear, the more danger they faced of losing everything they had worked for and earned from John Pearce.

He looked down onto the faces of his team – Arthur's unkempt hair and lightly whiskered jowls; the lively eyes of Shrimpton; the peaked cap of Gamble; the wandering gaze of Joseph White. The four of them sat in line to the front of the hall, a vacant chair beside them as prescribed for brother George. Sometimes, Silas could swear that he had seen their little brother sitting down with them; that he had felt his presence. Tonight was no different. It was as if he could hear George's plaint in his ears, importunate and unfading.

'Night men, mechanics, clearers and toshers...' Silas began. His voice was clear and confident in the resonant, timbered room. 'I've got a few things to say about our trade. As you know, for over twenty years we've worked hard and succeeded in that; a trade that we were given to by this city's finest, John Pearce...' he paused for effect, letting the crowd's approbation settle, 'for which we shall always be grateful.'

They owed the man everything – their position, their business, their house and home.

'Had it pleased the Almighty to have spared us John Pearce, he would this day have reached his sixty-fifth year.' He paused in reflection of their champion's life. 'Yes, you saw us good John Pearce...'

'And who are you then, all of a sudden; some great Lord of London?' the voice of an agitator came burling anonymously from the back of the hall. From scattered chairs laughter bubbled up like gas. 'You'd fall in a pool of shit and come up with a bag of gold, you would, Silas Hunt!'

'Lord Muck!' A second voice hitched itself on to the scorn of the first, raising more laughs.

Silas waited. 'You're right,' he agreed. 'Now's not the time to boast. We all know our business is organized. And profitable. But it provides a service too. A service without which this city of ours would be knee deep in it. A service to the farmers who want what we clear away.'

'Well, ain't you just the great philanthropist!' Again, laughter rose among the clot of agitators at the back of the hall.

Silas ignored it. He knew this field of faces well. The faces of decent men who worked hard for their living in unspeakable filth. The Mills outfit, the Reynolds team. The Barnett Boys. There at the back was O'Brien the giant. Theirs was indeed a truly benevolent circle. It didn't matter what the dissenters said. The work they did served everyone.

In the gaslight of the meeting hall, he could also make out the faces of other interested parties. John Grundy, their middleman; the dealer in manures, to whom they sold their nightsoil, but with whom no love was lost – the man was cheap and tardy with his payments. Beside him at the back, Silas kept his eye on a group of men, singular in their professional attire. Men with whom his argument was growing daily. Samuel Suddaby, Director of the new contractors, responsible for all these burgeoning sewers in the district. He was, without reservation, the richest man in the room. No, he wasn't Mr. Bazalgette – the brains behind the grandest sewer works in London – nor was he top brass, but Suddaby answered to the likes of Bazalgette. Beside him, Silas watched his officious little clerk, Mr. Peggs, and behind this pair the suited shape of Mr. Fleet of the local news. Better not go making lies up about our union tonight, he thought.

Silas lifted his hand and the audience quietened. He filled the silence and regained the listeners' attention. 'These new-fangled appliances,' he said, 'these water closets… they're putting men like you and me out of work. We've just laid off a horse. They're riding roughshod over us.' For a moment he thought of Bumble living out her days in some happy-go-lucky field. 'We've lost a quarter of the work we're used to.'

As he went through his speech, Silas picked out the faces of the other men who had spoken that evening. The moderates were nodding agreeably. The agitators huffing heatedly. He hoped to god they weren't going to start roughing people up outside once the meeting was over. He heard himself say 'water closets'. He heard himself say 'sewer works'. He heard himself say 'penguins'. And once he'd heard himself say it, he heard his audience's laughter.

Then he knew that his allotted minutes were drawing to a close. His speech seemed to be delivering itself and he was simply its vessel. Beside him the union secretary was already shuffling towards the podium, waving his aged hand. Silas drew to a finish, climbed down, and sat back beside his brother.

'Told you they'd find the penguins funny,' Arthur said approvingly. Silas nodded his head and pulled his lips into a tight smile.

Several speeches later, concerning routine matters of constitution and the unspoken boundaries of each team's rightful patch, the meeting drew to its conclusion. In unison, the Hunt brothers and their team raised themselves to leave.

'Fairly done, boss,' said Henry Shrimpton, buttoning up his overcoat. 'Here,' he said, 'what you said got me thinking. I was wondering... what's the difference d'you think between a penguin and a pimple...?'

'Do we have to joke right now, Henry?' his partner, Gamble, complained.

'Jokes makes this stinking work lighter,' the cartman said.

They shuffled towards the door with the crowd. A few men slapped Silas on the shoulder in approval. A few looked to the ground as he passed them by.

'It went well, boss,' said Gamble, 'don't you think?'

Joseph White, his fellow at the tubs, said nothing.

'As well as can be expected,' said Silas. They reached the back of the hall and waited in the throng of bodies pressing through the doorway.

'One of them's a blackhead,' Henry whispered to his mates, already laughing at his own punchline, 'but the other's a white.'

'What?' said Gamble. He had listened to Henry's jokes so often he'd grown oblivious to them. Just as he had to the stench of their work.

'Penguin and pimple,' the cartman said, still laughing to himself. His mate stared back at him, unmoved. 'Never mind,' said Henry. 'Hey, get a move on there won't you?' he called forward.

A few faces at the front of the queue turned back to look at them. 'Shut it, Shrimpton,' the voice of a troublemaker span back over the heads of those between them.

'Forget penguins,' said Gamble, seeking a distraction, 'what about carting animal dung as well? All them cows and pigs and sheep that's off to market?'

'What you on about?' Joseph White's face was predictably unimpressed.

'You've tried coming up through the city of a morning?' Gamble said. 'You can't move for livestock down there on market day.'

'There's countless geese and ducks too,' Henry agreed. 'Enough guano there for the nation. Dunno why they bother bringing it all the way from Africa and Peru.'

'And horses! Thousands of 'em. Gotta be a hundred thousand tons of horse dung on the roadway every year...' Gamble's voice trailed out into the street.

Silas followed it but, as he went, he felt a hand at his elbow, pulling him back. He turned to see the well-dressed figure of Mr. Suddaby at his side. The Director nodded at him politely. Silas looked down at Mr. Suddaby's gloved hand. The old scar on his shoulder shot him a sudden pang. 'You go on, Arth,' he said to his brother. 'I'll follow you home shortly.'

Arthur watched his brother step aside with the sewer contractor. He leaned over, half threateningly, but Silas nodded him on.

'If you say so,' Arthur said, stepping out to the street with his team.

Silas watched him pull his collars up around his neck and walk past the stirrers who'd gathered by the entrance. If they do anything to him, Silas thought; if they say anything out of line, I'll have them. He bristled as he watched Arthur exchange a few words with one or two of them. Arthur can tell those agitators himself where to go, he thought.

Mr. Suddaby coughed, and Silas turned back to the man who released his grip on Silas's arm. The two of them stepped further back into the room to let the remaining nightmen pass. Beside them stood the deferential figure of Mr. Suddaby's clerk, Mr. Peggs. The engineer spoke genteelly.

'An impassioned speech, Mr. Hunt,' he began, 'but ours is, of course, the best and only scheme. You *do* understand that? Install the WC across the city, with sewers beneath them. No question. No need for a cesspool. No need for,' he paused, choosing his words carefully, 'uneconomic clearances in the middle of the night. No smell. No disease. No cholera even, some say. Cheaper in the long term too. Flush the city's foulness away.'

Silas looked at the man in silence and nodded. 'You'll put us out of business,' he simply said.

'Come, come!' said Mr. Suddaby. 'Times change, man! We can't have hundreds of people sick and living in filth to save another man his singular employment rights. Your cesspools are hundreds of years old. Dilapidated. Overflowing. You know that. We can't have effluvia and noxious gasses leaking out everywhere. Have you not heard of the cholera? Miasma? Where have you been man!'

'Once *we're* all out of work,' Silas said, '*then* watch your cholera spread.'

'You'll find yourselves employed elsewhere soon enough,' Mr. Suddaby continued. 'Why not come and work on the sewers, the pumps, and the flushing? I've plenty of openings for bright, resourceful men such as yourself, Mr. Hunt. For men such as these,' he gestured towards the stragglers now pushing to the exit.

Silas's gaze followed them out. Arthur was still there debating those two Family fellers. Silas gritted his teeth.

'The money's respectable,' Suddaby went on. 'Bricklayers, six shillings. Tunnellers, five shillings sixpence. Labourers, three shillings sixpence...'

'For a ten hour shift!' Silas turned back to the Sewerage Director.

'Hard but honest work, Mr. Hunt! How about it?'

'You'd take the very bread from their mouths,' Silas objected.

'For the greater good,' said Mr. Suddaby. 'When have things not been thus?'

'A water closet does the work of gangs of men.'

'And what could be better? Nothing simpler than pulling the chain and, hey presto! It flushes away what it takes four or five of your men several hours to dig out.'

'You miss the point, Sir,' Silas said. 'Those men are then out of work. Your well-to-do homeowner's paying, what, several pounds they won't even miss for sitting their arses down on their comfortable appliances, while those nightmen themselves are unemployed and out on their own arses, to the tune of many pounds more. It isn't right.'

'I know you're just a nightman, Sir,' the contractor said in distaste, 'but there's no need for profanity. We can, at least, find it in ourselves to speak politely to each other, despite our differences, can we not?'

Silas returned his gaze blankly. The man seemed to be waiting for him to apologise. When several moments passed between them, the sewer contractor continued.

'As I said before then, Mr. Hunt. There's plenty of work for you and your men on the new sewer works. Think about it, won't you?'

'Better paid too,' Mr. Peggs interjected.

Silas stared at him indifferently. 'I doubt it,' he said.

'A Union such as this,' Mr. Suddaby went on, 'fighting to save a doomed trade, why, it'll end in nothing but trouble.'

'Respectfully Mr. Suddaby, Sir, our Union protects the lawful interests of our members. We've as much right as any working man to protect our trade. As much as doctors, lawyers... engineers.'

'We've seen the "rights" of "unions" before, Mr. Hunt,' the Director of Works retorted. 'Aggressive, unconstitutional, inflammatory groups. Doing nothing more than opposing their masters simply because they *are* the masters. Strikes and outrages. Provocative items in the press...'

Somewhere behind them, Silas caught the portly movements of Mr. Fleet from the local news, shuffling impatiently in the shadows of the lobby. What's he still loitering for, he thought. The man was muttering distractedly to himself.

'Why, you've even heard that agitation here yourself tonight,' Mr. Suddaby said.

'Nothing of the sort!' Silas raised his voice. 'We're properly constituted. President, secretary, treasurer. Monthly reports. Elected members.'

'That's as well as maybe, Hunt,' said Suddaby, 'and I hope it's so. A few navvies have been striking on the sewer works and what good has it brought them? They slowed us down and found themselves sacked.' The Director pulled his gloves on tightly and locked his fingers to push them into place. 'But striking's not going to get *you* anywhere anyway, is it now? You're your own bosses!' He laughed. 'Stop work in protest and you do nothing but harm yourselves...'

Silas knew he was right. Strikes were an unwanted evil for everyone and, in their own business, pointless. Not a man among them wanted to stop work and lose wages simply to prove a point of principle about new sewers. Not a man among them wanted to see their wife and family suffer in protest at the unbridled import of guano. But what to do instead? They stopped clearing cesspools and then what? The city's new sewers were already carrying half of it away anyway. They were powerless against the forces of change and sanitation that were cleaning up the city, street by street. Political agitation would only send them back to prison – and Silas wasn't going to betray George's memory with actions like that.

Mr. Suddaby clapped him on the back and strode out, his clerk in tow. 'You can't resist it, Mr. Hunt,' the contractor said with an authoritative air. 'It's the unstoppable wave of progress. Goodnight, Sir. You know where I am if you ever want to come and discuss working for me.'

As his voice trailed away into the general noise of the street outside, the well-built figure of the skulking editor, Mr. Fleet, stepped forwards from the shadows.

What now? Silas thought. He'd barely had time to consider Suddaby's proposal and yet here was something else. The editor approached him and handed over a calling card.

'I hope you don't mind me waiting? Couldn't help but overhear your interesting little chat there. But perhaps you'd like to come and see me first instead, Mr. Hunt? Why don't you?' Fleet's voice resonated in the close walls of the lobby. 'You never know, we might be able to come to some sort of... arrangement...' he lingered on the word, 'about printing the details of your story and the... difficulties...' again pausing, 'that you and your fellows now find yourselves in. A *cordial* article in the press would never hurt, eh?' He pressed a forefinger to his nose with a knowing nod.

Silas took the card and pocketed it.

'Think about it, Mr. Hunt,' said Mr. Fleet. 'You know where to find me. In return, I'm sure you could find it in yourself to reciprocate, if we understand each other?' With that the journalist disappeared back into the shadows as quickly as he had appeared.

As he stepped out into the street, Silas knew that he was caught between forces much greater than himself. On the one hand, there were honest debate, even newspaper articles and the liberal, common-sense politics that would see them all able to maintain their honourable trade in the face of these reforms. And, on the other hand, there were the radicals and agitators; those men with the gift of the gab who could stir up their fellows to believe anything they wanted them to believe and turn them to who-knows-what ends. Agitators who walked the precarious line of anarchy and unrest. He couldn't believe he'd seen Arthur even giving them time to speak just now. Then there were moderates – men like himself – who spoke in the measured words of their clubs and benevolent unions. They were the ones who truly stood for the working man, lifting himself from his plight by the strength of his own labour, the rightfulness of his cause and the solidarity of their numbers.

'George?' he said despondently to the night, 'surely that's got to be the right way?'

The following morning Silas sensed something burdensome on his brother's mind. Some lingering annoyance from the Union meeting, he presumed?

'A fair get-together last night?' he said as he came into the sitting room. His casualness tested the air between himself and Arthur sitting in his weekend chair.

'Fair enough.' Arthur ruffled his hand through his hair and stroked at his thin whiskers. On the floor between them, Scrap lifted a leg high in the air and began to lick at the inside of his thighs, working his tongue methodically down to the base of his tail.

'You mustn't worry, Arth,' Silas said. 'About the business. We'll weather it – the sewer works, the guano squeeze. I know business has slowed this year, but it'll all balance out. It has to.' He watched his brother's eyes lift from behind his paper.

'I ain't that worried,' Arthur said, nonchalant.

'Well, *something*'s up?'

Arthur returned his eyes to his newspaper. 'It's nothing.'

Silas paced to the other side of the room. 'I saw those wreckers from the Family stop you on your way out last night.'

Arthur shifted in his chair. 'And what of it?' he said sharply.

'Nothing. Just saying. You know I'd let them have it if they gave you any trouble...?' The question seemed to hang somewhere between the two of them.

'Well, there wasn't any trouble, alright?' Arthur cast his eyes down at Scrap. The creature evidently had neither interest in politics, nor brotherly questions. 'Anyway, I can handle myself, thanks very much.'

'We're talking about the Family, Arthur! You seen what they do to blokes they don't agree with?'

'You just got to stay on their good side.'

'Their good side!' Silas turned away. 'I'm only looking out for you.'

Arthur eyed his brother and his face softened. 'Anyway,' he said, 'what did Suddaby want with *you* last night? The two of you looked right chummy.'

Silas hesitated. He knew he had to tell his brother everything, if they were going to survive these difficulties. 'He offered me work, if you want to know.' He paused. 'Bloody cheek of the man!'

'You wouldn't?' Arthur lowered the paper onto his lap.

'What d'you take me for, Arthur! Chris'sakes!'

'Sorry.' Out in the street a brougham rattled by the back fence. 'What about that other bloke... Fleet, is it?' Arthur looked up from the cat. 'The newspaper man. I saw him lurking round too. What did *he* want with you?'

'He'll put something in the papers for us,' said Silas. 'If we pay him.'

'What sort of "something" in the papers?'

'I don't know. Something for our cause.'

'Oh! We got a *cause* now, have we? A cause! Lord help us!' Arthur's hand shot into the air. 'So *he's* the one stirring things up, is he?'

'Maybe,' said Silas. He watched his brother closely.

'Be cheaper to pay for adverts, wouldn't it?' Arthur thwacked the back of his hand against his paper, 'rather than throwing money away on some wheedling newspaper man.' The abrupt noise made Scrap jump to all fours.

'Can you not,' Silas said. 'Look at the poor thing.'

'Poor liddle Crap,' Arthur mocked. Scrap settled himself once again to his preening.

Silas had already decided for himself overnight that he would investigate Mr. Fleet's offer later in the day. A few words in the paper wouldn't hurt; an article on how these sanitation works were putting good working men like them out of business. It had to be better and cheaper than billboards and adverts.

'Well, *you're* clearly reading what he writes.' He flicked a finger out at Arthur's newspaper.

Arthur folded up the paper and put it on the table beside his chair. 'Still think advertising's better...'

'And how exactly do you advertise a trade like ours?' Silas asked. 'It's not like we're selling perfume.'

'Barber's got his pole,' said Arthur. 'Pawnbroker's got his golden balls. We could have a bucket of...?'

'Don't even think of it!' The tension between them broke into muted laughter.

'We could paint some boards then,' said Arthur. 'A hoarding.'

'There's not a brick wall anywhere, Arthur, that's not daubed with some business's branding.'

'Sandwich board then. Put Henry out with boards over his shoulders. He could walk the streets and get our name about while he's at it. He's got a good voice,' he paused, 'and he could tell a few jokes.'

Silas cocked a look at his brother. 'We do want *some* customers, mate.'

Arthur smiled. 'What about hand-bills then?' he said. 'You've only got to pay to have *them* printed. The boys and us can hand them out about town. Isn't that how we met old J.P. in the first place? Some card you picked up from the casual work stand? It's gotta be better than paying that fat old journalist to do your crying for you.'

As he buttoned his coat up, Silas considered his brother's advice. 'Maybe you're right,' he said, although now he wasn't so sure himself how to proceed. Perhaps the answer would come to him once he'd taken his Saturday bath.

'You off to the washhouse then?' asked Arthur.

Silas nodded.

'I'll go in after you and use your water. It'll only cost me tuppence.'

Silas laughed. 'Miser! Anyway, you can go in a couple of week-ends' time. Your birthday's coming up isn't it?'

'Very funny,' Arthur said. 'I'm not too proud to sit in a bath that's been used before, if it'll save me the readies. Look after the pennies, the pounds'll look after themselves. We might be doing well enough,' he added, 'but I'll still take it cold for tuppence. If I didn't think it'd freeze my balls off.'

'What balls?' Silas's voice echoed back down the hallway before the click of the front latch.

Silas's thoughts swilled around as his bathwater lapped at his chest and thighs. What were their options? Guano was coming into the country faster than water through the new plumbing systems, and farmers everywhere were using it instead of the old nightsoil manures. From what he'd heard, there were stockpiles of the stuff lying in shipyard warehouses from London round the coast to Liverpool. They couldn't compete with business on that scale. They could hardly give their muck away these days.

Last night at the meeting, the dissenters had shouted for disruption, but that was madness: sticking your oar in the sewer works could only mean one thing: prison. Deportation. Now Arthur wanted to go and advertise to bring in more business. But there wasn't any more business. Anywhere. There were more water closets in the city each day. People didn't want to pay to have their cesspools cleared. And the sewers were going in under the streets faster than you could name the streets themselves. No, Arthur was a gallon of dung in a half-gallon tub. Advertise! What was he thinking of? A complete waste of time and money.

Silas submerged his face, held his breath, and resurfaced. His hair lay flat to his brow. What would George do? He closed his eyes to conjure George's face but, as he lay there, one face alone materialised – the fat, self-satisfied features of Mr. Fleet. Ugly though it was, he had to go and pay the man a visit. Make their situation known. Get it into a public debate. Then perhaps someone might start thinking some common sense and get this mess sorted out to everyone's benefit.

When he arrived at the newspaper offices, a crowd had gathered outside to read the headlines of the first weekend edition, pinned up in the windows. Silas pushed his way to the front of the jumble and cast his eye across the copy. Mostly melodramatic banners from home and abroad – Oregon and Vietnam, wherever they were. Was there any local news here; news that Silas could believe in? On the evidence, would Mr. Fleet even care to publish an article about London's midnight mechanics and the downturn in their business? *CHARLES DICKENS' LATEST NOVEL ROARING SUCCESS.* At least that was something closer to home, but even the subject of this new book was French, so he'd heard. Wasn't there *anything* here to give him hope that events, as happened to Londoners, mattered to Mr. Fleet and his readers? His eyes lowered. In the corner he saw something more to his liking. THE *GREAT STINK. That* was what he wanted to see! *That* gave him hope that people were already talking about his problems. *We can colonise the remotest ends of the earth*, he read, as the crowd jostled for space, *we can conquer India! We can spread our name and our fame and our wealth to every part of the world, but we cannot even clean the River Thames.* Now that was something you could get your teeth into. Stuff that happened here. Maybe Mr. Fleet had his eye on the birdie after all.

He pushed past the faces at the window. 'Excuse me sir, madam,' he said, touching his cap as he went. Within a moment he heard the chiming of the bell above the doorway and the door closing softly behind him. Inside the hushed office, Silas stood before a large desk and an empty brass flowerpot. The clerk, a *Mr. Ernest Drinkwater: sub-editor*, as his desk-plate announced, stood by the bureau filing paper into compartments of various sizes. Above the bureau hung a line of business portraits, proprietors and editors from days gone by.

Silas coughed to make his presence known. Mr. Drinkwater looked up at him slowly. He was a lanky, long-limbed man, professionally attired, though ill-fitting. From the smell of the man, Silas concluded he must have been suffering a toothache for, as Mr. Drinkwater spoke, a strong aroma of cloves wafted across the desk.

'Yes?' asked the cloves.

'Mr. Fleet, if you please?' said Silas. 'I'm here to talk arrangements for an article.'

'Do you, sir... would you happen to have... Mr. Fleet is busy... have you made an...?' Mr. Drinkwater said fitfully.

'Appointment?' said Silas. 'No. I mean, we talked last night.'

'Oh, at the Union meeting?' said Drinkwater, well aware of the movements recorded by his superior's diary.

'That's right,' said Silas. 'We got to talking about an article.'

'Is that so?' said the cloves, wafting past him to open a door at the other side from which he had just emerged. Mr. Drinkwater leaned his tall body through, and Silas heard him murmuring into the hidden chamber. Shortly he turned around and returned to his position behind the desk.

'Mr. Fleet will see you presently,' he said, billowing aromatics Silas's way. 'Straight through,' he added, gesturing to the door.

Silas stepped through and turned to close the door behind him. 'I always use laud'num, myself,' he said as he went, patting his jaw. Bemused behind the empty flowerpot, Mr. Drinkwater stared back. 'Toothache,' Silas said, stretching a smile.

Inside, Mr. Fleet filled the chair behind his mahogany desk. 'Good morning Mr...' he offered quizzically.

'Hunt,' said Silas.

'Yes. Hunt.' The man was clearly calculating from where he knew his visitor. In a moment, the recognition dawned. 'Of course! The nightman. Last night. I didn't recognize you. You look so... clean!'

Was the journalist paying him a compliment, or not? Silas couldn't tell, though he took it as a matter of pride that cleanliness could make the editor mistake him for a journalist or a businessman.

'I wasn't expecting to be seeing you quite so soon,' Mr. Fleet went on.

'Times are urgent,' said Silas.

Although there was a vacant chair to the side of the desk, Mr. Fleet kept Silas standing. He found himself staring into the large mirror that hung on the wall behind the journalist's desk. Smart enough for business, he thought to himself. And your hands are cleaner than his. He looked down at the newspaper editor, whose palms were darkened with newsprint.

'Well. To the chase, shall we?' said Mr. Fleet. 'You may be interested to know, Mr. Hunt, that I am currently engaged in writing a court notice about a landlord who has been brought forward to explain a foul and offensive cesspool on his property. The landlord said it has been there forever, as if *that* absolved him of any responsibility!'

Mr. Fleet stood up from behind his desk and paced to one side of his office where a large globe sat suspended on a hardwood stand. He gave the ball a gentle spin and waited for it to come to a stop.

'I'd have cleared it for him,' said Silas in between the squeaks of the spinning globe. 'Would have been glad for the business.' He shifted awkwardly from foot to foot on the parquet flooring.

'Things a little... tight... at the moment are they then, Mr. Hunt?'

'You could say that.'

'Well, let's do say that then, shall we? *A little tight.*'

'Put me in touch with that landlord,' said Silas, 'and we'll sort it out.'

'Alas, too late,' Mr. Fleet said melodramatically. 'I'm sure you *would* have cleared it Mr. Hunt, given the opportunity but, the fact of the matter is, the said landlord was too parsimonious to pay to have the excrescence cleared. He should have installed a flushing closet years ago, like any decent sort... and be done with the problem for good.'

Mr. Fleet walked behind his desk to the other side of the room and pulled the long curtain to one side, peering out. 'So dirty everywhere these days, don't you think, hmm?'

'There's a quarter of a million water closets in the city now,' Silas said, 'and every one of them spilling their waste straight into the river. You've read your own headlines, haven't you? *The Great Stink*?'

'Indeed I have, Mr. Hunt! So pleased to see that *you* of all people have read them also.'

'They're flushing everyone's fortunes away. We could be feeding half the beggars in town, if only the farmers had their hands on all that wasted...' he checked himself, '*manure* for their fields.'

'So you suggest we keep things as they are, do you, Mr. Hunt? Keep everyone living in filth and squalor, just so you and your market-gardener buyers can feed a few mendicants, then line your own pockets with what comes naturally to the rest of us, eh? I don't think so! No, the WC is the way, Mr. Hunt. Flush, flush, flush!'

'There we beg to differ, Mr. Fleet.'

The two men considered each other a while in silence before Fleet sat himself down behind his desk. He picked up a pen, dipped it into the sunken inkwell and jotted a few notes.

Silas was tired of waiting. 'You mentioned last night you might be able to publish something in our favour?'

'It needs to be written first, sir. Written. Before we even think of publication.'

'Of course,' said Silas. 'I'm sure we could write it for you, if it speeded things up a bit and brought down the cost, so to speak.'

Mr. Fleet laughed explosively and then, regaining his composure, inhaled deeply. 'Mr. Hunt,' he said, in a torpid drawl, surveying his visitor with an air of scorn, 'I'm sure you are an honest working man, "so to speak", with at least a tolerably inclusive education, well-read, perhaps at least a little, in the popular literature of our times and capable, I have no doubt, of founding opinions for yourself on the salient news and matters of the day. I'm sure you might even be capable of conveying those opinions in unadorned and apposite syntax and even a little neat chirography if you put your mind to it?'

Silas stared back at the pompous man with unchecked distaste.

'In short,' Mr. Fleet went on, oblivious to anything but his own rolling address, 'I'm sure you may well even scribe the occasional well-turned epistle or draw up a working document or contract for your customers in suitable terms but, please, let's leave the wording of any *news article* to me!'

'It was only a suggestion. No matter.' Silas was almost ready to turn and leave.

'Well, let's hear it man!' the journalist suddenly exclaimed. 'What *is* this burning issue that everyone simply *must* read about?'

'You heard it last night, didn't you?'

'Yes, *that*,' said the newspaper man.

'Look. We're just normal working men, Mr. Fleet,' Silas began. As he spoke, the journalist took down a few notes. 'Men who can get seldom few people anywhere anymore to pay us for our labour. Not since your "flush" became the only sound they know. And like you heard last night, we can't compete with guano shipped in from Africa and Peru neither. This is the only work we know. Penguins don't have to earn a wage to clothe and feed their families. They dive in the sea and pull out a fish. But we have to feed and clothe ours.'

'Oh, I can see the headline now!' Mr. Fleet suddenly smiled, rising from his desk, and pacing back to his globe. He turned it carefully and it squeaked several times in its gyrations until he stopped it with his hand and placed a finger on the tip of Chile. 'Yes indeed!' he expostulated, jabbing at the *Tierra del Fuego*.

Silas waited for him to announce his brilliant idea, but the headline was not forthcoming.

'Well. That's good,' Mr. Fleet simply said, as though lost in some reverie. 'Let's talk about the price next time, shall we?'

Silas stood aback. 'Why's there a price when it's *me* who's bringing the story to you!'

'Mr. Hunt,' the journalist replied. 'Everything has a price!'

'But you'll be selling papers on the back of it! I haven't got money to pay for your news.'

'Mr. Hunt, Mr. Hunt!' the journalist cajoled. 'Who said anything about emoluments?'

'What?'

'There's no need for money, sir. You scratch my back, Mr. Hunt, I'll scratch yours,' he said. 'Let's call it... a favour in kind.'

'What sort of favour?'

'Let's just say that I have family, out in the suburbs. Setting up a large new concern in agriculture. They'll need a good load of fine grade manure to start them off and, thereafter, a reasonable deal when their stocks need replenishing. No point in them buying expensive guano, hmmm, when there's good value English nightsoil on the market?'

'I see.'

'*Quid pro quo*, as they say. In return, our esteemed paper will place a series of short articles about your... situation... in the press.'

'And where are these family of yours; we might be supplying them already?'

'I doubt it Mr. Hunt! They're to the south of the river.'

'Don't normally go that way,' said Silas.

'I'm sure,' said Mr. Fleet. 'But you could?'

'A series of articles, you say?'

'*Short* articles, Mr. Hunt.'

'I need to get my brother's agreement,' Silas said. 'You'll give me a number of days?'

'Certainly. Though I suggest we get your "news" in print, sooner rather than later. Who knows what other sanitary excitements are just waiting round the corner to knock it from its place as leader!' The man laughed mordantly to himself. 'Now, if that's all? Good day, sir.'

Out on the street the Saturday market was closing down. The traders, men and women, leant over tables and barrels smoking their pipes. On their three-legged stools, milk-girls sat watching the morning pass, their churns empty. Silas watched the scrawny children desperate for a final sale: match girls with trays around their necks; ragged girls with baskets of water cress; a pair of shabby kids hawking sticks of firewood. He thought of himself and Arthur, just out of the clink, in those hateful old days. How far away they mercifully seemed to him now.

'Nice new pair of shoes, sir?' a cobbler called up to him from the pavement. Silas looked down. An old man was guarding his rank of second-hand shoes, pulling at Silas's trouser leg. His hair dangled in lank tresses down either side of his face.

'No, thank you.' He shook his leg free from the cobbler's grasp.

'Boot-black then, sir?' the cobbler asked, prodding the boot-blacker who sat next to him, almost asleep, his box perched on the kerb.

'Really, no,' said Silas, more irritably this time.

'Just a penny sir,' the boot-black said, rousing himself at the prospect of business.

'Listen,' said Silas. 'Didn't you hear me? Which part of 'no' don't you get?'

The boot-black looked up at him, confused.

In that moment Silas disliked himself, but wouldn't these people leave him alone? All he wanted was to get home and eat that roast lunch. No doubt Nellie would be fetching it back from the cook shop right now.

'Leave him, Jack,' the cobbler said to the boot-blacker. 'He thinks e's above the likes of us.'

'Bleedin' toffs,' cursed Jack.

His business with Fleet and Drinkwater completed, Silas rode the omnibus back home. As the busy roads went by, he thought about his life's reserve of Saturdays. Now were the Saturdays of bathing and cleanliness and happy relaxation. Or happy in so far as these new dealings with Newspapermen and Contractors of Sewer Works would allow him to be. Once, there had also been those long-gone Saturdays of childhood when he and George and Arthur had run errands for the Jewish families around the block in New Jerusalem. When he had worked until he dropped, yes, but with coins in his pocket for his mother. Then the seemingly interminable Saturdays of prison – just a handful of them, but all the more memorable or, perhaps, forgettable for that – Saturdays picking oakum, treading the wheel and fending off the threats of scammers and dodgers. Then came the gut-wrenching Saturdays of hunger and scraping a living, followed by the Saturdays of odd jobbing and comfort at Belmerson's. And what of the Saturdays of John Pearce? Saturdays when he and Arthur were so exhausted from clearing cesspools that they could barely move by the time the weekend was through. Saturdays that had earned them their keep; that had set them on their path to their future... these new Saturdays when they were their own bosses. Saturdays when they relaxed in their own house, eating their own food and wearing their own clothes, with money enough to spare for hot baths and omnibus rides and paying the cook shop to do your roasting for you. Saturdays of something like a family once more, with Arthur and Nellie and workmates round to share the fruits of their labour. Saturdays when he could call, if she was willing, on the girl he hoped, one day, to marry. The Saturdays of Flora Street.

He dismounted from the knifeboard atop the omnibus and waved the driver off at the corner. 'Thank you, Potts.'

'You're welcome, Mr. Hunt.' Potts's voice merged with the birdsong, the rattle of wheels and the clacking of cobbles, dissolving into the air. Otherwise, the street was curiously quiet. Everyone must have already returned home from work and be sitting down to a Saturday lunch with their wives and families.

He pushed through the lattice gate to the front of his property and walked up the tiles to the front door, sidestepping one of Scrap's leavings.

Inside, he hung his cap carefully on the hallway stand. The front room was empty, he noticed – the snug front parlour with its fireplace, its cushioned wooden settle along the back wall, and its armchairs – although a fire had been lit and was now smouldering gently in the grate, ready for the usual after-lunch chat with the boys. Planning the week's work. He checked himself in the coat stand mirror and walked through the hall to the dining room.

Arthur was sitting exactly where he'd left him, inspecting a tatty piece of paper held up between his fingers.

Silas could hear Nellie clattering dishes in the back kitchen. 'You haven't moved.' He took his jacket off and hung it over the back of a dining chair. 'What you got there?'

'Nothing,' said Arthur, folding the paper and secreting it in his pocket.

'Nothing's nothing,' Silas said. 'Everything's something?'

'Aren't you the philosopher then,' Arthur sneered. Silas ignored him. 'Did you decide not to have a bath then?'

'A darn sight cleaner than you'll ever be.' Silas smoothed his hair back with his hand. 'What *is* that?'

'S'nothing.' He scratched at the back of his head. 'Just some thoughts I scribbled about advertising.' Arthur stood from his armchair and walked to the window. 'We'll talk about it later.'

Silas began to arrange the chairs around the table, watching his brother in awkward silence.

'Thoughts about advertising? I thought we'd talked about that?'

'Like I said, it's nothing,' Arthur repeated.

'Fine, Arthur, I gottit. Scuse me for asking!'

A voice called 'Hullo' from the hallway and the faces of their workmen appeared at the dining room door.

'...but was it *you* what told Reynolds I was mean with my money?' Gamble was asking his workmate in an agitated manner.

'Not me!' said Shrimpton. 'I always keep my thoughts to meself!' The cartman laughed and looked at Gamble, who offered him back a sarcastic smile.

'Fellers,' Silas said. Whatever tension might have existed in the air between him and Arthur now vanished in a flurry of handshakes. The pleasantries, however, were soon elbowed aside as Joseph White appeared disheveled in the doorway. Christ, he's three sheets to the wind, Silas thought.

'Morning Silas, Arthur. Mrs. Hunt.' Henry's voice carried through to the back parlour from which Nellie's voice came out to greet them in return. 'Afternoon boys,' it said. 'Take a seat, won't you.'

'Afternoon already, Mrs. Hunt?' Gamble looked surprised. Nellie came into the room and ushered him around the table.

'That Reynolds's so fat,' slurred White, rancorously returning the topic to where it had just come from, 'you could grease the axle of the omnibus with 'is shadow.'

'Thank you, Joseph.' Silas couldn't miss the lingering air of liquor on his breath. 'That's enough of Reynolds.'

Henry leaned into his boss's shoulder and whispered. 'He's only just taken a quencher, boss. He's totally half-n-half.'

'You're telling me.'

As White sat down, the extent of his drinking looked to be much worse. The man was morosely drunk. He slumped down into his dining chair.

'Don't.' Silas jutted his chin at the man. Everyone stopped and looked at him. In the pause, he raised his brow and index finger. 'Not today, please,' he said in a fatherly way.

Joseph White exhaled a short, sharp breath through his nostrils and consented. 'Certainly, boss,' he said.

'Heaven help us,' Nellie muttered, hurrying back to the parlour to collect the food.

As she went, Henry and Harry did as bid and sat down in a chattering burst at the far side of the table.

'Lookin' nice and clean today boss,' Shrimpton said once he was seated. 'As usual.'

'Saturday bath, Henry,' said Silas. 'You should try it one day yourself. Cleanliness does wonders for a chap's health and spirits.'

Henry laughed. 'Well, you know what the wise man says, don't you? *He who goes to bed with a filthy fundament, wakes up with fundamentally filthy fingers.* Ain't that just so?' The man roared inanely and, beside him, Gamble spluttered with foolish laughter.

Arthur turned his head to check that his wife was out of earshot. 'Not when Nellie's in hearing,' he ordered.

'Of course,' Shrimpton apologised. 'Sorry. Wasn't thinking.'

'Are you ever?' said Arthur.

'Where's your own good lady then, boss?' Gamble asked, his sniggers subsiding.

'If you're referring to Flora,' said Silas, 'she's elsewhere.' His workmen looked down at the table.

Henry fiddled with his cutlery. 'I...' he began.

'With her own family,' Silas added.

'You want to ask her one day soon, Silas,' said Nellie coming back into the room, a tray of steaming food levelled before her. 'Make her a part of *this* family instead. Can't have you a bachelor your whole life.'

'You need a bit of romance in your life boss,' said Shrimpton.

'I have romance enough thanks, Henry,' said Silas. 'We'll do it when we're both ready.'

'I got the best wife in the world,' said Henry. 'You've met her. She only ever hits me with the soft end of the broom.'

Gamble's shoulders once again rose and fell childishly.

'Marriage,' White contributed, 'is just a custom to keep women out of mischief and get 'em into trouble,' this wisdom arising from somewhere within his funk.

'You've already been told,' Arthur said stiffly. 'Mind your manners. There's a woman present.'

'A woman!' exclaimed Nellie.

'My *wife*,' Arthur corrected himself.

'Well, this has got off to a pretty start, hasn't it!' Nellie said.

'Are we ready to eat then?' said Silas, interposing.

'Be my guest,' Nellie replied dryly.

The beef was lifted from the pot, a dripping lump of tightened muscle, and placed upon the carving board. Silas took the plated knife and whittled away at the joint. It came away in rough chunks. As its smell drifted through the house, Scrap reappeared at the table legs, purring hopefully.

With a large spoon, Nellie divided the batter pudding. Both meat and batter were dished on to plates, with greens and peas placed beside by Nellie's hovering ladle. The gravy was poured. Knives and forks clinked in anticipation. Joseph White belched. Tentative talk of this and that hung over the table. Plates were filled, cleared in near silence, and removed from the table by Nellie.

Apple pie with sauce was served as sweetener. Approving noises made. Again Nellie removed the bowls and spoons, fetching in bread and celery on a shared platter. In sequence of the pecking order, hands reached out to take a piece of bread and a stem to crunch upon. And all the while, George's empty seat tugged at Silas's thoughts. I've done this all for you, he thought to himself and gazed up to the eyes of 'The Angel's Whisper'.

Nellie headed dutifully to the scullery, her job at least made easier in recent months, with water now laid-on to the terrace for such domestic chores. The water closet would never appear however, she rued, not so long as Arthur and Silas worked at this trade of theirs.

While she was clearing, the men moved into the snug room where the fire had now settled to a constant glow. They seated themselves at close quarters, to digest their lunch and talk about the coming week. Shrimpton, White and Gamble propped themselves up on the wooden settle. Arthur and Silas sat in the armchairs to either side of the fire. Each man had carried with him from the dining room a small pot of beer, save for Gamble who sat nursing a glass of water under the weight of his recent pledge.

Henry unpocketed his pipe and tobacco tin and began his loading ritual. He sucked hard on the pipe to clear it of any blockages. Whatever had been in there gave way with a loud *pop*. He then set to scraping the bowl with the blade of his penknife and rooted around in the stem of his pipe with a thin metal rod. Finally, he pinched up a mound of rough shag from the tin and tamped it down into the bowl, lighting the contents with a taper taken off the fire. Soon the room began to fill with aromatic smoke.

While he was at this business, Silas supped on his ale: his lunch was sitting comfortably in his stomach, but his thoughts were resting uneasily in his head. 'Just two closets to clear this week boys,' he finally said, once Shrimpton's pipe was blithely puffing. 'Tuesday night and Wednesday only. Sorry. Means wages will be down a little. There's nothing I can do.'

The three workmen sat and digested the news. White looked suddenly more sober. 'Time was, last year,' he said, in a dark voice, 'when we had five jobs each week. Every bloody week.'

'Like I said at the Union meeting,' said Silas, 'we're taking a knock at the moment. But things *will* get better.'

'I doubt that very much,' said White morosely. 'Things never gits bloody better.'

'You've got to work to make them better.' Silas took a swallow from his glass.

'I hate this fucking work,' White cursed under his breath. The room stiffened.

'Well, while you're working for us and earning your wages from us...' said Silas.

'And eating our food...' Arthur interjected.

'And eating our food,' Silas repeated, 'you'll like it well enough and watch your tongue and all. And if you don't like it, then you know who *is* looking for workmen.'

'Who's that then,' White replied.

'Suddaby. On the new sewers,' said Arthur.

'Or there's the underground train thing,' said Gamble. Silas threw him a sideways look as if to tell him 'enough'. Confused, Gamble prattled on. 'Trains in tunnels? Two thousand fellers they say, all with picks and shovels, underneath Westminster, can you believe it? Hundreds more at Earls Court 'pparently, baking bricks to build the tunnels. Thousands of people shuttling about underground like so many garden moles.'

'I ain't goin' underground for fucking no one,' said White, rising unsteadily from the settle. 'Don't have to do what no one says, I don't.'

For a moment the room went silent, each seated man wondering what the standing man might do next. Silas bristled in his chair. Slowly, White turned and shuffled to the door and pulled it ajar, stepping across the threshold.

'A man can go to prison for six months for refusing to work,' said Silas. 'You know that.'

'So what?' said White from the doorway. 'I don't give a fuckin' farden.'

'I've told you,' said Silas, 'watch your mouth!'

'Are you refusing to work?' said Arthur.

'Are you threat'nin' to shop me to the law?'

The men stared at each other.

'Thanks very much for lunch,' White said caustically and, like one of Henry's puffs of smoke, was gone. The front door slammed behind him.

Silas jumped from his chair. Arthur laid a hand across his brother's arm. 'Leave him.'

'Did that man just quit his job?' Silas asked when he had calmed.

'I believe he may have done just that,' said Arthur.

Gamble looked to Shrimpton and Shrimpton looked philosophically at the two brothers, a thin curl of grey smoke rising in front of his features.

'Well, that saves us some money,' Silas finally said. 'Two clearances this week suddenly looks more profitable for the rest of us.' He smiled awkwardly.

'If only he'd done it earlier, you'd have saved yourselves a meal as well,' said Henry.

'He'll be off to Suddaby's tomorrow, you mark my words,' said Arthur.

'If he don't kill hisself in the gin house first,' said Gamble.

'He won't find any work in that state,' said Shrimpton. 'He couldn't grow beans in a pile of shit, that wastrel.'

Silas came downstairs and sloped into the dining room. He threw himself down into a chair beside the table. Arthur was, once again, already warming himself by the fire. Nellie was in the kitchen. It was Monday morning, with no clearances until Tuesday and Wednesday night.

'That's all you do these days, d'you know that Arthur? Sit in that bloody chair.'

Silas's spirits were dented. Yes, they had a little work this week, which meant *some* pay at least, and manure to sell on to the middleman, Grundy. But what with their man White walking out over the weekend, business troubles were weighing heavily on him.

'Something up?' said Arthur.

Silas huffed. 'What's going on?'

'Nothing much,' said Arthur. 'The usual.'

'Can we talk about what we're gonna do?' He opened the small drawer tucked under the dining room table and pulled out a sheet of paper and pencil. Nellie came in with tea, a hunk of bread and two sausages.

'Silas,' she acknowledged. 'Breakfast.'

'Thank you, Nellie,' he said, slurping at the cup.

Scrap appeared on his never-ending quest for food. He butted his head against Nellie's shins. 'You want some Bags o'Mystery yerself do you, little one?' she said affectionately.

'Don't go wasting good sausages on him!' Arthur said, but Nellie had already stooped to pick up her pet and carry him through to the kitchen.

Tapping his pencil on the desk, Silas wrote down some numbers. 'What are the options?' he asked rhetorically, his teeth working the end of the pencil and muffling his words.

Nellie reappeared at the doorway.

'One: advertise. As you said the other day, Arthur.' Silas looked to his brother. 'Not my favoured option, but we'll include it.' He pointed the pencil's end at Arthur. 'You said you'd jotted down some thoughts?'

Arthur looked back at him blankly. 'Somewhere.'

'Well, when you find them. In the meantime, two: we team up with the middleman, Grundy, and branch out into manures.'

'Bet he's feeling the squeeze as much as we are,' said Arthur. 'We're selling half as much soil to him as we used to, since we ain't clearing as much out.'

'True.'

'He's probably selling out to the boys in guano himself.'

'Wouldn't put it past the bastard,' Silas cursed. To his side, Nellie blenched at his language. 'We're not falling for any more of his dodges. Bloody swindler. Never liked the man.' He scribbled John Grundy's name off his list. 'Which leaves us three: beat Grundy to it, sell up and start trading in guano ourselves.'

'Chance'd be a fine thing!' said Arthur. 'It's all tied up that deal, isn't it? Big companies?'

'There's millions in it,' said Silas, 'but is it gonna last? You might sell up here, jump ship so to speak, only to find yourself in worse off straits next year.'

'Selling up's not on the cards, is it?' said Nellie in surprise.

'Not if I can help it,' Silas replied. 'So, four: article in the paper. Mr. Fleet. Favoured plan for me.' Before his brother could reply, Silas moved swiftly on. 'Or Five: give up this whole nightsoil business for good and go and work for Suddaby.'

'On the sewers!' Arthur raised his voice. His brother stared hard at him. 'Sorry,' he said more quietly, 'go work on the sewers?'

'You can't admit defeat,' said Nellie.

'Just airing the options,' said Silas. 'But yes. Out of the question.'

'You had me going there,' said Arthur, shifting in his chair.

'So that's it then,' said Silas. The three of them formed a silent triangle.

Eventually Arthur spoke. 'One more.' He scratched his chin distractedly.

'What's that then?' asked Silas.

Arthur leant across the table and carefully plucked the pencil from between Silas's fingers. Bending over the piece of paper he wrote *Six: Direct Action*.

Silas stared at him hard and long. 'Join the Family!' he blustered.

'Wrecking?' Nellie's voice broke in a yelp.

'You can't be serious?' said Silas.

'They ain't doing nothing wrong, those boys,' Arthur said. 'They're just stirring things up a bit about the sewers. Someone's gotta do it, or we're all sunk.' His cheeks blushed under the sudden, sharp scrutiny of his brother and wife.

'Think of the consequences of getting messed up with them,' said Nellie. 'You'd be in for a long stretch of penal if you got caught doin' anything bad with the likes of them.'

'I dare say you would,' said Silas. 'You *do* remember what that's like, right?'

'They're not so bad,' said Arthur.

His brother looked at him in disbelief. 'How the hell would you know?'

'I just heard, that's all,' Arthur replied.

'Have you lost your mind, mate? Listen to what you're saying. D'you know what happened when the Chartists rioted years back? Hundreds imprisoned. Hard labour. Countless of them transported.'

'They were fighting for the rights of working men,' Arthur said defensively. 'Like us.'

'Pull yourself together, Arthur!' Silas rebuked him. 'People can't go round smashing things up and taking the law into their own hands.' He snatched the pencil back off him and threw it down on the table.

Wary of a fight, Nellie pointed to the paper with her index finger and made a scribbling motion. 'Cross it out, Silas,' she said. 'Quickly. It's not going to happen!'

Silas reached for the pencil still rolling towards the edge of the table. He seized it and, with a demonstrative sweep, struck through Arthur's writing.

The three of them stared at the paper in silence.

'I suppose you're right,' Arthur finally said.

'*Suppose*?' said Silas.

The standoff endured for several awkward moments. Scrap announced himself again at the hearth and sat licking his paws, wiping them across his nose and whiskers.

'So where does that leave us, Silas?' said Nellie, trying to settle the mood.

'It leaves us with just the one sensible option at the moment – going to get ourselves noticed. Which is Mr. Fleet. Agreed?'

'We ain't even discussed it yet,' said Arthur.

'We discussed it the other day and we're discussing it now!' Silas pointed to the paper. Mr. Fleet's name sat isolated on the page.

'Agreed,' said Arthur reluctantly, sitting back down in the chair beside the fire.

'Agreed,' said Nellie.

'In the meantime,' Silas said, 'I suggest we go and talk to Suddaby sometime soon and try to negotiate some sort of short-term security, while something longer term can be brought to the table. Right?'

'I'm not talking to that man,' Arthur said heatedly.

'Okay. Take it easy, Mr. Wrecker,' Silas said. 'You're happy to talk to the Family boys though, aren't you?'

Arthur stared back stubbornly.

'*I'll* go...' Silas went on, 'if it's going to be that hard for you?' He stood to leave the room. 'Let's concentrate on what we *can* do first, right? We got clearances to do this week. And you can get yourself out of that bloody chair for a start.'

'I don't spend all my time in it.'

'No, but what you *do* actually do is quite a mystery these days,' said Silas, leaving the room, his tea only half finished.

When he was gone, Nellie stared her husband down.

'What?' he said, returning her look.

'You're nothing but a fool Arthur Hunt, talking to your brother like that.'

'There's nothing meant by it, woman,' he said. 'You clearly don't know me if you think I'd...' He was suddenly interrupted by the sight of the cat, squatting in the corner of the room.

'Crap!' Arthur shouted, expecting a reprimand from his wife. But Nellie had already turned away and headed into the scullery. Behind her, Scrap's startled form shot out of the room in a dark blur.

A low bank of cloud sat over a moving sea of carts and horses. The carts had brought in brick, timber, and ironwork all day long and carted away equal amounts of earth and rubble. Great stacks of building materials lay piled between the wooden huts, draped in oiled tarpaulin. On top of one such mound of supplies stood a grave, unyielding figure – a gentleman in a tall hat and coat, waistcoat, and fawn cotton trousers held up by braces, a satin cravat held in place with a gold, jewelled pin, and a sturdy surtout coat to fend off the worst of the weather. Over his shoes he wore a pair of rubberized galoshes, the latest arrivals from America. He dipped his hand into his waistcoat pocket and pulled out his fob watch. 'Starting to come along on time Mr. Peggs,' he said, 'at last.'

Mr. Suddaby put his fob watch away and carefully lowered himself to the ground. There, a surveyor – an engineer from the army corps – was inclined over his apparatus, peering through the eyepiece of a theodolite, checking the angle of incidence to the ground across an open trench. The new sewer was being constructed in place of the old decaying one that had run here for two hundred years. Meticulously the surveyor called out numbers across the trench, where his companion raised a marker to the level indicated and cut a benchmark into the ground against which the angle had been measured.

'I'm assuming that this new branch can be put in before the worst of the predicted weather arrives?' Mr. Suddaby asked his surveyor.

The engineer raised himself from the eyepiece and turned to face the Director of Works. 'We're aiming to have it so, sir,' he said. 'The construction is in my hands; I'm afraid the weather is not.'

'Indeed,' Mr. Suddaby agreed. To their side Mr. Peggs watched carefully from within the confines of his long-coat and from beneath the brim of his tall hat, moving his head backwards and forwards in rapid signs of approval. It cast dancing shades over his clipboard maps and site drawings.

Heavy rains in recent weeks had put the sewer works behind schedule; the half-finished drains had already flooded on more than one occasion. If Mr. Suddaby was to fulfil his contractual obligations to Mr. Bazalgette and the Metropolitan Board on time, then there must be no more setbacks.

'No more hindrances, no more delays?' he said to the surveyor, as if willpower alone could make it be so.

'I certainly hope not, sir,' the man replied, although his voice betrayed his misgivings. There had been unfortunate accidents – acts of god, the surveyor called them – that had slowed down their progress this last quarter: a man dragged out from underneath a subsiding brick wall here; a small flare-up there, where gas from an existing connecting sewer had caught light from the lamps of the underground workers. The navvies had been hurried out to the nearest hospital with burned faces and singed hair. On other days yet more construction workers had been carried out of the tunnels unconscious, on account of the mind-numbing gasses underground. The workforce had needed to be replaced. All these things took time. Surely, the Director understood these kinds of pressures?

As the surveyor pressed his eye back to the theodolite, a gang of such navvies stood waiting to receive their new orders, with filthy cotton shirts open to their chests and red scarves knotted around their necks. 'He don't wanna do it like that,' one navvie whispered, scratching his head. 'Doin' it all wrong,' another specialist put in.

They needn't have worried about whispering, for their words were barely audible beneath the clanking chains and rattling pulleys and tackle. The mortar-mixer was churning and clattering, its operator carefully directing the outfall of his chute for the slurry to fall in the right position. Above, the emerging archways of the new sewers were held aloft by wooden struts and riveted steel formers. Vast spanning arches of brick. Red expanses curving up and over, the walls several courses thick and penetrated at junctures by adjoining branch sewers – a forking network of small conduits joined to larger, then larger still, until this sewer itself would come to join Mr. Bazalgette's massive intercepting sewer to this northern side of the river.

The navvies passed buckets of cement up to the apex where their mates were setting the newest rows of bricks in double skins.

Below the arches, excavators were digging out the earth by hand and hauling it away by bucket. Carpenters carved struts and joists; masons chiselled footing stones. In the cut-and-cover trench, a team of labourers pulled on ropes attached to carts further back in the tunnel, back there at the workface, where men with picks and shovels were hacking at the bedrock and clay, shoring it up with timbers. They loaded the residue into the cart, which now was being pulled out into the sunlight on temporary tracks.

Mr. Suddaby thanked his site engineer for his reassurances and moved on.

'Mr. Peggs!' he ordered briskly. The clerk lifted his eyes from his almanac and balance sheet and walked on with his superior. As he walked, he continued with his documentation of each brick laid, each human hour invested in the scheme: statistical reports on progress and costs, the million bricks, the so-and-so thousand cubic yards of concrete. The myriad tons of earth. Mr. Suddaby and Mr. Peggs walked away from the industrial anthill, picking their way through the mud until they reached their fiacre at the distant roadside, where they mounted and disappeared back to their clean, dry offices.

The working day was drawing to a close, and soon the workers would down their tools and abandon their labyrinth of tunnels and gantries, leaving it to be covered by the fall of night, just as the sewers themselves would, before long, be buried once again beneath ground, the works completed. Then the passageways and all the filth they were destined to siphon away would be finally hidden from view, the waste of the city flowing silently out to sea beneath the oblivious feet of the city's passers-by.

But whoever returned there to that industrious anthill at the stroke of midnight that same night, and who studied the tunnels and skeletal structures of wood might, just might, have detected there a very different kind of resolve at work. Who were those three furtive men dressed almost entirely in black? Black trousers and boots, black jackets and capes thrown across their shoulders, black caps pulled down to hide their purposeful faces.

What were these incognito figures doing here back at the anthill, now that the navvies had long since departed, drinking away their wages in a hundred steaming pothouses across the district? And what did those three figures intend with that rickety trolley and barrel that they were now easing down the slope and into the trench, leaving it to sit there beneath the overarching scaffold?

Whoever had been patrolling the worksite with a lantern held high and a guard dog leashed low, might have seen these three shady figures maneuvering their barrel into place and might, perhaps, have heard their whispered voices lingering on the night air, for tonight there was no clanking and rattling to mask the sounds that one man made to another.

'Shift it this way a little,' said one of the voices in a low rumble, its owner exerting himself to slide the barrel into place.

'Right there,' said a second.

'Underneath the crossbeam,' added the third, an expert it seemed in such sanitary matters. 'That's the one we want knocking out. Bring that portion down and the whole lot'll tumble like a house of cards.'

But whoever should have been patrolling the worksite didn't hear these utterances, for he was already comfortably asleep in his warm little watchman's cabin, his brazier glowing gently in the corner, his candle guttering softly in its holder, the flicker catching glossily in the half-empty bottle of brandy on his table. His guard dog also was just as comfortably asleep as his master, its legs twitching from dreams of the chase, his snuffles and snores combining with those of the sleeping watchman. Instead, the voices of those three secret agents simply floated up into the night sky to alight on no one's ears but their own. Which, for them, was just as well.

Once the barrel was securely in place, the chief saboteur urged his partners up and out of the trench. 'I dunno how long the fuse is on this thing,' he said, 'but you wanna get yourselves well clear.'

'Here,' said his partner turning back towards him in the shadows, 'you'll be wanting these.' He handed his associate a box of lucifers.

'Get going now,' said the first. 'Set yourselves behind those barrels there.' The man pointed up to the hulking shapes that rose above, casting their shadows down into the trench. 'I'll be up in a moment, once she's lit.'

The two black figures clambered quickly up the sides of the trench and, cloaking themselves behind the barrels, disappeared from sight. In the trench the remaining man struck a light, catching the match's acrid flare in his nostrils. He extended his fingers towards a fuse of twisted rag set in the top of his device and lowered the flame. Whoever had been watching would have seen the agitator's face in the flash of the matchstick and, perhaps, have recognized him later in a court of law should the man be apprehended, and the viewer be called in to witness. But the only witness was currently dead to the world in his work hut and this, the perpetrator hoped, was an act of sabotage that would go unnoticed. Unnoticed, at least, until the morning, when work would have to stop, repairs be made and, who knows, perhaps this whole endeavor of sewer building be abandoned, to leave the city to its old, time-trusted ways of disposal.

Carefully he introduced the flame to the rag and watched it catch. It sizzled and smouldered a little as he bent his face towards it to blow on the glowing rag. Within a second it caught and flared, and the man threw his head backwards to save his brows and whiskers. Quickly he turned and began to clamber up the side of the trench while the oil-soaked wick burned down to the top of the barrel.

A few moments later the barrel blew and the struts of scaffold supporting the archway erupted, giving way in a shower of brick dust, earth, and shrapnel. The earth below him began to collapse and, with a sudden effort, the incendiarist threw himself up and over the trench, covering his head as he cowered behind the barrels with his two companions.

Above them, a cloud of dust and debris began to fall, settling on their caps and shoulders, turning everything to grey. Behind them, the new section of sewer collapsed into powder and rubble.

It was then that the brick dam ruptured. A fountain of liquid, as high as a palace garden's, sprang into the air and showered down. Where only moments before had been fire and explosion, now came deluge.

They may have escaped the initial force of the blast, but the three cowering saboteurs now found themselves doused in a shower of the filthiest liquid. Foul, stinking water, ordure, and dung. The mire of a thousand households and street gutters rained down over the site and drenched them. They coughed and spluttered to void it from their eyes, their ears, their nostrils, and mouths. And then, like a passing summer storm blowing over a field, the shower halted, and everything subsided into magnified silence.

Tentatively the three men stood to look back at the destruction they had wrought. Wiping foetid liquid from their faces and spitting on the ground to clear their lips of rancid matter, they gazed down into the sinkhole. 'Bloody hell,' they said in unison.

'That ought to stop 'em,' the deeper voice said. 'Now, get outta here. On your own. We won't meet up 'til this thing has settled,' and, as secretively as they had come, the three dark figures vanished into the shadows of the night, melting back into the engulfing smut of the nearby rookeries.

Back in his cosy cabin, the night guard's eyes sprang open suddenly from a pleasant dream of dubious morality. At his feet, the eyes of his dog also leaped open from a pleasant dream of chasing rats. The two of them rose immediately to their feet by instinct. 'What the...?' the watchman said. His hound barked insistently.

The man stepped forward and turned the latch on the door, pushing it ajar. His head peered cautiously around the portal. His dog rushed out. 'Back, Topper!' the watchman commanded in a rough bark of his own, but Topper had already bolted. The guard watched him race across the worksite. 'Holy Jesus, I'm for the jump!' the watchman said to the night.

In the distance, above the speeding animal, an orange-grey plume was rising into the sky, followed moments later by a sky-high jet of water.

Samuel Suddaby's face wore an expression of appalled municipal dismay. The Director of Works was standing once again at the worksite in his rubberized galoshes and greatcoat. The top hat on his head defined his presence and his authority, towering over the ragged hole that had somehow appeared in the earthworks overnight.

Beside him stood Mr. Peggs, clipboard in hand as though, like a child with his favourite toy, he might have fallen asleep the night before still clutching it. Alongside stood the contractor's team of surveyors and engineers and an assemblage of helmeted policemen, their moustaches forming a broken line of fuzz that stretched horizontally between them from cape buckles to chin straps. Before these officials, the entire workforce was amassed – excavators, navvies, brickies, cement mixers, carpenters, and steelworkers – each man looking down at the ruin that had been wrought overnight on their labours. Their talk was as loud and dissonant as the grinding din of machinery the day before. But today the machines were silent, and it was the men themselves who churned the air in noisy, heated discourse.

Mr. Suddaby raised his hand. Slowly the crowd settled.

'I want, briefly, to talk to you about this... this outrage... and the threat that it poses to us.' His voice was as clear as a church bell at matins. 'I want to tell you how we, together, can keep this great capital of ours – a city of pronounced history and boundless progress – how we can keep it safe and civilised for one and all. What you see here before you,' he gestured to the damaged works, the scattered debris, and the deepening pond of effluent in the trenches below them, 'is a wilful act of destruction, with nothing behind it but the desire for anarchy. We are lucky that no one was killed. The police are still gathering the facts about what happened here last night,' at this, the rank of policemen to his side seemed to stiffen and stand tall beneath their capes, 'but here are the few things that we *do* know.'

Mr. Suddaby paused and looked to his right, catching the eye of the Chief of Police. Enumerating his points by emphatically slapping his gloves from one hand into the open palm of the other, Mr. Suddaby proceeded with his address. 'This wanton act was not committed by one of our workers.'

The crowd began to murmur in offense that anyone might suspect one of their own to be responsible for such an atrocity.

'*We,*' Mr. Suddaby smacked down his gloves, '*we* are all serving our fellow citizens, part of the great family that is London.'

At this, his troupe of workers cheered.

'No. This was evil work, done from outside, by those who would derail the engines of progress. Whether they are part of some broad conspiracy, or whether they are simply opportunists working on their own for some inconceivable and nefarious ends, we do not know.'

Here, the Chief of Police seemed to shuffle in his boots beside the speaker.

'But it *is* clear,' the Director emphasised, 'that whoever these men are, they have already lost themselves to the dark paths of chaos, embracing a perverted ideology that calls on them to keep us all living in the Dark Ages. Living in filth and in squalor. But we *will* not go back to the Dark Ages with them!'

*Smack*. Once more the workforce rallied and cheered at his pronouncement.

'This barrel bomb may have set our works back a few months, but they will not defeat us in our purpose. We *will* build our sewers!'

Another cheer. Another smack of the gloves.

'We *will* pursue these men until they are caught.'

A loud 'Here here!' from the Chief of Police.

'We may be confronted by their sickness,' the Director went on, stirred now by his own oratory, 'but we will not yield to their contagion. There *is* a cure, and we *will* exercise it rigorously. We will *not* give in to fear!'

Cheer. *Smack.*

'*That* is what these perpetrators desire. We will prevail by being resolute and completing the task that lies before us. Our law enforcers *will* hunt them down.'

Another audible 'Here here!' from the rank of police moustaches.

'And if *any man* here knows *anything* at all about the outrage instigated last night, I urge you to come forward to me, in confidence. We *must* work together in our hunt for the truth.'

At this the workforce hollered loudly and then, as if by some unspoken directive, suddenly stilled itself. For a moment, worker looked worker in the eye for the glimmer of knowledge, or betrayal.

'Now,' said Mr. Suddaby. 'Let us begin once again on our noble venture.'

'I thought you night-boys always went down the sewers in gangs?' Nellie's voice was fractious with complaint. 'Case one of you goes lost, or there's a swarm of rats or such down there?'

Arthur didn't respond.

'Get bitten bad by one of them and you're a gonner!'

Still Arthur remained silent.

'Perhaps you were bit by a rat, Arthur?' She swabbed at her husband's brow as he lay in bed, the sheets pulled up under his armpits, the pillows propped behind his head. 'Lord knows what filth they carry on their fur and teeth.'

Arthur's arms lay lifelessly on the coverlet. His eyes stared vacantly into the room. From the bottom of the bed his bare feet protruded, dirty ankles and toes jutting out of his nightshirt.

Nellie dabbed at him with a moist towel. His lips were pale, his skin pallid. Cold sweat shimmered at his brow and, gathering momentum, trickled down his temples almost as fast as his wife could mop it away.

'I wasn't... bitten... by no... rat,' he managed to reply weakly.

'Well how d'you get *so* sick all of a sudden?' she queried him. 'Don't sell me a dog, Arthur Hunt, I want to hear the truth.'

Casually she ran her fingers through his hair and, finding some matter stuck there, picked it from his scalp. She inspected the fragments between her fingers, before brushing them off against her apron. 'And filthy too! You were soaked through when you came home last night. And now this!'

'I... already... told you...' Arthur protested. The hesitations slowed his speech to a feeble trickle. 'Drinking... I stumbled... what's-his-name saved me... the river.' The exertion of speaking was more than he could bear, and he leaned to one side, retching violently into the chamber pot on the boards to his side.

'That's good enough to make a stuffed bird laugh!' Nellie folded her arms across her chest. On reflection, however, a headlong tumble into some branch of the river, or the canal, would seem the likeliest explanation. He wouldn't be the last drunk to do it. 'Well, I pray to the Lord,' she went on, 'that you haven't gone and fallen in and got yourself,' she faltered in her thoughts, not daring to voice their logical conclusion, 'a dose of the cholera.' Her sentence trailed off in the faintest of whispers.

Her husband barely seemed to hear what she said. The exertions of his retching, combined with his fever, had rendered him almost unconscious. She sat down in the chair beside the bed and watched him. Was cholera back in the city, she wondered. It hadn't been here for years, not since they'd taken the handle off that pump in the Golden Square. All those deaths. Then again, if it *was* back, there was nothing she could do, was there, but ease the coming torture? Lord help us, were these his final moments? Arthur's lips would be turning blue in a matter of hours, she panicked, and then the convulsions, the paroxysms and appalling diarrhea. The excruciating death. And if he *did* come down with it, then wouldn't they all get it soon? When cholera hit a house, it hit everyone didn't it? God damn this nightsoil business! If he hadn't spent his life crawling around amongst the very source of it, then this would never have happened. Why couldn't he be a clerk, or a regular mechanic like any other feller?

These worries plagued her as she tried to rest. Barely could she settle before they came back at her in waves. She dashed to the window to close the curtains and keep a shaft of sunlight from her husband's face. This done, she sat down again with her hands on her lap, trying to calm herself. Within moments, however, she was up, rearranging the pillows behind his head.

Arthur moaned in delirious sleep and Nellie brought the bedpan close to his chest. Nothing came. In the bottom of the bowl, thin watery matter swilled around. Its odour reached her nostrils, and she felt her chest and throat convulse. Quickly she took the bowl out and emptied it in the back yard.

It was several hours now since her husband had stumbled home in the middle of the night, soaked through, filthy and stinking to the heavens. Worse even than usual. As he woke her from sleep, he'd muttered something about stumbling drunk into the river on his way home from a night with the boys. He'd apologized to her profusely; too much, perhaps, she thought.

Not wishing to raise Silas from his sleep, Nellie had saved her barrage of questions and recriminations for the morning and Arthur, having swabbed himself down and dried himself roughly in the corner of the darkened bedroom, had slipped into his nightshirt and then into bed beside his wife. Nellie turned her back and buried her nose in her pillow, trying to keep the offensive smell at bay.

What followed had been a night of unusual disturbance. Within a matter of hours, Arthur had suddenly sat bolt upright, his eyes abruptly open, his stomach churning. Suddenly his cheeks puffed full, his lips shut tight on a rising column of bile. With this sudden flurry of movement, Nellie too had woken up to find her husband launching himself across the room to empty his mouth over the bedpan with a series of inhuman noises.

Now it was morning and she'd been swabbing his brow for hours, emptying the bedpan into the outhouse at intervals. How much water did a man have inside him, she thought? Would he not shrivel up like a dried prune if he kept on voiding it at this rate?

She was sitting downstairs now in the back room. Her blush-pink necktie emphasized her flushed and worried expression. With one hand she was idly stroking the black fur on Scrap's back; with the other, she massaged her own temple, in some attempt to ease a deepening headache.

Silas ambled in. 'How's the invalid then?' In face of his brother's stupidity, he thought, Nellie was managing to put on a brave face, despite her fears for cholera. If he *had* brought it into the house, then they were all as good as done for and everything they'd spent these last years building up would be ruined at a stroke. Silas had done it all for George but, if this *was* cholera, then Arthur was sabotaging everything for all of them. 'Keep giving him water,' he said, 'and keep his fever down. A cool, wet cloth. I'm not any doctor, but that's what needs doing. And brandy. Brandy's s'posed to help.'

'He's had brandy enough last night by the smell on him.' Nellie pushed herself up from her chair. Scrap flew from her lap, turned to give a look of displeasure, and padded disdainfully from the room.

'Oh Scrap,' she apologized to the vanishing tail, 'I'm sorry my dear.' She began to sob heavily.

Silas stepped forwards and put his arms around her shoulders, pulling her smaller frame towards his own. 'You're okay, sister,' he reassured her, holding her to his chest. She lay her face flat against it and howled, as much as from exhaustion as from worry. 'Let's get him better first. I'll give him his bollocking later.'

Nellie raised her face and laughed through her tears. 'Thank you, Silas,' she said. 'You're a good man. Unlike him. Rotten soak.'

'Well, I don't know where he went last night,' Silas said. 'He wasn't with me anyhow. I was with Flora. But the river'll have sobered him up, that's for sure. Swallow *that* down and, guaranteed, you'll be puking for a few days. There's not even fish can live in that water anymore. I know what gets washed into it.'

'Isn't that just the truth,' said Nellie. 'One thing's for certain, Silas, he ain't going to work with you tonight. He's not up to Dick,' she said. 'Can't even lift himself in bed. Let alone a shovel.'

'Just me, Henry and Harry then,' said Silas. 'Once we were five. And then there were three.'

Harry Gamble put down his last tub and stood leaning on his shovel beside the honeycart. He wore a shabby coat, tied at the waist with an odd piece of string. Its sleeves and breast were grimed with sludge as he'd raced the buckets back and forth between Silas down in the cesspool and Henry at the honeycart. He had had to run twice as fast as usual, for his one-time partner at the tubs had gone. Goodbye Joseph White and good bloody riddance, he thought. Harry had cursed him through the night, feeling that extra burden in his own muscles. Gratefully he handed over the final pail and watched his teammate climb the ladder at the back of the honeycart to load the muck into the barrels.

'Last one,' he said.

'Til next time,' Henry observed shrewdly. The cart man upended the bucket and watched the muck tumble out. This off-load done, Henry descended the ladder and stood back in his oilskin jacket and trousers, a long-tailed hat pulled back on his head to save the dirt from falling down his collar. He un-knotted the white necktie at his throat, besmirched with filth, and wiped his brow before beginning his smoker's ritual. Pipe from pocket with one hand, tobacco pouch with the other. Scrape, fill, tamp down. A swift flick of a lucifer. Flame. Contented puffs of smoke were soon emanating from his lips like the wisps from a steam train's funnel.

As Henry stood smoking, Silas's head emerged from the underworld. Poking up through the manhole, his face appeared in the flickering lamplight. It glistened with a thick slick of black liquid that streaked his features from brow to chin. His hair lay matted to his forehead and the whites of his eyes shone with an unusual intensity, the only lightness in his filthy face. 'Born again, me old muckers,' he said.

'Aw, boss,' Henry said mid-puff, 'you got something all over yer sleeves. How'd that happen?' His self-amusement made his pipe smoke sputter.

Silas lifted his hands out of the manhole and into the soft glow of the lantern. A dark black liquid ran down his arms. 'So I have,' he said. 'Isn't that a mystery.'

Easing his shoulders up through the opening, Silas placed his hands on the cobbles at the rim. Everything about him, from fingernails to the tip of his nose was black and soiled. He pulled himself up, a human cork releasing a cloud of vapour into the night air. Gamble bent over to assist him, hooking his hands beneath his boss's arms to give him leverage. Silas popped out onto dry land and shook his arms down, sending trails of muck spattering to the floor.

'Cloth,' he requested.

Henry flung him a yard of fabric from the back of the cart to swab himself down. He worked the cloth over every inch of his face and head, exploring each crease and crevice. When he had finished, he kicked himself out of his oilskins and pushed the iron cover back over the manhole with his boot.

'Job done boys,' he said. 'Let's get this gold pile home.'

'Bloody missed Joe tonight,' grumbled Gamble, flexing his back and shoulders.

'Did a better job without him,' Silas said dispassionately.

'Missed Arthur too,' said Henry. 'Could have done with another pair of hands.'

'Well he's got the shits, hasn't he.'

'Let's hope it don't run in the family.' Henry laughed, considering his pipe.

The three midnight mechanics threw their buckets and shovels onto the back of the cart. Silas climbed up to the driver's seat. Henry walked round to the horse's head. He removed the bag from Queen Bee's nose, unhitched the tether and flung the loose end up to Silas, before climbing up beside him. Harry checked the ground to each side of the cart for any tools left lying, then climbed the ladder and sat on the containers to the rear, holding his lantern high to cast a beam.

'Walk on girl,' Silas said, flicking the reins. Between the vehicle's shafts, the mare lifted her disinterested head and ambled on, pulling the wheels over cobblestones and paving setts as they returned their precious freight to the yard.

'Bloody bad news about the bombing, eh?' Henry drew philosophically on his pipe and steamed into the night air.

'Those anarchists'll stop at nothing.' Gamble spat over the side of the cart. His phlegm caught on his thick lower lip, and he wiped it with his sleeve. Moments later he spat again where he had just left the taste of the cesspool.

'I heard there was shiploads of 'em coming over from the continent.' Henry inspected the glowing tobacco in his bowl.

'You don't want to believe half of what you hear.' Silas urged the horse on, and the team settled back into reflective silence. Some distance down the road, Henry asked about the rest of the week's work.

'Same again tomorrow night, boys,' Silas said.

'Where'bouts?' said Henry, sucking on the embers of his pipe. He turned and knocked out the ashes over the side of the cart. Short-lived flecks of orange fell through the dark and extinguished themselves on the wet roadway.

'Round the corner,' said Silas. 'Once we're done, we'll cart it off to Grundy's on Thursday. When he's paid us, I'll do your wages.'

'You mean we get paid for all this pleasure too?' Henry laughed. 'I knew there was a reason we did this.'

'Always the joker,' said Gamble.

As if by order, Henry seemed to take this as his cue. 'Here... how d'you use a public convenience in winter?'

'Dunno' said Gamble.

'For the record,' said Silas, 'I never used one myself, winter, nor summer for that matter.'

'Well, when you do,' Henry said, 'do it bloody quickly.'

Quietly the tumbril rolled on, the clop of hooves beating in time with Henry's self-satisfied laughter.

By Thursday morning, Arthur had not died. His lips had not turned blue. He hadn't lost half his body weight to the watery dejections of cholera. Whatever it was that had briefly struck him down, it clearly wasn't that king of diseases. People simply didn't recover from that. As she made him a cup of beef tea, Nellie counted these, her small blessings. She fetched down a jar of beef extract from the parlour shelf, unscrewed the lid and scraped around the insides with a teaspoon. There was just enough there to begin the makings of a single cup, which she simmered gently on the stove. While the drink brewed, she sat flushed with worry and gratitude – gratitude that she'd been spared a husband; worry that work troubles were pushing him beyond himself. When and why had he taken to such heavy drinking?

When she took the beef tea upstairs, Arthur was sitting up in bed, starting to look hale again, she thought. Scrap followed her into the room and jumped onto the foot of the bed, turning himself in circles and pawing at the blanket with pummelling footsteps before he settled himself in a self-enveloped spiral.

'Well, look here,' she said, a spry lift in her step, 'if it isn't Lazarus back from the dead.' Whatever anger and annoyance she'd felt towards her husband was tempered now with relief. They'd been spared the scourge of disease in their home.

'I thought you were a goner,' she said. 'Thought you had the cholera. Truly Arthur. I never thought you were going to live to see this coming birthday of yours. I mean, it's not like we can afford a fancy coffin, is it?'

Arthur smiled weakly at his wife's mordant humour. She'd forgiven him. 'Is that beef tea I smell?' He tried to make his voice as remorseful as he could.

'You need to get your strength up,' Nellie said affectionately. 'You been off your chump. Time to get back to work when your strength's up.'

'What day is it?' he asked, gingerly taking the cup from his wife.

'Thursday,' she said.

Arthur made to raise himself. The beef tea slopped on his wrist and scalded him. 'Dammit,' he said, mopping at the spillage. 'Thursday? But that means I've been...'

'In bed for days. Yes!'

The cat, unwilling to give up his comfortable spot, remained unmoved.

'Be careful with that cup of tea, won't you?'

'But we're booked to take the muck to Grundy, Thursdays.'

'Silas has gone already. Now, stop fussing. Sit back and drink.' She eased him backwards and joined her hand to his, lifting the restorative brew to his lips.

As Silas pulled the cart up outside Grundy's yard, the chill of early morning seemed to be coming not so much from outside but from within him. It was as if his spirits were frozen and stilled inside him, leaving him numb; incapable of caring about much at all, least of all a slipshod, drunken brother. He'd cost them time and effort, laid up there in bed for days while he and the boys had been out slaving at clearing these last two cesspools. He deserved all the shits he got.

His feelings about business were also confused. One moment the voice he could hear inside his head was his own. The next, all he could hear was George calling 'Clean me, Silas!' And then that familiar voice was replaced by the smug tones of Mr. Fleet. 'We can come to some arrangement, Mr. Hunt, hmmmm?' More troublingly, his feelings for Flora lay buried beneath it all. He hadn't seen her for days now and, what with these setbacks to business, he was beginning to doubt he might ever impress her enough to give her the things she wanted – her fine house in the suburbs, her bedrooms, her piano. Her nursery. Don't mention the WC.

For now, however, his feelings towards the man with whom he was about to do business were absolutely clear. Neither Silas nor Grundy had ever lost warmth between them. It wasn't that they were enemies – business was business after all – but their dislike of each other was elemental. To Silas, Grundy was an unscrupulous man who'd sell his own family for profit, or sell-out on his business partners if he thought there might be something in it for him. And to Grundy, Silas was a man beyond his station. He'd laughed at him publicly in the past. 'A preening nightman,' he'd called him once, 'who bathes and trims his nails and dresses as though he was better than everyone else. Thinks he's a gentleman!' Grundy had laughed like a drain. It had been as much as Silas could manage to stay calm.

Grudgingly then – for this *was* the middleman with whom he was forced, by history and necessity, to trade his nightsoil – Silas tethered Queen Bee to the post outside Grundy's yard. He walked through the gateway. The middleman was already there to meet him, dressed like a waggoner in a country smock, breeches and leather gaiters tied below the knee. He wore a doorknocker beard and moustache beneath a parish pickaxe of a nose.

'Hunt,' he grunted curtly from underneath his bowler.

'Grundy.'

The two men sized each other up. Grundy was the first to show his colours. 'No finery today then?' he said, looking Silas's working clothes up and down. 'Apparel'd like the rest of us, I see.'

'What business is it of yours?'

'The way you usually dress up, well, it's butter on bacon, ain't it.'

'The way I usually dress is no concern of yours.'

They stood watching each other, as though this was the start of some wrestling bout in the upstairs room of a shady drinking den. 'What you got for me this morning then?' Grundy broke the silence.

'Two clearances worth,' Silas said matter-of-factly. 'Twelve barrels, out on the cart. What'll you give me for it? I make it a ton, give or take.'

The middleman stroked his doorknocker chops and pondered the matter deliberately. Silas waited for a figure he knew would be laughably low.

'Got to pay the turnpike toll to get out of town,' Grundy looked away. 'Out *and* back mind you. Take that off your price.'

'Take it off your profits,' Silas parried. 'I got to pay the boys for working, you know. What am I gonna pay 'em with if it all goes to you for carting?'

'I heard you lost one of 'em last week?' said Grundy with a knowing look.

'Word does spread fast, doesn't it.' Silas looked up over the middleman's head. A magpie was taking off from the eaves of the outhouse with something bright in its bill. He followed the bird until it disappeared. Had Joseph White already come running to Grundy, looking to make up his work with this conniver instead? 'We can do the work with four just as well as with five,' he said. He wasn't going to have Grundy thinking *Hunt Brothers* couldn't manage its own business.

'Nightman earns a pound a week' said Grundy. 'You're pulling-in good tin. You can live like Royals on that.'

'You got to be joking man! There's no earnings like that in it anymore and you know it. Prices rising makes it more than most folk can afford to empty a cesspit. They're just leaving 'em full. Less work for us.'

'Cut your men's wages then,' Grundy suggested. 'Simple as that.'

'How they going to live then?' said Silas. 'Rent. Coal, unless you want them to freeze to death. Bread, milk. Tea. Clothes, washing...'

'Does it always come down to baths and washing with you, Hunt?' The middleman laughed. 'Look, I don't need a shopping list, nor a fashion show.'

Silas ignored him. 'Ain't any change, not even from a quid a week, for all that.'

'I got my costs, Hunt. You got yours. You'll have to pay them less and, if they don't like it, they can go out of collar. If they don't like what you pay 'em, they can go and dig train tracks and sewers. Like your man White seems to have done.'

'Don't mention him, nor the bloody sewers,' said Silas. 'It's them that's putting us out of business in the first place.'

'That's what the anarchists are all saying,' said Grundy. 'Heard there was a bit of a blow up.' He picked a fingernail and flicked something away. 'Then, you'd know all about that already.'

Silas stared the man down. 'What you saying?'

'Nothing,' said Grundy. 'That's quite a few fellers out of work though, thanks to some maniacs with a grudge.'

'They'll get over it,' said Silas. 'Anyways, we can't go on strike like builders can.'

'Not my problem,' said Grundy bluntly. 'You're the one with men to pay in your team. You cut your costs. I ain't got no way of cutting mine. Turnpike's a fixed cost and I got to pay it.' He paused and seemed to be considering how he might yet further rankle his visitor. 'You're a bit of a handy man, anyways, aren't you Hunt?' he said. 'You can fix a clock or mend a shoe; frame a door or hang some shelves, can't you? You should turn your hand to something practical – start working for the other side, you know. Don't be too proud.'

Silas could feel his ire building. Don't rise to him, he thought. But was he to be squeezed from *every* side? Like it or not, there was an uncomfortable truth to what the middleman was saying. The city seemed to be getting larger day by day, with new housing developments sprawling outwards in every direction. The suburbs were swelling. It was like the market gardens were creeping further and further away from those who supplied them with manure, or further yet from the costermen who traded those vegetables back into the city markets. How could Grundy afford to transport manure to the market gardens when his own returns from selling it were becoming ever slimmer?

'I'll give it you on scrip,' Grundy finally said.

'You'll give it to me in bloody money, or you ain't having it at all.' Silas knew that Grundy would quibble at the cost, whatever it was. He seldom paid fairly. The man gave no quarter in business, and he brooked no rival. How to do business with a man like that? You never knew where the next bit of trickery was coming from.

'There's precious few farmers who want it at the moment, Hunt. Fact is, it's cheaper to buy in bird shit. Even from Africa, or Peru. You know that.'

Silas closed his eyes and laughed softly to himself. Grundy had him in a corner. He'd have to take the 'I owe you' and wait for Grundy's money once he'd sold-on the muck. How he was going to explain that back at home was something else but, for now, on scrip it would have to be.

'Okay,' he said. 'But I'll be back next week once you've sold it on. I want my money.'

He drove the cart back from Grundy's and stopped on the top of a steep hill under the shade of an old tree. Dismounting from the seat, he nose-bagged Queen Bee, letting her enjoy her champ in the shade of the branches. The barrels on the honeycart were empty and his pockets emptier than he could have hoped. Was there any profit at all left *anywhere* in this trade of theirs? What had been two-pound-a-ton was, today, not even half that. The only people making money, it seemed, were the guano importers and the contractors of sewers. Yet the former were doing nothing to clean up the city, and the latter were putting him and his boys directly out of work, which only made matters worse – the cesspools still existed, after all.

It had turned into a fine morning and from his vantage point he felt as if he could see for miles; the vast panorama of the city stretching out beneath him like a welling black bruise on either side of the river. Where the hill sloped down to the stretching field, there stood little knots of cattle and sheep put out to graze. The swathes of grass were cut across by lines of post-and-rail fences and the darker lines of hawthorn, hazel, and buckthorn hedges. From out of these rose, every hundred yards or so, the crown of an oak jutting its branches high to spread itself full canopied. Silas's eyes travelled over the fields beyond, to the outskirts of the city itself, where the streets stood lined by large, expensive houses with slated gables and mansard roofs, garret windows, their white facades punctuated by the open eyes of frames and windows. Dark clusters of swelling trees protruded between them. Above the roofs his eyes followed a line of birds in flight, leading back into the hazier distance, to the smoke that rose from city chimneys and the smog that settled back down over the buildings like the heavy serge blanket on his bed. In the very distance, the city stretched away to a unified blue-grey smudge.

He refocused his eyes and tried to pick out his own home. He could see the general area, but there was so much building going on around that it was impossible to make out individual streets. He wondered how long it would be before the fields here would be dug up and turned over to housing and industry. And where amongst all this construction, he wondered, where amongst this forest of water towers and church spires, where was Flora Street at this very moment? She was a lost individual in an ever-swelling mass. Would he ever win her to live in a house like one of these out here in the suburbs?

He studied the river, shining like a sheet of glass between the two halves of the city, its burnished surface broken here and there by the towers of bridges, the spires of dockyard cranes and a thick forest of masts on the hulking black shapes of the steamers and trading ships. Far out at the distant mouth of the river he could just make out the convict hulks moored up in the middle of the flow. What a sorry place that must be to end your days.

Beside the river, Mr. Bazalgette's intercepting sewers were going in at an unparalleled rate. New railway works were going in beside them. He could make out the new, wide thoroughfares being built in the place of the old rookeries. Where had all those displaced people moved to? Swallowed up by the ever-growing body of the city. Everywhere he looked he saw a town in reconstruction, the old parts failing and falling, the new parts burgeoning, with fresh works springing up overnight like mushrooms on a midden.

He dipped his hand into his jacket pocket and fetched out two apples. He unhitched Queen Bee's nosebag and fed the mare one of the apples. 'There you go girl,' he said, patting her neck as she crunched the fruit down in two bites.

The second apple he tossed into the air and caught again, before sitting himself at the base of the tree. The skin was a soft, brownish-green, covered by a scarf of russeting. As he felt the juice hit his tongue, he dreamed a little and savoured the flavour, nutty and sweet. He crunched slowly and gazed into the branches above him, watching a squirrel cling to a vertical branch high above. Sensing him, the squirrel froze, looking straight back. Silas let his eyes blur. The face of the squirrel blurred with them, through the dappled leaves. He stared harder still until, the more he stared, the newer and stranger the squirrel became: the creature's face seemed to transform into a human face; the branch into a human body, until, sitting there in the canopy, swinging his pint-sized boots, was his brother George, his familiar features glowing in the buttery sunlight.

'Thousands of men, all working hard, all earning decent wages, Silas,' the boy said.

'You mark my words, George,' Silas said to the air, 'it'll all fall away, all come to an end and *then* what are they all gonna do for work? Some of them back off to Ireland, others back up north to Tyneside and the docks up the Clyde. But the rest of 'em are going to stay, and *then* you got a problem on your hands.'

'Charity will help them, Silas,' George replied.

'Charity won't do anything! Charity encourages beggars and false cases who ain't deserving of nothing.'

'Building up the city is good for others.' It was as if Silas could hear his brother's voice inside his own head. 'Good for shop-keepers and traders. Landlords too. The builder's living is the shopkeeper's loaf. One dependent on the other.'

'It'll be a fine thing when man starts helping man in this city, George.'

'The building's a good thing, Silas. Sewers too.'

'Sewers my arse!' Silas blustered.

'They clean the city, Silas. One day you'll see. Honour bright.' With that, the refrain he'd imagined so many times across the years, Silas suddenly started up. His rapid movement made the squirrel dart to one side and vanish. He tossed his apple core away and watched it roll into the nook of a risen root. Bewildered and drained, he rubbed his palms against his face, then gritted his teeth and shouted a pained call into the branches above him. 'I don't know what to do, George! Tell me what to do!' Beside him Queen Bee whinnied in slight alarm.

But the boy was gone and Silas turned back to his cart. He mounted the ladder and flipped the reins.

'On girl.'

Queen Bee stepped forward and the honeycart began to trundle down the hill, back towards the city. Behind them, the squirrel descended the trunk of the oak and sat in the nook of the risen root, gnawing on the core of Silas's discarded fruit.

Silas woke and slid himself up on the iron rungs of the bedstead. At his feet, Scrap sat on his hindquarters, his two front legs held straight down beneath him like the columns of a doorway, his eyes gazing straight forward. 'Morning Crap.' Silas interlocked his fingers and stretched up above his head. The aches of his week dissipated through his fingertips. 'Not so much as a "Good Morning" back, eh Crap?'

He reached a hand forwards, but the cat remained sitting statuesquely at the foot of his bed. 'You're a cold creetur, Crap. Nothing but stony silence. You'll be wanting breakfast from me though, wontcha? Does a master get no rest, even on a Saturday?'

At the mention of breakfast, the cat stood and shook a shiver through his body from whisker tips to tail. Silas swung his legs out of bed and pulled his trousers on over his long johns, and his tunic shirt over his head. Scrap had left the door ajar in the night.

'Come on then,' he said. 'Let's see what we can find you downstairs,' although Scrap was already leading him through the doorway and out onto the landing.

Downstairs, Arthur was sitting in the chair beside the fire.

'It's alive!' Silas said, making little effort to disguise his displeasure.

'Look, Silas, I'm...' Arthur began.

'Save it, Arthur,' Silas said. 'I'm not in the mood.'

He walked towards the kitchen where he could hear Nellie making breakfast, but stopped himself in the doorway. 'No, come to think of it,' he turned back to face his brother, 'I'm going to say my piece and clear the air and, when it's said, perhaps we can just get back to normal, alright?'

From his chair, Arthur opened his palms towards his brother and shrugged.

'You come home drunk,' Silas began. 'Not a crime, I'll admit.

But you fall in the river. You come home drunk, soaking wet, stinking and covered in muck. You spend the whole night shitting and puking and causing Nellie untold worry. In fact, you spend the whole week at it. You cost us work and money and you leave *everything* for me to do.' He was trying to control his voice, but anger was ringing at its edges.

Arthur was staring down at his knees.

'We've got a business to run, Arthur. A living to make. We gotta keep good time. Together. We can't be slipshod. Jesus Christ, times are hard enough as it is! This whole wave of "progress" is against us. Middlemen ripping us off. If we don't stick together, mate, this business is going down. *We're* going down.'

Still Arthur didn't raise his eyes. He was either lost deep inside his own shame or plotting his excuses. Hadn't he been acting strangely before? Silas thought. Secret scraps of paper in his pocket; no one knowing where he was some evenings; cock-a-hoop notions about advertising hoardings to save the business. All this laziness, slouching about in that bloody armchair. Talking with the Family. What had happened to the brother he knew and had trusted all these years? What had happened to plain old hard work?

Silas shifted his tone. 'Look, I'm just letting you know where we stand, Arth. I'm not angry. Well, not so much. But you got to face facts. I only got half the money from Grundy this week. Half!'

'What!' Arthur sat upright in his chair.

Silas thought about the IOU note in his pocket and wished he didn't have to lie. 'We lost White too. You started drinking like him as well, have you? And now there's been some blow-up on the sewers. The whole place is guessing the who-what-and-why of it and there *you* are, washed up in your sick bed like some homeless drunk.'

Arthur fiddled with the hem of his waistcoat.

'A bombing, they reckon,' Silas said. 'Sabotage. The bloody Family at it again.'

'How'd they know it was a bomb?' said Arthur finally.

'The flippin' sewer exploded, Arthur! What else could it be?'

'Sewers often flare up,' said Arthur. 'Coal gas. Sewer gas. You know that. Explosions aren't uncommon.'

'What is it with you?' Silas raised his voice. 'You gonna quarrel about *everything*? Look, it was a bomb, alright! They found what was left of the barrel, traces of explosives. These things leave a trail.'

'Okay, okay, keep your hair on...'

Silas pointed at his brother. 'This sort of thing can't happen, right? We need each other. Now more than ever.'

Arthur stood up. For a moment, Silas was unsure what might be going through his brother's mind. Was he considering the consequences of his sickness; how it had affected Silas and the boys? Lost workdays; lost money. Arthur could see that, couldn't he? Perhaps he was too ashamed about what had happened; was thinking of how to save face. Should he offer him a way out? Then again, how would Arthur have felt about it, if Silas had done some stupid thing and left all the work for others? No, all that was required was a simple apology. Just say you were wrong man, Silas thought. Show us some hint of remorse.

Eventually Arthur spoke. 'I admit what I done was wrong, Si,' he said. 'I can't explain it, but I was wrong. It won't happen again. I promise.' He proffered his hand and, cautiously, the brothers shook.

He sounded sincere, Silas thought, but still Arthur wouldn't look him directly in the eye. He didn't entirely believe it, but Arthur had apologized and, for now at least, that would have to do.

'Nellie?' Arthur called to the kitchen.

Warily his wife peered round the doorjamb, hoping that whatever quarrel there might have been was now over.

'I'm sorry, Nellie,' he said. 'Truly I am. Won't you both forgive me?'

Silas looked to Nellie and Nellie looked to Arthur. 'Forgiven,' they said in unison and, together, from the distant points of their small domestic triangle, each sent to each a wan, forgiving smile. In the kitchen, Scrap whined softly for his breakfast.

Come Saturday, Silas stood in the haze of his bathhouse cubicle, one white towel wrapped around his waist, another draped across his shoulders. The suds and water were spiraling down the plug-hole, leaving a black ring around the bath.

'One for you Johnson,' he said to the steaming ether, imagining the doorkeeper down on his hands and knees scrubbing at the tub with lye and a brush.

He turned to the mirror and swiped his hand across it. The sink rippled with hot water. Lathering his face with soap and bristle brush, he flicked open his razor, pulled the skin of his cheek taut and began to scrape at the week's growth. Foam and dark stubble came away in a series of deft sweeps. As he lifted his arm, the raised red line of his scar seemed to move on his skin like a worm in the soil.

Already he'd told Arthur and Nellie that he wouldn't be home for lunch. Those two still had things to make up together and, what with Grundy cheating him over the load mid-week, there was precious little money today for joints of beef, nor lunch for the boys, or those that remained of them. Instead, he'd go to Mr. Fleet and seal this business of the news story. Then, lunch with Flora. What better thing was there to look forward to, he thought, as he pushed up his nose to remove the sprouting moustache. What better thing than to take his girl out for Saturday lunch, a drink in the pub and an afternoon together in the park? 'It's been a bloody wretched week,' he said to his reflection, patting his cheeks dry, 'but things, at last, are going to come good.'

Bidding a good day to Johnson, he stepped into the street, clean, trimmed and feeling like a new man in his weekend best. He called into a breakfast shop where, for a couple of pennies, he took a fill of coffee, bread, and butter. The place was full of men – labourers in working clothes and cloth caps. You might just be a nightman, Silas, he thought, but it doesn't mean your standards have to be low.

There wasn't a woman among them – the girls were all outside on the street, flower women like his mother had been, basketwomen, washerwomen, the wives of these labourers and mechanics. 'I'd let you sit with me though, Flora,' he said under his breath, and warmed himself on coffee and the thought of an afternoon with his girl.

Stepping out, he sidestepped a muffin man, his goods covered up in his basket, his bell ringing. 'Muffin, sir?' The vendor wiped his hands on his white sleeves to pick out a hot one for his potential customer. But Silas had already moved on.

A short while later, the bell chimed above the entrance to Mr. Fleet's office. The door swung closed behind him. Inside, the domain of Mr. Drinkwater was much as it had been when Silas had last visited, a hush hanging over the empty brass flowerpot. At the chime of the bell, Mr. Drinkwater rose from behind the desk, as though he'd come up through the trapdoor of a theatre. His sudden arrival startled Silas, who flinched under the gaze of the portraited proprietors and the dusty bronze carving.

'Ye-es?' said Mr. Drinkwater. He raised a spindly arm to his brow and flicked a lank tress of hair from in front of his face. As the scent of cloves hit him again, Silas considered the sub-editor's ongoing ailment.

'It's just a quick call on Mr. Fleet,' he said, waiting to be shown through.

'Oh yes,' said Mr. Drinkwater. The man gyrated his shoulders in a slow and bizarre manner. 'Mr...?'

'Hunt.'

'Yes. Mr. Hunt. The nightman, isn't it?'

Silas nodded.

'I'm afraid...' Drinkwater began, 'that Mr. Fleet is no longer in a position to discuss these matters with you, Mr. Hunt.' His arms came up onto the desk one by one, moving like a spider's, his fingers interlocked in a fist and his elbows jutting forward on the desk.

'Not in a position?'

'I'm afraid we have a problem... a conundrum... you might say,' Drinkwater went on, 'concerning your story.'

Silas was bemused. What possible reason could Fleet have for defaulting on their agreement?

'But it was just last week,' he said, 'we...'

'Indeed,' Mr. Drinkwater interrupted him. 'But the territory has shifted somewhat in that week, wouldn't you agree? Surely you've heard of what happened with the sewer works?'

'I heard there was a blow-up on the new section,' Silas said. 'What's that got to do with anything?'

At that moment, the door to Mr. Fleet's office burst open and the journalist came barreling through, already blustering about some matter. 'What does it have to do with you, Mr. Hunt?' he stormed. 'What does it have to do with you!'

Taken aback by the force of his entry, Silas retreated. Behind the desk, the limbs of Mr. Drinkwater seemed to be climbing up onto the counter like some predatory creature.

'I'll tell you what it has to do with you, Sir! Firstly, news of an explosion on the sewers *trumps* your piffling story of hardship in the cesspits. No one wants to read your hard-luck story when there's news of sabotage and explosion on the sewers. And, secondly...'

Silas could see the man building up a head of steam that was about to knock him right off track.

'Secondly,' the journalist continued, 'the constabulary have just app-re-hen-ded one of the protagonists.' He spat out each syllable with a piety that would have made Silas laugh had he not been so shocked by this rebuff.

'Protagonists,' echoed Mr. Drinkwater.

'And?' Silas snorted.

'*And,* Mr. Hunt,' the journalist emphasized with his finger, 'it seems that the culprit has been only too willing to share information on the identity of his accomplices.'

Silas was at a loss. What the confession of some agitator from the Family had to do with him was anyone's guess. 'You aren't making any sense,' he said.

'Let me make it simple for you then, Mr. Hunt. Although they don't have names,' said Mr. Fleet, 'the allegation is that one accomplice was...'

'Was what?' Silas raised his voice.

'If you are going to shout, Mr. Hunt, you can turn around directly and go back to that cesspool from whence you came!'

Silas bristled. 'One accomplice was what?' he said, trying to contain himself.

'Was a nightman, sir!' The word hung in the air between them like a bad smell.

For a moment, Silas considered the journalist's proposition. The idea was absurd. He knew all the nightmen in the city and not one of them would have involved themselves in an act of sabotage like that. 'That's ridiculous!' he said. 'What evidence have they got?'

'The police have all the evidence they need,' said Mr. Fleet. 'The bomber has as good as confessed and turned the rest of his conspirators in. I don't doubt the police will be making arrests before too long.'

Silas looked from Fleet to Drinkwater. Both men seemed to be eyeing him with great disdain. 'Wait a minute?' Silas laughed. 'Surely you're not suggesting?'

'*We* aren't accusing anyone,' Mr. Drinkwater suddenly put in. He was almost on top of the desk now, leaning his sinewy limbs forward.

'The matter is, however, plain, Mr. Hunt,' said Mr. Fleet.

'Whether you, or your men, had anything to do with this outrage is...'

'Wait a minute!' Silas banged his fist down onto the desk. Mr. Drinkwater's arms shot upwards.

'...is for the police alone to discern,' Mr. Fleet continued. 'For our part, our business together is, henceforth terminated. All previous arrangements hitherto discussed are, as from this moment, null and void. You cannot seriously expect us to conduct affairs with the likes of you while suspicions are abroad, and the matter is under police investigation? Now, good day to you sir!'

Mr. Fleet span on his heels and bowled back through the door as dramatically as he had entered. Behind the desk, Mr. Drinkwater lurked, bobbing at the heart of his imaginary web. 'Good day to you too, sir,' he said, watching calculatedly as Silas stood seemingly lost in the foyer.

Slowly, Silas turned and walked towards the door. Between them, the doorbell rang a jangling farewell.

To try and stop his thoughts from spinning out of control, Silas stepped into a nearby chophouse to take stock and something to eat to settle his nerves. The place was full of clerks taking a slap bang lunch, cheek by jowl in their wooden booths, gnawing on chop bones or diving in to boiled beef and carrots with dumplings. Now that he could smell it, however, he didn't seem to have the stomach to eat anyway.

What the devil had Fleet been talking about? So, they'd caught some ne'er-do-well responsible for blowing up the sewer. Big deal. He could have blamed anyone. Who was to say it was a 'nightman' who'd done it with him? It was his word against the next man's. And who but a desperate police chief would believe a criminal like that anyway? No, they were clutching at straws. Why would a nightman want to destroy a sewer? They had worries enough of their own at the moment – how to make an honest living in these wretched days – without resorting to actions like that. And who among them could have done it anyway? It certainly wasn't him, or Henry, or Gamble. Arthur was out of the question.

'You can have chops and potatoes, fish in sauce, or steak in oyster sauce,' the owner said in a flat, bored voice. 'Shilling each. Beef and carrots is off now. I haven't any left. Vegetables and bread and butter is a penny extra. You can finish off with cheese for tuppence.'

'Pardon me?' Silas's thoughts were wandering. He knew the owner must have been detailing what the menu had to offer, but his words seemed like nothing more than the babble of water from his bathhouse tap.

The owner seemed to change his mind. 'Come to think of it,' he said, 'we're down to hot eel stew, spiced with pepper and vinegar. Threepence a bowl.'

The dish when it came did nothing for Silas's concentration, or his spirits. He left half of it still swimming in its bowl, his short tower of pennies piled beside.

By the time he reached the *Old Bell* where he'd arranged to meet Flora, the Saturday sky had clouded over, and a light storm was threatening. Even a walk in the park with his girl was looking doubtful now. Outside the alehouse, three brawny draymen were unloading barrels from a high-sided cart, heaving the cargo down onto their leather-aproned bellies, then letting the barrels slide down their fronts to bump onto the ground. From here the landlord was helping roll them into the dark cellar whose trap had been opened to receive the load.

Silas pushed the *Old Bell's* door and stepped inside. Two bartenders were standing behind the bar in drab grey waistcoats and white cotton aprons, their sleeves rolled up in a business-like manner. One was uncorking a bottle, bent over at the waist with the bottle between his knees. The other was pulling ales from the row of white-handled taps atop the bar. A woman in a long black dress, held tight at the neck by a satin band, was clearing away handfuls of dirty pint pots and glasses.

Silas pushed through the drinkers and stood at the bar. To one side a man in a Homburg hat was downing a tankard, the ale spuming on his beard. To his other side, two battered Toppers were disputing some matters of questionable commerce. Beside them, a shabby mother was thrusting her fingers into her baby's mouth in some attempt to make the infant hush.

Silas ordered a double measure of gin and drank it down quickly. It bit at his throat and gave his lips a sour twist. He then took a pint of warm ale to wash the bitterness away and retired to an empty booth beneath the window. As he downed his pint, he wondered again who among them could have resorted to such desperate means. The name of Joseph White bubbled to the surface of his mind. If anyone, it could have been him. White had left them drunk enough that last weekend, hadn't he? Drunk enough to go and do something stupid like that; angry enough to join the Family, just to make a point? It must have been him. Thanks for nothing, Joseph.

He didn't know how long he'd been sitting there drinking, matching each pint with a chaser of gin, but he was about to embark on another round when Flora finally appeared. When he saw her, he realized that the gins and the ales had done their worst by him. He looked up blearily from his glass to see her standing there, a dark blue cloak wrapped around her shoulders with a lighter grey mantle tied around her neck and a pork-pie hat with a striking little feather.

She gave him a reproving look. 'You been wetting your clay,' she said.

'God I'm right poked up, Flora,' he apologised, trying to mask his embarrassment. 'Sorry, I...'

'How long have you been at it?' she asked, trying to work out what state he was in.

'Just one or two,' he lied. Did she believe him? 'Here,' he said, 'take a seat. Let me get you summat. I'll stand you a treat.'

'You certainly will,' she said. 'Looks like I've got a deal of catching up to do.'

'What's your poison then?' He felt himself sway a little as he stood. Awkwardly he lifted himself from behind the cramped table.

'I've had my lunch already,' she said, 'so I'll take a glass of wine. If you don't mind.'

He returned from the bar and slid a glass towards her. They sat drinking together, a distracted, sorrowful look on his face. She asked him what was wrong, and he subjected her to a lengthy diatribe on the ills of the day. By the time he'd finished, she was done with her drink and looking around for a way out.

'I'm sorry to hear it,' she said disinterestedly, rising from her seat, 'but I could do with some fresh air. And so could you by the look of things. You may take me to the park now.'

Outside, the afternoon storm had still not quite arrived, making it dry enough for a quick turn around the green. They set off together in silence. Silas was still preoccupied with Mr. Fleet's turnaround, and barely spoke a word. He turned his mind to Joseph White's involvement in the blast and, with that turn, their chances of conversation were as good as over. Flora clipped along beside him in displeasure, though Silas barely seemed to notice.

At the park gate there were the usual fortune-tellers, jugglers, contortionists, and bird sellers. Someone had set up a temporary roundabout and swing upon which children were turning excitedly through the air. A pavement scrivener was drawing chalk landscapes on the paving stones. One of them looked like the view from the oak-topped hill where he'd stopped and talked with George, or what he thought was George.

Inside the park a group of workmen were dousing themselves in the pond, their working week over. Two or three were splashing each other like children, letting the grime of work seep away to mingle there with the mud and the muck at the bottom of the pool.

'I take mine at the bathhouse,' Silas boasted.

'What do you want,' Flora said, 'a medal?' It was the first thing she'd said since they left the *Old Bell*.

On a park bench a cluster of working girls sat watching the half-naked workmen wash themselves. The women called out crude remarks. Each was dressed in extravagant satin trimmed with soiled and torn lace, their threadbare shoes filled by drop-down stockings, hardly a fichu between them, and neither bonnet nor mantilla to cover their heads.

'There's a bunch of gay ones,' Silas said. 'Look at 'em hoisting their petticoats.'

'Silas!' Flora complained. 'I'd rather you didn't if it's all the same with you?'

'Listen to that one there,' Silas pointed, ignoring Flora. He indicated the loudest of the slatterns. 'She's a right church-bell that one. Mad as hops, I bet.'

'Ain't there nicer things a chap could point out to his girl, Silas, than the night-girls of the town?' Flora complained. 'You've been nothing but morose and unseemly since the moment we met.' She arched her eyebrows at him.

'I'm sorry,' he said, rubbing the heel of his palm against his forehead. The germ of a headache was already forming behind his eyes.

They walked on in silence past the tea garden, where men and women were drinking from china and picking at winkles and whelks, cracking crab claws and passing their time more congenially than Silas and Flora seemed to be doing. Their children turned wheels on the grass beneath the chimneys of smoke rising from the pipes and cigars of their elders.

'It must be such a pleasure to be a mother,' Flora observed rather mawkishly, Silas thought.

'I doubt it.' His reply could hardly have been blunter. 'It weren't for mine.'

'It must be for some though.'

'Ma, she was loving, yes. But she was sickly. She's gone now anyway.' His voice was slurred with drink. 'Pa too. He died from the tannery. Poisons and whatnot from chemicals. She died, straight after...' his voice trailed away.

'After what?' Flora asked.

'I don't want to talk about it...'

'Suit yourself. From the mood you're in, it's not going to be a pretty tale anyway.'

He ignored her. 'I think it was the shock that killed her.'

'Well, *I* think it must be a nice thing,' Flora said. She pushed on past the tea garden and headed straight to the southern gateway. A line of horse and carriages stood waiting at the kerbside. Before he had a moment to protest, she pulled herself up onto the back of a chaise and leaned across to Silas.

'If you're always going to be like this, Silas,' she said accusingly, 'then you can stand me the treat of the fare home as well.'

Automatically, he dug his hand into his pocket and fetched out a fistful of small coins. 'You can't just go,' he said.

'Watch me.' She leaned across and helped herself to a shilling. 'Don't you dare spend the rest of that on drink.'

'But when will I see you?' he said. For a moment he felt like a lost child.

'That,' she said, 'depends.'

'Tonight?' he said hopefully.

Flora laughed. 'I've made...'

'...other arrangements.'

'You might say that,' she said.

He felt the smart of rivalry. Brusquely, he exhaled. Could his day get any worse? Always some other secret relation going on. He didn't know why he bothered with her anymore.

Flora was staring down at him expectantly from the back of the carriage. In front of her the cabbie turned impatiently. 'Where to?' His voice was like the bark of the crows in the branches above them.

'Look, it's Arthur's birthday mid-week,' Silas said, ignoring the cabbie. 'You are still coming, aren't you? Please Flora? I'm sorry,' he said again.

'We'll see,' she said determinedly and, leaning forward, gave the driver his instructions.

The skies had been promising to open all afternoon and, as she disappeared into the distance, it began to spit with rain. Silas watched the cab vanish, then turned and walked home, the late-afternoon sky darkening with the shadows of evening, the rain-drops bursting on his shoulders like wasted dreams.

'A cup of 'ot elder wine this 'orrid evening, sir?' a hopeful vendor called as he walked past.

A potboy standing nearby added his voice to the petition. 'Ale, porter, stout, sir? Lift your spirits this awful season?' But Silas walked on, oblivious to the world around him, his mind locked on the thoughtless sabotage he'd unwittingly enacted on his affair.

'There isn't going to *be* an article in the paper, Arthur.' Silas exhaled in exasperation. He was sitting behind the parlour table, his legs stretched out beneath it, his fingertips resting on the edge like a reclining pianist, except the music he was conjuring was anything but harmonious. His headache was swelling and tugging at his right temple.

'I don't get it,' Arthur said, pulling himself forward on to the edge of his seat. 'Last week you set it all up, then today?'

'You heard about the blast on the sewer works, didn't you? Or were you too busy dying of the shits to notice?'

Arthur slapped his hands onto the armrests of the chair and threw himself upwards. 'We been through that,' he said. The cat, who'd been sitting at his feet before the fire, sprang and landed on the table, his hind-quarters pointing directly at Silas's face from beneath its vertical tail.

'Godsake Crap, you vile creature!' Silas pushed the cat away and spat air through pursed lips. The cat stole indignantly from the room.

'I heard what happened,' Arthur said. 'You don't have to bully me on every goddamn thing.'

'Well, thanks to whoever did it, Fleet won't write his article now. Says blasts against the sewer works "trumps" our hardships.'

Arthur stared down into the fireplace. 'Bugger,' he said.

'I heard that, Arthur Hunt!' Nellie's voice raced in from the kitchen where she was washing the dishes after eating with her husband. Arthur raised his eyebrows to the ceiling and exhaled deeply.

'What *is* interesting,' Silas began, 'is what he said about the bloke the bobbies caught.'

'And what's that then?' He was standing looking at the fire, his back turned to Silas.

'Apparently, the man they caught confessed it was himself what did it and...'

'And what?'

'And said he'd been working with others.' Silas paused. 'A nightman.' He let the fact hang in the air. 'What d'you think of that?' He studied Arthur carefully for the slightest reaction. Impassively, his brother stood before the fire, toasting the front of his legs. Eventually he turned around and sat down. 'Well?' Silas asked.

'Impossible,' Arthur said eventually. 'It weren't none of us and we know all the other boys in the city. They were all at the meeting recently. And they're all on our side. Mills' and Reynolds' teams. The Barnett Boys. O'Brien. Whoever the police have caught, he must be making it up.'

'But why?'

'Damned if I know!' Arthur protested. He sat back down.

'Arthur!' Nellie's voice screeched in again from the parlour like a shovel on stone.

'Damned if I know either!' Silas shouted. He calmed himself. 'So you know nothing about it?'

'How would *I* know?' Arthur objected. 'What you saying, Silas? Just a minute ago you were kicking me for being sick. Now it's *me* what done it, is it?' He laughed explosively. 'Is *that* what you're saying?'

His hands gripped the carved wooden ends of the armrests. His knuckles shone white.

'I never said that. I just thought you might know something.'

'Well don't go having no bloody conniption, alright? I don't know nothing about it!'

From the kitchen, the sound of crockery chinking in the sink carried between them. Silas rested his elbows on the table and placed his forehead in his hands, smoothing his fingers back over his head. He scrunched his hair with his fingers, then brought them together, pressed to his lips as if in prayer. 'I thought it might be White,' he said calmly.

Arthur studied his brother and huffed. 'I'm sorry. I thought you were...'

'Accusing you?'

'I'm sorry, alright!' Arthur smiled wryly. 'But White? Really?' He reached out a hand as Scrap ventured back into the room and headed towards his armchair. 'I suppose if it's anyone, *he's* the man with the motive.' He paused. 'You know what,' he said, clapping his hands together, 'I bet it was him. The bastard.'

'Arthur!' Again, Nellie's voice raced into the room. The brothers stared at each other long and hard. Finally, Nellie came in. She gave them both a withering look. They dropped their heads.

'Well, that's *that* job done. Again!' She directed her complaint directly at Arthur.

He seemed to let it pass without notice. 'What next then?'

'I said, that's that job done,' Nellie insisted. 'Don't you...'

'Thank you, Nellie.' Silas acknowledged his brother's wife. Arthur nodded.

'Fine lot of thanks that is.' Nellie moved to the window and arranged the greenery in the jardinière.

'Well, the newspaper story's a no-go.' Silas flicked his head up.

'I guess that means we're advertising. Where's that list you were making?'

'What list?'

'Last week. Your little scrap. You said it could wait?'

Arthur stared at his brother. 'Oh, that?' he said. 'I chucked that away.'

'What d'you mean you chucked it away?'

'I dunno, Silas! I haven't got it, alright? P'raps I used it to light the fire or summat. What does it matter?'

Nellie turned back into the breach. 'Enough!' she said. 'Can we do without the fighting. Please.' Silas and Arthur stood silenced beneath the gaze of Nellie and the figures pictured in *The Angel's Whisper*.

'And how was Flora today, Silas?' Nellie finally asked. 'She coming to this cusser's birthday celebrations mid-week?' She pointed a finger at Arthur, who had crossed his arms and legs in the armchair in a defensive ball.

'She might,' said Silas. 'I dunno.' He rubbed his temple where the afternoon was knocking on his nerves. 'She left in a hurry. It was raining.'

'Well, I'm sure she will,' said Nellie. 'I hope she will anyway. Who'm I going to talk to otherwise?' The question hung unanswered between them. 'I wonder what'll she wear?'

Silas and Arthur were looking to different corners of the room. She stepped between them and rocked herself up onto her toes as she gripped the back of a dining chair. Scrap purred his way in a figure of eight between her raised calves.

'I could do with something nice to wear,' she voiced to the room in general. 'Arthur?'

'If you want a new dress, Nellie, go get it from the tally shop,' her husband replied. 'I can't afford to pay for things like that up front. Not any more.'

'Go to a tally man!' Nellie's voice rang with astonishment. 'Lord a'mercy,' she said, 'has it really come to *that* already?'

'It's weekly payments or nothing,' Arthur said firmly, 'if you want something new. That's the end of it.'

'New?' Nellie cried, dropping her heels to the floor. There was a sudden howl as Scrap went flying towards the door, the end of his tail pulled swiftly from under his mistress's descending heels.

In the back room saloon of their local inn, Silas and Arthur gathered to mark the younger brother's birthday. Harry and Henry were present, Nellie too and, to Silas's relief, Flora, who had deigned to grace him with her presence.

'It's going to be like a twopenny hop,' Silas said as he surveyed the room. Some twenty guests – men and women, friends and workmates – to drink and talk and dance to the fiddle and, for a night at least, leave the pressures of their working days aside.

'Like a free-and-easy!' Arthur said, his voice lifting. He was leaning lightly on his brother's shoulder to speak closely in his ear. Whatever differences had come between them recently had been put by, at least for the day.

'Only, better performers than you'll get at one of those.' Silas laughed. He'd arranged for a small band of musicians who, for the price of a meal and a drink, had welcomed the invitation to air their talents on a willing crowd.

The pillars of the room had been decorated with cotton swags and a wreath of greenery from a costerman's cart. The tables were covered with coloured bunting. On the walls the lanterns were lit and the fire to the middle of the room flushed with a benign glow. A table had been set with a moderately generous supper.

'We can't afford it,' Nellie had protested the day before. 'It's you who keeps telling me that.'

'You can't let no one know that time's are hard,' Arthur had said. Consequently, there was a platter of trotters with jelly packed around them. Cow's cheek. A platter of pies and puddings, cut into slices. Shrimps potted-up by the half-pint.

Whelks and watercress. A plate of eel, and a crock of pea soup, mopped up with potatoes and bread.

Around the edges of the room, low stools and benches had been arranged for their guests, while the varnished boards to the centre had been left clear for dances. A low platform had been raised for the musicians at one end of the room – a podium of planks laid across the bottoms of upturned brewery crates.

The early arrivals had already set themselves up in groups. These were the men – and their partners, or wives – who had supported Silas in his Union speech just recently. At one table, a couple were already intertwined with each other, the woman sitting across the nightman's knees, his smiles and carefree voice filling that corner of the room. Another man in a shabby jacket and cravat had his arms draped around two women, both holding a glass of hot negus – one girl's glass lifted up to her chap's lips, the other's raised high in the air above her head. She was leaning back in her long cream dress, to whisper something in the ear of an enormous man standing behind them. O'Brien. Beside them, on the table, sat a large bowl of punch, behind which sat another man and woman already engaged in intimate nose-to-nose conversation.

Henry was propping up one of the saloon walls, puffing contentedly on his pipe and drinking a glass of punch. Beside him Harry held a glass of water, muttering censures on the evils of drink.

Nellie leaned forward in front of the fireplace and touched her companion on the arm. 'I'm so glad you could come, Flora,' she said. The lace of her new bonnet and dress shone in the light of the fire.

'Is that a *new* dress, Nellie?' Flora asked. 'I don't think I saw it before. Such a pretty colour for you. It matches your eyes.'

Nellie blushed. Although she was glad of it, she hadn't expected anyone to comment on her frock. It had, after all, only recently been freed from the tallyman's shop.

Around them the room was already ringing with high spirits.

The party had been underway just under an hour, but the punch-bowl was almost empty. The sound of laughter and conversation, jokes, and carefree chatter, bounced over their heads. The land-lord hopped in with a glad glow of business on his lips, carrying a new bowl of punch to replenish the first. His red and white striped jacket only partially hid the stains of the swilling liquor. Beneath his feet, two nightmen from O'Brien's team were playing at cards on the floor, one watching his pile of pennies grow while the other's pile diminished.

As yet, the musicians were still sitting outside in the street, perched on a bench with their instruments clutched close, trying to come to a final agreement on the list of dances they would play: a fiddle player in a velvet coat and pair of chequered pantaloons, a Turk's turban on his head; a fierce looking double-bassist, partially bald and taller than his instrument; a waist-coated guitarist in a paisley cravat, and a dark-haired mandolinist in unlaced boots and knotted belcher neckerchief. As they muttered to each other about their running order – one moment in harmony as to what they might play, the next in discord – the landlord's wife stepped out of the doorway in her long skirts and dark bonnet.

'Might yers yet be ready to come in and begin?'

The players took their cue and rose together, gathering their instruments. The woman followed them into the saloon, her spaniel yipping at her heels.

On the platform, the turbaned fiddle player struck a long, single note with his bow and, taking it as their standard, the ensemble fine-tuned their instruments. For a moment the room was filled with the cacophony of strings pitched higher, then lower, each twist of the pegs bringing the notes closer and closer to resolution until, finally, the players stood ready to strike up their first number.

As the jig began, guests started to tap their feet on the boards and the voices round the room rose higher to make themselves heard. Arthur and Silas stood locked in trivial talk of work with O'Brien, Henry, and Harry.

'There's nothing I haven't found thrown down a privy,' the giant was saying. 'When I been in luck, I've had valuables, jewellery, a silver spoon.'

'I pulled out documents once,' said Silas. 'A will.'

'Fat lot they must have thought of the family,' Henry laughed.

'Dead dogs. And...' O'Brien paused, 'the body of an infant. Newborn.'

'They gotta dispose of them before anyone knows if they were ever in the family way,' Arthur observed. 'The babies.'

'That's the vilest, most un-Christian thing I ever heard,' said Gamble.

'Some lasses get caught,' said Henry. 'I 'eard one went down for two years, just the other week. Concealment of birth.'

'She killed her child?' Gamble protested again.

'Jury said the child was born dead. Makes it more palatable for them believing it was so.'

'She's lucky the doctor didn't kill her,' O'Brien put in. 'Poisonous herbs. Most of 'em gets wounded when they, you know...'

'Fellers!' Silas raised his voice. 'It's a party – what sort of talk is this?'

Around their circle the men nodded. 'Sorry Silas, Arthur,' said O'Brien. 'Must be the punch getting away with me.'

'A little less of it on all counts,' Gamble said under his breath.

By now the song was in full swing and the noise of clapping palms, hooting mouths and clacking dance shoes was making the taproom echo. More guests arrived. The rest of the Mills outfit and the Reynolds team. The Barnett Boys. They may have been competing for the ever-dwindling number of clearances, but they were of a breed and stuck together, in both celebration and hardship. Tonight, their bearing was bright and, what with their spruced-up clothes, they looked like men who were working hard against their changing circumstances.

Arthur and Silas greeted their guests and showed them over to the punchbowl, ladling glasses from the jorum. Their pleasantries made, each group of men then took to a bench and sat to watch the dancing.

Silas watched Flora as she swayed and turned in front of the fire with Nellie. He liked the sparkling aigrette in her hair, and the way that it was bunched in ringlets to the sides. Her neck was unadorned, descending to the décolleté of her bust. One day he'd buy her some pearls to hang there, but for now that dress of hers was showing the best of her figure, and her forearms were peeping from her sleeves. What he wouldn't give to hold her to him in dances tonight; to win her to him for good and give her the future she'd so often told him she dreamed of. What with the noise of the band and the swirl of the punch and the heady atmosphere of the room, he could feel his passions rising. Standing here with his workmates any longer simply wouldn't do. He put his punch glass down and moved across the room to the fire, taking her by the hand just as the players began a new dance. He kissed her fingers.

'May I?' he asked in a semblance of gentility.

'Why, sir,' she played back.

He pulled her to him more forcibly and kissed her mouth. Flora yielded to him. Silas felt his spirits rise. Beside them Nellie turned away, a broad smile on her face.

Together Silas and Flora stepped into the middle of the room, his right hand holding her left, each with their best foot pointing forwards, the anticipation of the dance poised in their limbs. Behind them, a line of partnered dancers followed suit – Arthur and Nellie, a few fellows, and their women. At the back of the column, Henry turned Gamble around by the shoulder and pushed him forwards to the floor. 'You'll have to do,' he said.

'Take it away,' cried Gamble. The players launched themselves into the new dance.

Holding hands, the couples formed a circle, and the movement began. Bow to the partner. Curtsey to the men. Reels to the right and reels to the left. Women and Gamble to the centre, swapping partners. Passing crosses. Men now facing new partners and taking their hands. Chain link walks around the circle. Gamble going the wrong way then re-joining the ring, to much laughter. Women in a right-handed star. Men clapping in line as they waited. Gamble taking the wrong steps and scurrying back to his place. An arch at the end for the couples to duck beneath, back to the top and start again. Gamble lifted from his feet and twirled through the air. Skip to the left with whoops and cries and stamping heels...

From the end of the room there suddenly came a hammering.

To begin with it blended with the music as though the band had been joined by a percussionist, but slowly it took over until the music began to peter out. As it died, the loud and drunken figure of Joseph White burst in through the saloon door. Where just moments before had been music and laughter and gaiety, now came disruption and chaos. The instrumentalists slowly stopped playing. The violinist scraped a final searing note.

For a moment everyone stood still. Then the dancers scattered. Stools were knocked over and tables crashed into. Glasses flew to the floor. Punch spattered on the trousers and dresses of those standing nearest by.

'So you're havin' a party and you didn't think to invite little ol' me?' the intruder drawled. White was in the middle of the dance floor, the revelers arranged around him in a ring. 'Appy birthday to me,' he shouted. 'Or is it you, Arfur?' In silence the carousers looked on. 'Cat got yer tongues?'

To the fore, Flora gritted her teeth and darted her eyes at Silas. 'Go on!' she said urgently. Silas stepped forward and moved towards White, standing far enough away to dodge a punch.

'Silas Hunt,' White began. 'The greatest nightman in Lunnun. And his little trollop.' The room inhaled sharply. 'Where's yer other boyfriends tonight then Flora?'

'You piece of scum!' Flora spat at him, her hair working loose as she threw herself forwards. Silas flinched and flung his arm out to one side. Flora latched her arms over it, fuming.

'You gonna let him talk to me like that?' She slapped a palm against Silas's chest then threw herself back through the crowd in tears to Nellie's waiting shoulder.

'You're gonna regret you ever said that, White.' Silas took a step forward. In front of him White extended his arm and faced his palm towards Silas, his fingers fanned outwards in a shield.

Arthur also stepped forwards, leaning himself over his brother's shoulder.

'And little Arfur too,' White said, moving his palm first from one brother's face then to the other. 'Well, well, well. Word has it you been a very naughty boy before your birfday, Arfur. A very naughty boy indeed.'

'Shut yer bloody trap White, or you'll cop a beating.' Arthur's voice wavered unsteadily.

'Go to the Devil!' The drunken newcomer stood his ground. 'You can try an' blacken my eye if you want,' he said, 'but it's you what's got a blackened name.'

'What the hell are you talking about?' Silas said. 'I'll give you to the count of five to get out of here. There's twenty of us here who'll show you what for. Now, g'it!'

From the circle came shouts of support. O'Brien pushed forwards and stepped into the ring. Suddenly White dipped a hand in his pocket and pulled out a short-bladed knife. He thrust it towards O'Brien and sneered. 'C'mon then big boy!' he shouted. The hulking man stopped. 'That's right,' said White. 'You stay there, digger O'Dell.' He turned back to Silas. 'Twenty of you?' he scorned. 'You're a bunch of bloody meaters.'

'I'll knock your fucking ivories out for that.' Arthur strained forwards trying to reach beyond his brother's arm. Despite his bluster, Silas held him back.

'Woo-hoo,' White mocked him. 'Who's the big man now?' Slowly he started to pace sideways like a crab, so the brothers too were forced to move in a new, more threatening kind of dance. 'But you wasn't so big the other night was you, Arfur?' White went on. 'Not when you had barrels and gunpowder to hide your cowardly little arse behind.'

Slowly, the meaning of White's accusation dawned on Silas. He too was charging Arthur with the wrecking.

'You're talking shite.' Arthur's voice burled into the ring. 'I got nothing to do with it and you know it. Fact is, I heard it was *you*.'

White threw his head back and laughed aloud. 'That's rich!'

A silent scream erupted inside Silas's head. Was this really happening? The party blighted. White accusing Arthur, deflecting the blame. The coward. 'You got five seconds to take that back,' he said. Calmly he stepped forwards. 'After that, we're gonna teach you a lesson you ain't going to forget.' He began counting.

White slashed his knife wildly before Silas's face. 'Keep back,' he warned. 'I ain't taking it back. It's true. You'll find out soon enough. All of you!'

The man began to walk backwards, swishing his knife randomly through the air. Behind him, the silent circle parted to give him clearance, the knife passing before them too. To the far end of the hall, a startled player let his instrument fall from his grip and the room rang with the clatter of wood and the echo of strings. The crowd turned to look. When their faces turned back to White, the intruder was gone, the saloon door slamming firmly shut behind him.

The party was over. The musicians were seated in a line along the back wall of the inn. The bass player held his instrument in his arms like a lover, wrapping them around the viol's wooden shoulders, his head slumped forward against the fingerboard in a moment of disillusioned drowsiness. Beside him the violinist also sat with his eyes closed, his instrument laid across his chequered lap, his turban now removed to reveal a pate of thin hair slicked down with sweat. His shoulder was weighed down by the head of the guitarist who'd slumped beside him, a ceramic jug of ale at his feet. The mandolinist sat with his arms crossed, his feet splayed wide in a lazy vee. 'That was the worst bloody jig ever,' he said. 'I couldn't even hear what I was playing.'

The celebrations were done. Silas sat beside the fireplace, his head hanging. Flora had gone. Arthur had taken Nellie home. The landlord and his wife were irritably clearing away half-eaten food and unfinished drinks. Their spaniel was cleaning up scraps from the floor.

That night, Silas slept fitfully. His mind rattled through his thoughts like beads on the old abacus. The biggest bead was Flora. How wonderful she'd looked tonight. And how good it felt to be dancing with her. What he wouldn't give to finally win her to him; to give her everything she wanted, and more. She wouldn't have to trudge down to the market in the mornings to fetch meat. No, he'd have a house where she was comfy, and the butcher's boy would knock on the door in the morning: *What did she want to order*? She could have whatever her heart desired. *A side of pork, liver, ox heart and tail, a pig's head*? Give her the lot. And by noon the boy would be back again with the meat piled up on his tray and the servants would cook it up and there'd be lunch laid between them like you'd never seen. She'd have whatever she wanted by way of a house. Dammit, he'd even give her that water closet.

But then the bead on the abacus came shuttling back. Would she even have him? Their last few meetings had been disasters. Now this birthday bash, ruined by White. Accusations against his family. And Flora taking off before they'd even had the chance to say goodnight. He might ask her to be his, only for her to say no. What prospects did he have anymore? It was all going down the pan. He'd have to jump ship and work with the guano importers – that was where the money was – but could he do that? Wouldn't that go against what he'd told Arthur and Nellie? Wouldn't that betray George's memory?

And then there was the other abacus bead: Arthur. What was going on with his brother? First, Fleet's suggestion that a nightman had done the wrecking. Now White casting aspersions.

Was it thinkable even that Arthur *hadn't* fallen in the river that night? That he'd been there when the sewer was blown? Drenched in shit like that, no wonder he'd got sick. He could have swallowed a gutful in an explosion and... No, it was absurd. Arthur would never get involved in such business. He'd always been a good brother. The best. An honest man. A hard worker. He wouldn't go and join the Family. He'd lose everything. White was a bloody liar; a knife-wielding wretch. It would be *him* that was heading to gaol. It was *him* who'd wrecked the sewers, and now he was trying to shift suspicion. Getting in his accusations before the police came looking for him.

In this way the restless hours played out in Silas's brain, trying to tally these extraordinary reports and events. When sleep finally came, it was equally troubled. He dreamed he was standing at night in a maze of courts and back roads. There in front of him hovered his little brother George, his boyish body barely lit by the few lamps in the windows of the grottoes. Beckoning him on, George guided Silas through the cholera dens of the city. Here were the hovels of paupers, their faces haggard and wretched, scratching a life for themselves from the muck: a chummy boy, a chimney climber, sleeping in a corner. A tinner putting new bottoms into old tin pots smeared with grease and filth. Rag gatherers picking scraps from the steaming open drain that ran with mud and filth. A scrawny furrier sitting by an unglazed window sewing unspeakable pelts together – the nightmarish furs of cats and dogs lifting themselves to stand and screech beneath his bony fingers. Here were dustmen unloading their muck in mounds in the same spot where sweet-stuff vendors and penny-ice men were hawking their confections. George floated past a warty gutter merchant, with wens on his face like chicken eggs, his tray piled high with quack remedies. They passed on towards a lean-to; a dilapidated abode with broken windows, the panels of the doors kicked-in where a drunk stood yelling. The handle, the number and knocker had been stripped away and sold for scrap. Inside, Silas and his ghostly guide floated up a rickety staircase, looking down through broken boards, to enter a damp, unlit penthouse. In the corner, a man lay on a pile of damp sacking. He was dressed in a long coat, patched trousers, and a double-breasted waistcoat, ripped open at the neck. The blue of his skin told the story at once. A tale of cholera. When he lifted his face and turned his gaze to Silas, the dream shattered. The face was Arthur's staring right back at him.

Silas sat bolt upright. His hair was soaked in sweat. His breathing was fast and shallow. Confused where he was, his eyes finally alighted on the soft figure of Scrap at the end of his bed. 'Crap,' he said wanly, puffing his cheeks and exhaling, 'everything's turning to shit.'

The cat looked at him impassively and then flicked his head to the door. 'Is it always food with you, you little beggar? Silas cursed. 'Alright, I'm coming.'

Somehow from his fevered calculations he had decided what he had to do today. Downstairs in the kitchen, he tossed a cold sausage to the floor for Scrap and talked himself through his plan. Tonight they had a clearance, but that was at midnight. First, he would visit the offices of Suddaby & Co. He wanted to know what they knew about the bombing. And to clear himself – and Arthur especially – of suspicion. Then he'd go to the docks. If the only choice left open to him was working with the guano men, then he needed to talk with them pronto. Price's guano warehouse was the one he knew, his advertising hoards were posted up all over this part of the city. He'd visit there and check out their operations before he went making decisions about the future of his own business. Then home, prepare the honeycart, Queen Bee; check tools, buckets, shovels, barrels; then out tonight to clear a brimming cesspit at the end of the neighbouring terrace.

First, however, he needed to make sure he was dressed in his finest – there was no point in visiting Suddaby and the guano man, Price, if they wouldn't take him seriously from the start. He went upstairs and changed into his Saturday best.

Standing in the Office of Samuel Suddaby & Co., Silas found no answers.

'While the matter is under police investigation,' Mr. Peggs the clerk was saying in his unctuous manner, 'there's nothing more to divulge. The police have a suspect, helping them with their enquiries. The blackguard's already confessed. This much we know. Whatever else may or may not be known is strictly confidential, you'll understand, Mr. Hunt. I'm not at liberty to say.'

'It weren't no nightman that did it!' Silas protested. His words came out in a tangle of anger and denial.

'That remains to be seen,' said Mr. Peggs.

'It just doesn't make sense,' Silas calmed himself. 'We're all the same. Nightmen, sewermen, toshers and gleaners. What would a nightman have to gain from doing it? Nothing. No, we're all the same: tradesmen, managers, foremen, clerks.'

Mr. Peggs threw Silas a disparaging look. For a moment the clerk appeared confused at the well-dressed nightman standing in front of him. '*We*,' the clerk emphasised, 'are most definitively not the same as the anarchists who tried to blow up our tunnels just a few nights ago! *They* are trying to bring the city and works to a standstill. *We* are trying to save the city. Reckless! How many people have to die from disease when the sewers are razed to the ground?'

'The city's grinding to a halt already,' said Silas. 'Ferries and steamboats have put the watermen out of work. Toilets and sewers are putting us out. Hundreds of fellers been put out.'

'But others in! Others in!'

'You're pitching man against man.'

'Mr. Hunt,' the clerk implored. 'How many times must we go through this? We need a water pump and working sewer in every quarter of town. In some forsaken districts you'll find close on twenty thousand dwellings with no water and no sewerage laid on at all, or people drawing water from standpipes they share with thirty other houses.'

Silas thought of the filthy lanes where he had grown up, the shared outhouse, the water butt in the yard.

'What's worse,' Mr. Peggs continued, 'the water they're drawing lies spoiled by effluent from ancient cesspools barely able to contain their waste. You've seen them. You know what they're like. Think about it, man. What disease have we not seen around here? Diphtheria, yes. Typhus, yes. Scarlet fever carrying untold babies away, yes. Diarrhoea, pneumonia, and influenza, yes. Cholera, well, it goes without saying!'

It was clear that there were no answers to be had here this morning. At least Mr. Peggs had not mentioned the name of Hunt in connection with the crime. They'd have to wait until the wrecker's trial, coming soon no doubt, to find out the truth of the matter.

Silas said his 'good days' and turned from Mr. Peggs. Next stop the guano wharf beside the river. Perhaps there might be something there to get to grips with; some way of negotiating a slice of business before the guano importers swamped the manure trade entirely, leaving him and his nightsoil high and dry.

He reached the river and walked past the white-lead, tar and candle factories, over to the Golden Wharf – *wharf* for its function, *golden* for the riches that came pouring through it. This much he knew. Tethered to their bollards, the flat-bottomed scows that carried merchandise up and downriver bunted each other dully at the dockside. Through that dull knocking, he could hear the hobnailed boots of the dockers clattering over the cobbles. It was late morning, and fishmongers in cloth caps and smock frocks hanging over their brown cloth trousers were knocking up pots of shrimp and cockles for the dockers to eat at lunchtime.

He walked by a group of such men, already into their elevenses. Coopers, carpenters, cordwainers and shipbuilders. They sat in their moleskin trousers, heavy boots, sleeved waistcoats and felt hats, their strapping chests showing at the necks of their cambric shirts. It was a different world down here to the one

Silas knew. His was a closed world of underground cellars, tunnels, and cesspools, dark and airless. Here, where the breeze whipped up off the water, mudlarks and coal whippers busily worked the river's low-tide edge. He'd spent a bit of time here as a boy, straight out of lock-up, trying to scrape a living. But that was all water out to sea now.

Out on the river, passenger ferries, steamers and flotillas of wherries blew their whistles as they plied back and forth between the pontoons. Sturdy lightermen navigated their barges and steamers along the open highway of the river, to line up their vessels and moor them alongside the trade ships docked in parallel, laden down with burgeoning goods: builders' bricks and stone shipped up from Kent. Hay and straw floating in on barges with the tide. Steamers bringing northern coal. Three-masted clippers gliding in on trade winds, bringing tea and spice and merchandise from around the world. Not least African and Peruvian gold – guano.

Silas followed his nose. Guided by the tang, he found himself standing outside the warehouse and offices of *Thomas Price & Co. Guano Importers*. He looked about him. Here were knots of sailors, their tarpaulin hats masking their eyes, their whiskers framing their jaws like bushels of steel wool. The boats were making a din as the halyard ropes rattled against the masts. Anchors were rising and falling to the clank of chains. Captains were shouting a chorus of call and response with their crews. Barrels boomed as they rolled emptily over the cobbles onto the dockyard.

He pushed the warehouse door and stepped inside. Behind the desk stood the trading clerk, a fat man whose features bulged out from beneath his stovepipe hat. Beside him stood a naval type – a man in Guernsey-shirt and straw boater, a knotted handkerchief around his neck, and a pair of blue canvas trousers rolled up at the bottoms over his bare feet. His ears glinted with the wink of golden rings. He was handing over docking papers and awaiting receipt to take back to his ship.

As the seaman left the offices, the door to the rear flew open and a businessman came striding confidently through, followed by a team of clerks and scribes, each carrying a pile of ledgers and dockets. Silas took the man for Price. He seemed to be of average stature, ordinary features, with a cleanly shaven face. His salt-and-pepper hair was shorn tight at the sides and matched his fashionable tweed suit, snug at the shoulders and pleated at the waist, studded with fancy buttons and a breastpin in the shape of a lucky horseshoe. His patent leather boots mirrored his shiny hat, which perched on his head, its broad brim undulating like a wave of wash on the Thames. Not just any old businessman, Silas thought.

'A commodity of great import…' the man said, and the gaggle of scribes and accountants laughed at his pun, 'of very great import indeed,' he continued, 'for the improvement of agricultural lands in the realm.'

'The Peruvians have certainly found it so for centuries,' the nearest accountant said.

'Important for what?' Silas heard himself say. The group of men before him stopped and stared.

'I'm sorry,' the businessman said casually. 'And you are…?'

'Silas Hunt.'

'And your business here, sir?'

'I'd like to meet with Mr. Price, if it pleases you,' he said.

'Would you now?' the businessman asked rhetorically. 'I wonder if that might be arranged? And to what does your enquiry pertain?'

Silas shuffled uneasily on his feet. 'Nightsoil.'

'Well!' said Mr. Price. Beside him his entourage laughed into their collars. 'If it's as important as all *that!*' he laughed, 'I wonder if *he* might be in to meet with *you*?' The businessman turned to the portly clerk and looked at him quizzically. 'Is Mr. Price in the office this morning to receive Mr. Hunt?'

The clerk, slightly confused by the joke, blustered in response. 'Yes Mr. Price, sir.' Silas stood bemused.

'It seems you are in luck then, Mr. Hunt,' he said. 'Mr. Price will see you in his office *tout suite*.'

Price beckoned Silas forward, the entourage parted and together they disappeared behind the door of his private office. The businessman seated himself at his desk and indicated for Silas to sit.

'To answer your question, Mr. Hunt,' he began, 'as to why our product is of import, it's simple. Turnips mostly. Hops, clover, barley. Beans, wheat, potatoes. But I'm sure you know all this already? And you are in... nightsoil you say? I have to say, looking at your attire, sir, I find that rather hard to believe! You're a trader? Manure manufacture? Are we already engaged in business of some kind, perhaps? What is it man? Speak up.'

Choosing his way carefully, Silas laid out his position. The pressures on his business. The seemingly inevitable progress of sewerage. The pressure of guano. 'I've run the best nightsoil operation in the city for years,' he concluded, 'but I'm starting to believe it's over.' He watched Price – the man was listening intently. Interested. Sympathetic even.

'Your nightsoil's never going to compete in this market, Hunt. You do know that? The landscape's changed. I know a manufacturer of different manures in every town in Britain, from guano to saltpetre, farmyard manure, to desiccated compost. Nightsoil's had its day, sir. It's more economic, I'll wager, to bring the guano up from Africa, or over from Peru even, than it is to cart your nightsoil from Tower Bridge to Hampstead.'

'I don't doubt it.' The face of John Grundy flashed into Silas's mind.

'I can get a bag of guano out to a hill farmer in the north,' Price said, 'and he'll have returns on that for a whole season. You could never get your horse to pull a cart up those mountainsides.'

'Don't need to sell to the north,' said Silas. 'My market's round London.'

'The point is academic, man. My costs are low, my returns are high. With you it's the other way round. Simple economics. Why dig English dung when you can dig African and Peruvian at a fraction of the cost? *And* transport it halfway round the world!'

This analysis aside, Silas knew he had intrigued the trader for now. Unbidden, the guano man began to expound the details of his business. Digging and freighting costs. Docking, warehousing, insurance. 'Used to sell as high as eighteen a ton,' he concluded, 'back in the heyday. Now we're at thirteen which, by anyone's reckoning, is still £7 profit on each ton we import.'

The figures were impressive. Inside his head, Silas could hear George's voice. 'You're in the wrong business, brother.' If he could only make the move and work for Price, his business problems would be solved; his prospects sealed with Flora.

'We are, quite literally, turning birds' muck into gold, Mr. Hunt. The sums add up in our favour.'

Silas rubbed his chin thoughtfully. The day's stubble was already rough against his palm.

'And how are you with sums, Mr. Hunt?' Price asked.

'We've done alright these last twenty years.'

'But you'd like to do better?'

'Goes without saying.'

'The governments in Africa and Peru demand a high price, naturally. Contractors receive commission on gross sales.'

The capitalist paused. Silas understood he was being tested. 'So they shift large volumes at low prices?' he offered.

'Indeed! The conflict in the trade, as you can see, begins at source.'

Silas could see his way in. Impress the man now and, who knows, he might offer him work of some kind. A foot in the door. It couldn't be that different from selling nightsoil. Shit was shit, birds' and men's alike. 'So you got to forecast in advance,' Silas offered cautiously, 'what farmers might need, say, six months down the line?'

Price's lower lip protruded. He nodded.

'And that makes chartering ships a gamble,' Silas went on. 'You don't want your dockyard filled with unwanted stuff.'

'Exactly!' Price leaned forwards over his desk. 'And there I was thinking *what could a nightman possibly know of this business?*'

'You shouldn't be fooled by appearances, Sir.'

'It seems, Mr. Hunt, that there are more similarities between you and I than might meet the eye. 'Listen. Tell me what you think of this.' He beckoned Silas forwards. Silas hooked his thumbs into his trouser pockets and dipped his shoulder. The two men were huddled over the desk, almost conspiratorially.

'There's a rash of small-scale speculators trading in West African guano, bringing it in to small ports. We can't get our big ships in. They can. Damned nuisance for our trade. Nonetheless, they won't be able to compete with the big players for long. It's an economy of scale.'

'Bring it all into London and distribute it from here?' Silas said.

'Perhaps. But that pushes prices up. Direct cargo to the provinces means cheaper products.'

'So you have to sell more.'

'There's no way of telling which way it'll go,' said Price, 'but one has to be provident, Mr. Hunt. Take a long-term, balanced outlook.'

Mr. Price leaned back in his chair. From outside, the sound of clanking anchor chains and rolling barrels came in through the windows.

'I wonder if you're a gambling man, Mr. Hunt?' the businessman suddenly asked speculatively, touching the horseshoe tiepin at his chest.

Where had the question come from? Where was it going? 'I don't have money to gamble,' Silas said.

'One has to venture something to win extraordinary rewards, Mr. Hunt. What would you say to a little wager? Your long-term future against my short-term gain?' Price pulled a silver shilling from his pocket and rolled it through his fingers.

Silas watched the coin move, as though he was watching a

conjuror perform some slight-of-hand. 'What d'you have in mind?'

'Heads, you come to work for me. A job. Good pay. Better than you're earning now. Better conditions, certainly.'

Silas stood amazed. 'Truly?

'Why not man?'

'And tails?' Silas said.

'Tails...' Price silently balanced the equation in his head, 'tails you come and clear our warehouse cellars whenever they fill up with... well, you're quite aware what cellars fill up with, Mr. Hunt. You never know, one toss of a coin and there might be an opening for a man like you, eh?'

Silas weighed the improbable proposition. On the one hand he was being offered the dream ticket; the job in the business that would buy him and Arthur out of trouble; the job that would finally win him Flora. On the other hand, he stood to lose – what? – a few days' work each year whenever Price's cesspools needed clearing. They'd soon enough be connected to the sewers anyway and then he'd be relieved of the burden. In the meantime, once he was down here, he was as good as in with the man anyway. The odds were in his favour.

'You sure?' he said.

'Wager's a wager, man!' Price said. 'Either way, I win.'

Exactly what I was thinking, Silas thought. 'In that case Mr. Price, Sir, heads.'

Before him the businessman let out a throaty laugh. 'That's my man!' Hurriedly he thrust his hand forward. Silas took it and the two men shook. In an instant the silver shilling was sitting on Price's knuckle awaiting the force of his thumb.

Silas watched the businessman flick the coin upwards to begin its spinning ascent. It seemed to rise in slow time, each turn of the coin revealing the Sovereign Lady's face. She appeared with every revolution to more and more resemble the face of Flora Street: 'A hallway with tiles,' she said with the first turn. 'Two reception rooms,' with the second. 'A lounge and a dining room,' with the third. 'Three bedrooms for us and our children,' with the last revolution in the air.

The coin reached the apex of its journey and hung there, where the face on the winning side seemed to wink. In that short interval, Silas heard his own blood drumming in his ears.

The silver shilling then began its descent. With each descending gyration, Silas saw the tumbling figure of Britannia on the losing side of the coin. 'Have you completely lost your mind?' she asked with the first turn. 'You're selling out,' with the second. 'This way to ruin!' with the third. 'Clean me, Silas, clean me,' with the last. Silas felt the old wound on his arm shoot a nervous pain from shoulder to fingertip.

The shilling landed. Price clapped it down on the back of his left hand with his right palm. 'The suspense is delicious, is it not Mr. Hunt?'

Silas made no reply. His feelings were a void. His heart was racing. Had it all come to this moment of madness; to the toss of a coin?

Slowly, Mr. Price lifted his right hand up, and proffered his left forwards.

Beyond the window, the commerce of the docks died away to nothing. The seagulls, garrulous until now, stopped their squawking. The wind no longer rattled the halyards against the masts. Even the river itself seemed to stop in its flow. The world stood still. And in that pause, it was as if Silas sensed an angel float above him and whisper.

'It seems your luck is in, Mr. Hunt!'

What had been worry and tension only moments before suddenly became clear. Everything was resolved. It's all yours, Silas, he thought to himself.

When he gathered himself, Mr. Price was staring directly at him with a congenial smile. 'Look Hunt,' he said. 'We're having a business supper. Next week. In town. Building up the business, new market opportunities, that sort of thing. If you're going to come and work for Price's, well, you'll need to come along.'

Silas hardly knew what to say. 'I... yes... thank you.'

'And dress sharply won't you, there's a good fellow,' Price paused, 'although I see you clearly do already. Extraordinary. Extraordinary!'

He came out from his side of the desk and gestured towards the door.

'Now, if you'll forgive me, I have other business to attend to. The Clerk will furnish you with the details.'

Silas smiled to himself. 'Thank you, Sir,' he said. 'Thank you,' and with that was shown from the office.

He walked along the wharf and rested himself against an iron bollard. Leaning back and sighing a breath of relief, he stood looking down at the water. Things at last had taken a great turn for the better. His speculations about the guano trade had paid off. And the gamble. He laughed out loud and raised his eyes, closing them contentedly in the breeze. When he opened them again, the slight wind and the sunlight on the river's surface made the water shift in a mirage of a thousand mirrors. Dark greens, light greens, blacks, whites, silvers, and untold shades between, glistening in an undulating sheet. Across this jewelled surface, paddle steamers puffed their way, releasing airy plumes. They rose and cut across his vision of the bridge in the distance, mixing with the pink-tinged clouds. It was as attractive an apparition of the city and the river as he had ever seen; sailboats pulled up to the wharves, a red sail flapping gently here, a broad white sail further along.

And there he would have stayed, for once enraptured by the city in which he lived; at last convinced that, yes, there was perhaps a way out of the mess their trade had fallen into. The morning seemed so faultless now that he would have stayed there watching the river and her populace, but for one small detail encroaching at the corner of his eye. Was that John Grundy – unmistakably, it must have been – approaching the offices of *Price & Co* further back down the dock? He turned and stared back at the small figure now walking up to the warehouse doors. How could he mistake him? The waggoner's smock, the breeches and gaiters, the doorknocker beard, and that pick-axe nose. What the hell was that bilker doing here? Was he too going to talk with Price? Had Grundy already signed himself over and quit his own trade in manures, to shift his business interests to the more profitable trade in guano? Had he beaten Silas to it already?

A wash of fury overtook him. Why the hell should he let Grundy cash in on this, if he could do it instead? In that instant his decision was confirmed. Guano and Price had changed him from midnight mechanic into a new kind of dealer.

A low full moon bathed the streets in bright metallic light. Henry Shrimpton sat at the driver's seat of the honeycart preparing his pipe, its bowl soon glowing with the intense orange-red of a crucible. All around him the world was doused in moonlight, a silverness glittering off railings and doorknockers.

'The phantom shitter was 'ere, by the look of things,' the man laughed philosophically, sucking on his pipe. He was surveying the barrels of nightsoil lined up on the honeycart's deck behind him, calculating their worth. 'A few quid's worth there,' he noted as his workmates joined him. They clapped each other on the back.

'Not as much as you'd reckon anymore,' Silas said.

'Two quid a ton?' Shrimpton said.

'Half it,' Silas told him. 'Take off a little. That's what I'm getting from Grundy these days.'

'The man's a bloody thief,' the smoker complained.

'Well, we're bypassing him this time,' Silas said. 'Selling straight to the buyer. Hi girl!' He flipped the reins and the honeycart rolled away into the early hours of the morning, a mere shadow of the old profitable days.

By the time the sun had replaced the moon, the Hunt brothers, Gamble and Shrimpton were already out of the city, past the toll gates and out into the surrounding countryside. There was no point in paying Grundy to cart their nightsoil for them; that was just throwing money away. They would make their own deliveries today. It meant a longer night's work and morning too but, in the end, it was saving their business something. And that mattered more than anything right now. Anyhow, this might be Silas's last clearance and then he'd have to find a way of telling Arthur what he had agreed with Price. How was that going to play out, he wondered?

While he'd counted on himself and his boys working solidly through the night, however, what he hadn't counted on was the tiredness of the cart itself. As they neared their destination, the honeycart's wheel hit a deep rut in the road. Somewhere beneath them came a bone-cracking shudder.

'What the bloody hell?' Silas moaned as the cart lurched violently to one side. To the rear the barrels of nightsoil shifted suddenly. The right-hand wheel splintered at the rim. Unable to bear this newly distributed weight, the rails that held the barrels in place gave way, snapping noisily. First one and then a second barrel slid from the deck and smashed open on the ground, spilling their cargo in a spreading slick. Cursing whatever and whoever came to mind, Silas jumped down from the seat and inspected the damage.

Arthur followed quickly behind him. 'Shit.'

'Exactly!' said Henry. Beside him, Gamble thought better of laughing and checked himself.

'Henry, Harry,' Silas said, gauging the extent of the damage, 'you'll have to go on to the farm. She's going to need a new wheel.'

'It's further than you think,' Henry began.

Silas gave him a withering look.

'We'll be directly on our way then,' the carter amended.

'So you will,' said Silas.

'We can't all go.' Arthur pushed his fists against the rail and the honeycart rocked. 'Someone's got to stay.'

'Which is why *we'll* stay put, brains.' Silas clapped his brother on the shoulder.

'Better get shoveling then,' said Henry, pointing to the spillage. Arthur too cast him a reproving look. 'Right,' said Henry, 'we'll get going.'

He set off up the road with Gamble at his side. By the time they'd turned the bend in the distance, Silas and Arthur had already shoveled up a good deal of their spillage. They barely spoke. Queen Bee stood blithely nose bagged.

When they'd finished shoveling, they stood with their backs to the honeycart. She had broken down on a road that cut through green pasture whose boundaries were marked by thickets and copses. To one side, the new railway had been cut through the fields, the parallel steel rails running away to a distant vanishing point. At weekends the new carriages brought the middle-classes out this way and a constant freight leaving the city for transport through the country.

'We ought to bring Nellie and Flora out at the weekend,' Silas said, trying to drive his frustration away with thoughts of what the line might offer.

'I never thought of it,' Arthur said brusquely. 'S'pose so.'

'In fact, I can hear one coming now.' With the excitement of a young boy, he pulled himself up onto the deck of the cart to look back down the rail lines. 'Yes,' he said, 'here's one coming.'

As it hove into view, he caught a trail of steam lifting from the approaching shape of an engine. The rails began to whisper of the train's approach. 'Told you,' he said. He'd never had reason to take the train himself, but to see one pass by now would take some sting out of their breakdown, these lost hours and shillings.

'Big deal.' Arthur kicked at a tussock beside the cart.

'Suit yourself.' Silas wasn't going to let his brother's sullenness spoil the moment. As the train hurtled across the field towards them, he could feel the ground begin to shake. He stood on the back of the lopsided cart and waved an arm. The steam billowed and wafted in a long trail. The rails hissed and rattled. The trees shook. In a moment of rushing pleasure, Silas felt the air sucking at him and buffeting him as the train passed.

The carriages flew by and then, as they became their own sound and vanished, slowly his smile began to fade. As he stood watching the carriages recede, he realized what they were transporting. On the side of each boxcar, the transporter's name was emblazoned in bright lettering on taught canvas panels: *Thomas Price & Co., Guano Importers and Suppliers, Golden Wharf, London*. How would he ever tell Arthur? He stood in silence, confusion and resignation vying for control of his heart.

Within the week, the trial at the High Court was underway. The nameless agitator whom the police had been holding was being tried and sentenced. His fellows remained at large. Outside the courthouse a large crowd had gathered to hear the verdict. Most were sanitary workers, toshers and nightmen, men with vested interests in the underground workings of the city.

Among them stood Arthur Hunt. He had his collars pulled high and his cap down low, a scarf around his jaw. He shuffled from foot to foot, nodding to the men he knew, but keeping himself to himself. He didn't want to draw attention to his presence, for there were also agitators gathered there – disillusioned Family men, unemployed workers, and political stirrers. There were also men of little cause at all: coarse streetwalkers and beggars, street fighters, roughs and navvies who'd joined the number solely for the prospect that things might turn ugly and here was a chance for a good old-fashioned ruck. 'Up the mob!' The man beside Arthur was shouting drunkenly, waving a fist. He turned to Arthur and clasped his forearm. Two of the man's fingers were missing. 'Right brother?' he said.

'Right,' said Arthur, pulling himself away. Don't call me brother neither, he thought. He already had one of those. But where he was could have been anyone's guess. 'I got no interest in the fate of the anarchist and good luck to him,' Silas had told

Arthur that morning. 'He'll get whatever he deserves. And by the way, wasn't that the very man who tried to involve your name in this business, Arthur?'

After that, they'd argued once more. Arthur accused him of giving up hope on the future of their business. 'At least I still care about the issues, Silas!'

'You know what? I'm beginning to think that he – and White – just might have been telling the truth about you.'

At that, it had very nearly come to blows. 'You wouldn't know the bloody truth if it bit you on the arse!' Arthur cursed him, storming from the room.

The moment for resolution was gone. Would it ever be possible to sit down calmly together and for Silas to explain the offer from Price; that he'd won the wager; that there was a way out of this slump after all?

Now Arthur was standing alone outside the courthouse, buoying his spirits on the rumble of the gathering mob. When the doors finally opened, a procession of officers, of legal men and sanitary inspectors, came out onto the steps of the courthouse beneath the high entablature and shining columns of the civic edifice. At the forefront stood Samuel Suddaby, flanked by his legal aides. Below him, at the foot of the steps, a line of carriages had drawn up to take the dignitaries away. The horses were shying nervously at the swelling noise rising from the crowd. Their drivers held tightly to their reins with trembling fists.

'Guilty!' Suddaby suddenly exclaimed over the heads of the crowd. 'Transportation for life. No less than these anarchists deserve. We are cleaning up this city street by street, sewer by sewer, criminal by dwindling criminal!'

With this verdict and valediction delivered, he descended the steps with his entourage and the doors of the carriages were opened.

It was then that the brewing resentment of the crowd began to spread from man to man to woman and boy, like a rapid, rapacious contagion. Whisper turned to shout. Shout turned to roar.

Roar turned to surge and, before the dignitaries had even had time to comfortably seat themselves in their coaches, the ruffians and thugs, the political agitators and co-agents of the condemned man, had broken the cordon and fallen on the vehicles in a fury.

Mr. Suddaby pushed his dismayed head through the carriage window to shout instructions to his driver. No sooner had he done so than the Director's top hat was dislodged by a missile and trampled underfoot. Quickly he pulled his head back in and tugged the window up for protection. The footman leaned over the roof rails, striking down on the heads of the assailants with his horsewhip. At the foot of the carriage, the rioters began to heave at the wheels, rocking the vehicles back and forth. Policemen rushed down from the courtroom steps and dove into the fray, striking out with truncheons to bloody the rioters' foreheads. The horses shied and the drivers struggled to keep them under control.

It was then that a decision appeared to have been taken. Mr. Suddaby and entourage suddenly abandoned their carriages, ran back up the courtroom steps and barricaded themselves inside. Four terrified policemen stood on the street-ward side of the massive, bolted doors. Slowly the crowd advance up the steps towards them, while the carriages below took off at speed, their open doors flapping as they jangled away. Some of their furniture was being set alight in the street already.

With the bolting of the doors, the noise in the street rose to lawlessness and reverberated that way for some time before the doors of the courthouse suddenly flew open again and a Justice of the Peace stepped out commandingly.

This representative of the law could not have looked more distinct from the mob: his legs were stockinged, his head was wigged, his belly was pushing at the buttons of his ceremonial cloak. 'Our Sovereign Lady the Queen,' he began with all the force of a town crier, reading the protestors the Riot Act. 'Our Sovereign Lady chargeth and commandeth all persons, being assembled, immediately to disperse themselves.' But where his voice had begun with force, it now began to be lost in the clamour, '...unlawfully, riotously and tumultuously assembled...' it came in fragments, '...contumacy...' fitfully flying over the rabble's heads, '...must disperse within the half hour. God save the Queen.'

A barrage of offensive insults and missiles began to rain on him, and the man quickly disappeared back through the doors, his terrified officers following swiftly behind him.

The street was now the rioters' own. For a moment there was a deafening hammering on the courthouse doors as the trouble-makers tried to break their way inside. When this proved futile, the rabble turned away and set their sights on causing whatever disturbance they might. Linking arms and wielding crude weapons – bludgeons and work shovels, broken off pieces of carriage, jagged bottles pulled from a pocket – they descended the steps and joined in procession to the square at the far end of the street. Small gangs of hotheads united with them in one welter. The great crowd marched along the street in an irrational hulla-baloo, ranting and chanting. Those bored youths who'd tagged along with them began to throw stones. Windows were broken. Street vendors' stalls were overturned. Their owners ran away in fear. Soon the road was clear, save for the mob.

They reached the square at the end of the thoroughfare. Facing them there, two carriage-loads of officers were waiting. They dismounted their wagons and formed an impregnable line. For a moment, the two forces considered each other.

Arthur felt himself pushed on from behind by an undefined force. His neighbour's elbow banged into his ribs, and he let his breath go in a strong huff. Behind him, the breath of the fellow at his shoulder was warm at his neck. He turned his head to cast a glance at the man. His chest was pressed into Arthur's back. His nose, red and inflamed with ruptured vessels, was inches from Arthur's cheek. He turned back and pulled his cap down firmly on his crown. To his left, another man close-at-jowls complained at Arthur's raised elbows. Arthur gave the man a blunt look. 'What?'

At last, it struck him that he had become involved in corrupt, unlawful matters; that he should have listened to Silas; that this path of agitation was leading him nowhere but to a rude appointment with the law. The air around him began to ring with the shrill blast of police whistles as the unit of officers advanced, pushing the herd back.

Now they found themselves sandwiched into the square between two police forces, for the officers from the courthouse had also rallied and pursued the mob from behind. What followed was a free-for-all, a chaotic melee. The police struck out with determination and truncheons. The mob dispersed in panic, some stopping to fight in small clusters across the square, others fleeing to escape injury or arrest. The police formed cordons at entrance and exit to stop the crowd from spilling out into the neighbouring streets. They charged in a din of whistles and a cloud of dust thrown up by hundreds of boots on the roadway.

In the morass of the revolt, Arthur defended himself and those around him. To his side, a policeman had his fist gripped tightly on a young man's collar, yanking him to the ground. Arthur pushed and shoved at the policeman but was pulled away by other officers. Around him the multitude's confused fury was spending itself in pointless skirmishes. Where once before their spirits and their confidence had been high, now their cause was looking lost. They were outnumbered.

More police arrived on horses, pushing the rioters further back. The horses whinnied and stamped. Their mounted riders struck down at the heads of the rabble with unrestrained resolve. A sea of cloth caps and battered bowlers swayed this way and that under the assault, the shoulders of the men hunched down, their hands raised above their heads as they ran to fend off the worst of the blows. The mounted police gave chase.

It was then that Arthur fell. He had reached up to grasp the arm of a rider and pulled the sergeant down. Before he dropped, the helmeted man looked down in great surprise, the whites of his eyes shining in alarm between the brim of his helmet and the strap on his chin. As Arthur pulled, the rider tumbled and both men began to plummet. He tumbled backwards and watched the unmanned horse rear up and bolt away. The caped torso of the sergeant seemed to loom above him like some dark angel slowly descending.

Arthur could feel himself falling, seemingly forever. Then, at his back, he felt the ground rise to meet him. He landed, spine down on a street strewn with stones and broken bottles, dropped weapons and a hundred hats and caps. His head hit the ground with a whiplashing blow. And then, with a thump that knocked the wind from his chest and the consciousness from his head, the dark angel landed on top of him.

'He's going to be doing penal!' Nellie screeched. 'Transportation Silas! For life! I ain't never going to see him again...' Her last word trailed away like the horn of a train into the distance. The woman was inconsolable.

'He is.' Since his brother's arrest, Silas had spoken barely a word. Truth was, he was in a terrifying slough. He could barely think. Blankly he stared up at 'The Angel's Whisper' hanging above the fireplace.

'Don't you care, Silas Hunt? Your own brother! What'll become of him?' Again, Nellie dissolved in a heap of wretchedness, her head laid on the table, her fist beating a slow, steady toll. With each thump, Scrap adjusted himself by the fireside then, standing no more for this disruption to his routine, slunk from the room.

Silas sat in silence. It was as if a curtain had descended in his skull and blocked out all light, all avenues of thought and reason. His mind was utterly blank. In his lassitude he could feel nothing. It was as much as he could do to stay sitting in the room without thinking he might succumb to madness or explode from the pressure within.

Eventually he spoke. His voice was strangely neutral. 'I've

made up my mind Nellie,' he said. 'I'm selling up. Harry and Henry can take the business over if they want it. They can buy it off me by stages. I don't want it anymore. I've had enough. I'm going to work with Price, in guano.'

'Where in the Lord's name is Guano?' Nellie said irrationally, crying ever louder now.

'It's not a place Nellie! It's fertilizer. Penguins. Bird shit from Africa, Antarctica. That's where the money is.'

'Africa! Antarctica?' Nellie cried. 'That's farther than Arthur!'

'I'm not going there, woman!'

What good had this business ever done him, he thought. Working thanklessly in the nation's muck for next to nothing? He'd had it. He was done. What he wanted was something regular – eight hours' work, eight hours' sleep, eight hours' play. Proper pay. If Arthur could jeopardise them all and toss their life away like that on a whim, then he could change it all on the flip of Price's coin. What in god's name had his brother been thinking of?

He sank himself back into the depths of his chair and his self-comforting silence.

'And what's to become of me then?' Nellie sobbed, burying her face in her handkerchief, 'once he's gone for penal and you've sold up? Tell me that. You think of no one but yourself. You never have done. You're all bluff, Silas Hunt. You're hardened by that stony heart inside you. You're allus so... stolid. No feelin' at all!'

If Silas's anger had locked him inside himself, Nellie's was kicking down her own walls. Surely, she didn't mean it? He'd done everything for her. Lord knows no one was forcing him to share his house with his brother's wife.

'One thing's for certain,' she said. Her voice was trembling, on the verge of screaming. 'I won't be doing all *this* for you no more,' she flung her arm wildly around the room, 'to keep you in the fancy ways you're accustomed.' Her voice now pulled itself back to a strong resolve. 'You'll have to marry Flora, Silas. If she'll even *have* such a cold-hearted monster as yourself. Get *her* to do the feeding and the clothing if you can. I'd like to see you try! The washing. The mending. All them domestic duties that just seem somehow to get magically done.' She paused and collected herself. 'Gwarno? Flippin' bird shit? I thought it was bad enough with people's. You've been a martyr to that. But birds? You're off your flippin' mind.'

From somewhere within his fug, Silas considered her verdict. Was he really that bad; cold-hearted? Why was this *his* fault? She was just being irrational. Angry at everyone. He'd tried to do the right thing all along. And he wasn't going to be casting Nellie out of home now on account of Arthur's stupidity. Yet, equally, how could he keep her here? She seemed to detest him. She blamed him for Arthur's actions. How could he ever make a household work again between them?

'How're *you* going to earn your keep then, Nellie?' he managed. This wrangling between them was as much as he'd said the whole week. 'You got to bring some brass in somehow...' he paused, wondering if Flora would even accept him now. 'When Flora moves in, she'll be working for her old man doing books. Business doesn't run without books. And you're welcome to stay with us. Of course.'

From across the table, she looked at him with bleary eyes.

'Arthur or no Arthur,' he said, 'this is your home.'

Without answering him, she burst once again into a blur of dissonant wailing. Sitting in the armchair where his brother had so often recently sat, Silas massaged his temples. Slowly, Nellie's grief-stricken howls quietened to a softer, occasional snivel.

When she had gathered herself from her fury, her eyes were drier. 'Might do some piecework then,' she said wiping away her tears. 'Broidering braces for gentlemen, or dressmaking. Or some nursing in hospital. I ain't working on the foul ward though.'

'Won't have no woman in *my* house doing that,' Silas cajoled her.

'No, but you'll have us washing your filthy work-clothes won't you, you bloody nightman.'

'Guano man,' he said.

Between them they pulled two tight-lipped smiles.

By the Monday, Price's business meeting came around. The guano trader, sartorially impressive in his tweed suit and tiepin, gave Silas's outfit the general seal of approval – he'd bathed and shaved and dressed himself finely for this, his first business meeting.

'A very good look for business.' Price ushered Silas into the meeting hall. 'Some small talk of commerce,' he said, 'new partners and relations, then dinner.'

Silas found himself standing in front of a line of young hopefuls. Price waved his hand along the line, in an all-purpose gesture of introduction. 'You've all been invited here tonight for what you might bring by way of new energy and expertise to the company,' he said to no one in particular and then, singling Silas out, 'this is Mr. Hunt, gentlemen. Mr. Hunt is,' he paused, 'a maven in manures.'

'Really?' said a thin business-like fellow.

'He'll be joining us shortly,' Price said, 'under exceptional circumstances.' He seemed to wink at Silas, the way his coin had winked during their wager.

Silas mumbled and smiled tentatively at the line of men. He was honoured to have been invited and, having been asked, didn't wish to waste his opportunity. For close on half an hour, he stuck to Price's shoulder, finding himself introduced to dockyard managers, the charters of ships, accountants, and distributors. By the time it came for official business, Silas felt he as good as belonged in their number.

Respectfully he took a seat to the side of the room and tried to pay attention to the minutes and accounts, the reports and the figures, the proposals for expansion, appeals for new appointments in the regional offices. When it came time for dinner, Price ushered him to a seat with the other newcomers.

'I'll take my leave of you now, Hunt,' he said. 'Report at the docks, eight, Wednesday morning. In the meantime, I hope you've found this introduction useful?'

'Thank you, Sir.'

'And before that,' said Price, 'try and enjoy your supper, eh? Don't want to go to all this expense for nothing.' He let out a sharp burst of laughter and turned away to the high table with a team of fellow businessmen.

Silas seated himself next to a hungry clerk behind a tall silver cruet-stand. The clerk was barely as well dressed as he. 'Me, I'm making the move from retail into commerce, you know,' the clerk boasted. He flipped out his napkin with a flourish and smoothed it onto his lap, too late it seemed, for already the man had spilled the juice from some item down the front of his nankeen trousers. 'Hoping to strike a deal or two yourself, are you?'

'You could say that.' Copying his neighbour, Silas repeated the motion with the napkin. Its weave felt foreign in his hand.

The two strangers sat awkwardly, shoulder to shoulder. 'Oyster?' his neighbour asked, pushing the plate towards Silas.

'Don't go in for oysters much,' he said. 'Thanks all the same.'

'Don't like the taste, or the texture? Which is it? It's always one or the other.'

Silas laughed to himself. 'Have you seen what they swim in?' He pushed the plate back towards the clerk. Looking down on the opened shells, his neighbour screwed his face up in distaste and pushed the oyster dish away.

'Perhaps they'll serve some pickled fish instead,' he said. 'Last fish supper I attended, they served us bloaters, salmon, sprats. Finished off with claws. Finest spread I've ever seen.'

Silas had to admit it – oysters aside, the meal was as good a feast as any he'd ever been to. There were anchovy toasts, dishes of meat, fresh and crisp vegetables, soft boulders of potato. Fruit for afters. Coffee. Cheese. It put Arthur's birthday spread in the shade. If this was what guano money bought you, well, sign him up for more of it.

He closed his eyes and let his mind drift back to that perfect morning just past, with the offer from Price done and dusted. He pictured himself leaning back on a bollard at the dockside, watching the sunlight play in hopeful patterns off the water. Yes, he could have stood like that in the sunshine for ever...

'Silas? Silas!' The voice he heard in his dreamlike state was George's. 'Silas? It's me.'

Still warm inside his reverie, his eyes firmly closed, Silas saw the face of his brother before him. 'Don't just stand there dreaming on the water,' George said. 'Come look over here, quickly.'

Dreamily in his imagination, Silas followed the guiding hand of his brother, pointing him away from his bollard on the dock, through the masts and rigging of the trading ships and out to the current-stirred depths of the river. There, in line, he saw the massive shapes of the prison hulks fixed at anchor. Their dark, foreboding holds were custodians of wretched prisoners; men like Arthur, waiting in limbo until transportation.

Silas tried to open his eyes but couldn't. He felt as though he'd been drugged, like soporific laudanum for toothache. He wanted nothing more than to bring himself back to the room, to Mr. Price, to the promise of his new employment, to more dinners like this. But his mind was now locked on the immovable hulks with Union Jacks, pennants and prisoners' shirts flapping between their unrigged masts.

The vessels sat some hundred yards from shore, where dockers and traders and coal-store workers were going about their daily work, at liberty to come and go as they pleased. But what a difference those hundred yards made. What a difference to that work-gang of convicts now finishing their forced labour – clearing the riverbanks and digging embankments – and marching now back down the steps of the brick-built pontoon, traipsing as best they could, their ankles chained with rattling shackles. He watched their sorry figures boarding the rowboats and sculling out across that short stretch, their freedom falling away to drown beneath the surface of the Thames. After a short, strenuous pull on the oars, driven on by the voice of the sergeant and the crack of the bosun's whip, the prisoners pulled their dinghies alongside the prison hulks. Their flanks were marked by rows of portals, where the old guns had once poked through, now boarded and barred.

What a dark, forbidding interior awaited them. Silas watched the prisoners mount the gangway and disappear beneath the broad decks, into the vast galleys and the airless hammock-houses. If only he could open his eyes on his own freedom. But his lids felt heavy like tombstones and George's spirit would not let him look away. 'Come look in here,' his brother was saying, leading Silas in past rows of bunks that hung in double rows behind iron bars. Behind them, the faces of hungry prisoners stared gauntly. Sentries and warders paced the boards, their bulls-eye lanterns sending dim shafts of light into the gloom as they jangled their keychains. The faces of the prisoners were striped in shadow.

'Here,' said George. 'Here he is,' and whether this was dream, or real, or some wild imagining, Silas found himself looking down at the lost-forever form of his other brother. Arthur. He was sitting on his hammock bunk, his blanket pulled up around his shoulders, his feet pulled up beneath him. His shoes had fallen from his feet to land on their sides on the boards beneath his hammock. A cockroach crawled from the tongue of one into the mouth of the other. Cradled in the caul of his canvas, Arthur was nursing his head in his palms. Already, in just a week, it seemed as though discomfort, mean rations and a strict regime had worn his spirits down to nothing but a shapeless residue. Here, on the lower decks, where all the lifers were held, awaiting long passage to distant colonies, Arthur looked a broken man. The air was stifling, unbreathable, shared as it was between the lungs of five hundred, their wrists shackled, their legs dangling over the sides of their bunks kicking to and fro – damaged men marking time like so many swinging pendulums. Silas choked on the airlessness...

'I say, are you alright chap?' The eager new clerk was leaning over, patting Silas on the back as he coughed vigorously beside the table.

'What?' Silas twisted to face the clerk. Suddenly he felt a shooting nerve in his shoulder. He winced, coughed one last time and opened his eyes in wide discomfort.

'I said are you alright, chap? Good Lord, I thought you'd been taken funny there for a moment.'

Silas checked himself. How long had he been sitting there in his daydream? There was Price at the head of the table. Here was the clerk. The uneaten plate of oysters.

'Lost you for a moment there!' The clerk grinned awkwardly. 'You alright?'

'I'm sorry,' Silas said, standing. 'I just need to get some air.'

'Be my guest,' the clerk said. 'P'raps it was something you ate? It is awful stuffy in here.' He nodded to Silas and then turned to the man sitting to his other side. 'Oh well,' the eager clerk said to the other new fellow. 'Hoping to strike a deal or two yourself, are you?'

Outside the meeting hall, the air of the street was fogged and misty. Mechanically, Silas traipsed from one street to another. Nobody would miss him back at the hall now. Price had already dismissed him. 'Eight, Wednesday morning.' The directive was chiming in his head like a new alarm clock. That gave him a day.

Around him as he walked, crowds of folk were ebbing and flowing down side streets and thoroughfares like the mist itself, hanging in the corners and crannies of crowded bye-streets, pushing at doorways and rapping at windows. From around their feet, vapour was climbing from the pavements, up the wrought iron lampposts. Misted flecks of light glinted off the bonnets of the black lacquered coaches as they rattled over bridges. The mist was driving the populace home, a steady flow of human traffic, knocking at their doors now to be let in, entering their houses, their courtyards and hovels, slamming the door fast to keep the bad air out, to keep the stink at bay. Silas strode past them with one burning resolve lighting his way.

He didn't know how he got there, couldn't remember the route he had taken, but he found himself standing in his own back yard. His walk had been automatic. There before him was the outhouse door, ajar in what was left of the moonlight. The privy door seemed to be calling to him like the entrance to his worst nightmare. He didn't want to go towards it, but he couldn't resist. He was drawn on and appalled in equal measure. There, beneath the ground, lay the whole street's effluent. It gathered here in the sump beneath his very own yard. 'If you want a cesspool anywhere, make sure it's in the midnight mechanic's yard,' the phrase he'd touted out so many times now seemed to taunt him.

Buried there beneath the outhouse boards was everything that had shaped his life. That had taken George and his mother away from him. That had brought them to John Pearce. That had given them their business. That had now taken it all away. He owed everything to it, and he hated it more than anything.

Beside the outhouse, leaning against the wall, stood his shovel. Next to that, two nightsoil buckets. Within moments he had thrown his jacket down, rolled up his sleeves and seized the shovel. Already now, as though they were nothing more than sheets of paper, he prized up the floorboards of the midden. There beneath him lay his devil's gold. It was everything he'd ever needed to make good his promise to George. To make himself wealthy for Flora. To give Nellie a home. To bind him and Arthur together. He'd sold his soul for it. Now he hated it for what it really was. Filth. Miserable, abject waste. He never wanted to dig another cesspool again in his life. This would be the last one. Ever.

Feverishly he began to dig, slopping the waste into buckets. He couldn't smell it anymore. For anyone else the stench would have floored them. But Silas was immune to it. He gritted his teeth and battled on.

Throwing himself out of the hole he ran the buckets back to the barrels at the rear of the honeycart, then dove back into the ditch to dig again. Indefatigable. Where four men usually strained and heaved past midnight, he performed the task alone. He was holeman, ropeman, carrier and cartman all rolled into one. It was his penance. The shit was thick. His own. This was muck of his own making and he would clear it all. His muscles burned with a hellish pain. The scar on his arm burned like a farrier's brand. His head was dense with fog. He was caked in muck from head to toe. In every crease of his clothing, every orifice – his eyes, his ears, his mouth, his nostrils, were plugged. But he didn't care. He wouldn't stop until this final task was over. And then he'd be done with it forever. He needed neither to see, nor to think about what he was doing. He did it all by instinct.

While his arms flailed maniacally at the dung heap and his legs pedalled him back and forth between barrels and cesspool, his thoughts ran between two other posts; between the two people who meant the most to him. Arthur and Flora.

Oh Arthur! Silas had stuck by him every day since they were kids. Hadn't he always looked out for him? In the clink. At Belmerson's. When they'd held nothing between them but two rotten shillings. When they'd been forced to live on the streets and on their wits. He'd stuck fast with his brother. They'd done all this together: working for Pearce, building a business, building a home. Lord knows he'd even given up half of that home to Arthur and his wife. And this was how he repaid him! It probably *was* him, the raving idiot, not White at all, who'd got involved with the Family. It probably was him there that night when the sewer blew. He was bloody well there when the riot kicked off, wasn't he? Who was to say that he hadn't actually gone and bombed the sewers with them in the first place? How could he do this to Silas?

Then again, wasn't this all his own fault? The chain of blame went all the way back to their childhood and bound itself to his, Silas's, wrists. He was the one who'd dreamed up the dodge of stealing pure. He was the one responsible for taking George across the roofs. It was him to blame for George's death. His lifeless corpse lying there in the moonlight in the knacker's yard beside the middens, mired with every kind of filth you could imagine.

He, Silas, had let his brother down. And he'd been punished when god took him away. He, Silas, had let his mother down too and, soon enough, she was also taken. He deserved everything he got. Now he'd lost not just one, but two brothers. He'd failed Arthur dismally. He should have been there to protect and guide him. He should have seen what was happening and stepped in to stop it. He, Silas, should never have been so blind to Arthur's private schemes. It was obvious, all along. Why had he done nothing? The secret pieces of paper. The silent brooding in his armchair. The week in bed from falling in the river. *Falling in the river?* Had he been blind! If only he hadn't been so obsessed with schemes for saving their business. For winning Flora. He should have been looking out for Arthur. And now he'd failed him. Now he was gone. Now he was being transported.

And Flora. What was his fancy with her anyway? Why was he doting on her all the time when he hardly ever saw her? These past months they'd barely spent more than a couple of days together and, when they did, he'd been in his cups, or they'd argued, or she'd fobbed him off for someone else. When he wasn't with her, who knew where she was? He was fed up with hearing her say, 'Don't ask questions, Silas.' Fed up with her telling him it was a girl's right not to be watched-over day in, day out. 'So what if she walked out with other chaps; didn't he trust her?' Well, if it was all so innocent, why wouldn't she tell him where she was going and with whom?

But then there was her smile. Her laughter. They brought some light into his dark, underground world. He would have given anything to see that crescent of sunshine that was her grin; to hear that babble of birdsong that was her laughter. He thought of her independence. Her spirit. She was a different kind of girl. She wasn't chained to the parlour, to the dishes, like Nellie. She seemed able to come and go as she pleased. He adored her ambition. Her longing for that house in the suburbs. What was it? A butler in the basement and a maid in the attic. A drawing room, piano and bathtub. God damn it he would personally build her a water closet! Who cared for nightsoil anymore? Flush it all away! He was moving into guano. He was going to make a mint on the Golden Wharf.

As dawn broke, a small crowd had gathered to watch. Word had spread that the nightman had lost his mind 'on account of his brother.' The local peddlers had gathered as they made their dawn walk to whatever street corner it was they worked from: street barbers, crossing sweepers, shoe-shiners and barrow boys. The residents of the street were still asleep indoors. Nellie's curtains were drawn. But the street folk were up and about their business. And this morning they had something unusual to watch.

When he was done, Silas emptied the last of the nightsoil into the barrel and dropped his bucket. He wandered to his gate and stared the crowd down. 'There,' he said. 'Show's over folks. It's all done.'

No one spoke. He was faced by a line of disbelieving faces, sad-eyed and open-mouthed. He stood before them utterly besmirched. It was the worst of his nightmares to be seen like this. He was a clean man. A tidy man. A man who took great care of himself. To be seen like this, as he really was – filthy and base and corrupted – was the absolute bottom. You couldn't go any lower. But he *wanted* them to see him like this now. This was his forfeit. These were his amends. Arthur had paid his price, now he was paying his. 'Go on,' he said. 'There's nothing more to see here. We're done now. Go on with you all.'

Slowly, the gathering began to peel away, muttering between themselves. Behind them, he stripped himself to the waist and turned to the standpipe at the back of the house. The raised scar on his arm had reddened with his exertions but now, in the cold morning air, it began to settle down to a faint pink line. He ran a finger along its length then turned to spit on the ground.

'Clean again,' he said. 'Time to get clean.'

Now was time to wash the past away. To wash himself. To wash the whole damn place clean for the future.

#### Acknowledgments

A novel is never a solo enterprise and I wish to thank those who have helped me. Firstly, Rob Magnuson Smith, whose enthusiasm kick-started me into writing, and whose technical advice on early drafts, and final re-shaping, was game changing. Also, Jacob Ross, whose insight into narrative form was invaluable for me, and whose editorial eye is unmatched. Thanks also to Bysshe Coffey for his passionate and insightful comments on the earliest draft, and to friends and colleagues at Exeter University, including Virginia Baily, Vesna Goldsworthy, Corinna Wagner, and Professor Mark Jackson who supported the initial research for this novel (and a wider project on waste and water) with seed funding. Thanks also to the University for granting research leave in which to complete this novel and related projects, and to Shola Charles for help with proof reading.

Specific thanks to my mother, Ruth Brown, who gave my early draft what she calls "an everyday reader's" response but who, more importantly, first gave me the gift of reading and who never tires of discussing books. Finally, incalculable thanks to my wife, Natasha Charles, who sat and listened patiently and enthusiastically while I read the manuscript aloud during the early stages of editing. Natasha helped me see what needed to be cut and what needed to be developed, with an acute storyteller's eye and ear, providing all the support, encouragement, and inspiration I could ever need.

I'm indebted to a raft of technical books, histories, collections of photographs and paintings and, of course, Victorian novels too numerous to mention here. My greatest debt is unsurprisingly to Dickens, for which I also owe an as-yet-unacknowledged debt of gratitude to Philip Hensher for starting me on my quest to read the *Complete Works* – a task he may be mildly pleased to know I have completed.

So far as the history and geography of this story are concerned, I have deliberately kept things ambiguous. There are many excellent academic and popular history books about London in this period, to which the reader can turn for geographical, political, social, medical, and other historical facts – mine remains a work of the imagination. The newspaper headlines in the window of Mr. Fleet's offices, however, place the later events of the novel near the end of the 1850s – the quoted article is adapted from *The Illustrated London News*, 26 June 1858. All other words are of my own questionable invention. The development of the new London sewers is, as we know, the crowning legacy of Sir Joseph Bazalgette, not Samuel Suddaby, and the latter is not meant to represent the former in any literal way. Finally, the attempted sabotage of the sewers and the subsequent riot after the trial of the perpetrator is entirely fabricated – it is simply, as all fiction perhaps tries to be, an attempt to examine a set of pressing circumstances through the speculative lens of 'What if...?'

# About the Author

Andy Brown has published numerous short stories in international journals. *The Midnight Mechanic* is his second novel, his first being *Apples & Prayers* (Dean Street Press, 2015), a novel of Tudor rebellion. The author of over twenty acclaimed books of poetry, he also co-edited the major medical poetry anthology, *A Body of Work* (2016) for Bloomsbury, and other critical works. Bloomsbury recently published *The Tree Climbing Cure*, a pioneering study of the relationship between tree climbing and wellbeing. A former Centre Director for the Arvon Foundation at Totleigh Barton, Devon, he is now Professor of Creative & Critical Writing at Exeter University.

# About the Press

Sea Crow Press is an award-winning woman-run independent book publisher based on Cape Cod in Massachusetts committed to amplifying voices that might otherwise go unheard. In a rapidly changing world, we believe the small press plays an essential part in contemporary arts as a community forum, a cultural reservoir, and an agent of change. We are international with a focus on our New England roots. We publish creative nonfiction, fiction, and poetry and our books celebrate our connection to each other and to the natural world with a focus on positive change and great storytelling. We have been building a literary community since 2020.